THE HORSES

THE HORSES

Janina Matthewson

WILDFIRE

First published in 2024 by
WILDFIRE
an imprint of HEADLINE PUBLISHING GROUP

1

Lines from Edwin Muir poem 'The Horses' © Faber & Faber

Cataloguing in Publication Data is available from the British Library

Hardback ISBN 978 1 4722 9981 9
Trade Paperback ISBN 978 1 4722 9983 3

Typeset in Scala by CC Book Production

Printed and bound in Great Britain by Clays Ltd, Elcograf S.p.A.

MIX
Paper | Supporting
responsible forestry
FSC® C104740

Headline's policy is to use papers that are natural, renewable and
recyclable products and made from wood grown in well-managed forests
and other controlled sources. The logging and manufacturing processes
are expected to conform to the environmental regulations
of the country of origin.

HEADLINE PUBLISHING GROUP
an Hachette UK Company
Carmelite House
50 Victoria Embankment
London EC4Y 0DZ

www.headline.co.uk
www.hachette.co.uk

For Tineke, fellow reformed horse kid

Late in the evening the strange horses came.
By then we had made our covenant with silence,
But in the first few days it was so still
We listened to our breathing and were afraid.

– 'The Horses', *Collected Poems* by Edwin Muir
(Faber & Faber, 2003)

Prologue

It was almost dark when they came.

The last curve of the sun sat above the horizon, but its light and warmth were long gone. A dead chill had set in and the world was grey and lifeless.

And then . . .

At first, it was just a feeling. A thrumming vibration through the ground, almost like a heartbeat. Before long, though, it was a sound. Rhythmic, primal, a pounding on the earth, fast but steady.

For a while it seemed like the sound would stretch on forever, never becoming anything more. Then, all of a sudden, there was a crowd of them, wild and proud and godlike, manes streaming behind as they ran.

They came over the fallow fields and on to the sand, meeting the dark ocean in recognition, as kin, before continuing down the shore.

After a year of solitude, the horses came.

Summer

So it had been like this.

A storm that lasted longer than any storm should.

Planes seen careening drunkenly through the air.

A sky stained with an unnatural hue.

Radios that fell silent. Phones that were dialled but never answered.

A ferry that no longer ran.

A small village of farmers and fishermen that had always felt cut off from the rest of the world – isolated, peaceful – found itself truly alone. Removed from the rest of civilisation by the sea, the residents of Black Crag were left to speculate when the world around them fell silent. Something had happened – something disastrous.

And this small island could only try to imagine the unimaginable, and wonder if whatever had silenced the mainland would eventually reach them too.

No one seemed to know or care when people had first settled on Black Crag, and no one was sure why they had. Some claimed that people had come here at first in search of coal, but no mine had ever been dug. If there had ever even been a survey conducted, no one knew where on the island it had been done.

Some claimed the village was started by people fleeing

society, fleeing the law, fleeing the plague – which plague was never quite agreed on, either.

It seemed such a strange place for anyone to settle. Inconvenient. It was not an island, not technically, but it might as well have been. It was connected to the mainland by a long, curving isthmus, which stretched down to the south before arcing back through the ocean towards the shore. It must have been a wider, more reliable stretch of land when the village was first settled. The road that stretched along it must have been used regularly enough to warrant gravel paving once upon a time, despite the endless hours it took to traverse it. But these days getting to the mainland by road seemed absurd, when it was so much easier to go by boat.

In any case, it had been decades since anyone had used the road, and longer still since there had been any attempt to maintain it.

Those who had their own boats could, of course, travel to the mainland at their leisure, but most simply timed their visits around the ferry that came twice a week. The crossing was still slow – five hours or so each way – but life was slow in Black Crag. That's what those who lived there wanted.

On the other side of the ferry crossing was another village. It was an hour's drive from there to get to a larger town, and another two before you came to the nearest city. The city had a name once, as did the towns and villages that surrounded it. The streets that led from one to the other. The farms that spilled over the fields between them. All these places had names, before. But in the afterwards, no one spoke them.

Perhaps it felt like a violation to pronounce the names of places where everyone was dead. Perhaps invoking those places brought to mind too clearly the people who had lived there. Perhaps calling them to mind too often would have made it impossible to get out of bed in the morning. We all need something to help us keep going, and sometimes denial is all we have.

Whatever the reason, the world shrank to a small, would-be island, and no one mentioned what used to be except in the vaguest terms.

And the world that was left was beautiful. The world that was the size of a small island, the world that was home to three hundred and fifty-seven souls.

The cluster of cottages and bungalows that made up the bulk of the village centre carved a semi-circle around a sandy bay. It had a long jetty that at any time would have fishing boats docked beside it. The sand stretched away to the south gently, but to the north it was cut off by the low beginnings of a range of hills that spread around the entire northern border.

If you approached the island from the north, you would see the black cliffs that gave it its name in their full splendour, plunging like shorn glass into the rough waves below. Of course, you wouldn't approach from the north, because there's nowhere in that direction to come from. You would approach from the east, sailing into the heart of the village. The cliffs seen from this side seemed gentle. Green hills sloping up at a deceptively relaxed pace, looking down over the fields below with a gentle majesty quite unlike the harsh judgement they showed to the sea beyond.

The small cluster of houses around the heart of the village soon thinned out, giving way to farmland in all directions. At one time, the farmland was varied, a range of crops and animals designed to support the village itself. The farms used to be worked by oxen and traversed on horseback, but it was decades now since most work animals had been replaced by machines. Tractors replaced oxen, quad bikes replaced horses – cheaper to run after the initial cost, and more reliable.

The nature of the farms changed as well, and now there was more wheat than anything else. A more lucrative use of the land, growing something to be purchased and sent far afield, processed into products that lined supermarket shelves and fed people thousands of miles away. So where once you would have walked by the verdant green of vegetables, now you would see the swaying gold of wheat.

Eventually, the farmland to the west gave way to a shaded fen that itself grew into scrubby bushland.

To the south, there was empty, rocky grassland, interrupted only by the long – and long-ignored – road. It was cracked and faded, with wildflowers pushing up at it, slowly reclaiming it. The road ultimately jutted out into the sea, subject to the tides, washed by the waves.

That winter had been particularly harsh. There had been snow in the village for weeks, which was unusual this close to the sea. The snow had stayed on the hills throughout the early days of spring until it was finally displaced by drizzle. Now, as summer drew near, the clouds had parted and warmth had spilled across Black Crag. The ocean sparkled under azure skies and the air felt rich and alive.

It seemed inappropriate that things should go so wrong when the weather was so beautiful. Such dread and grief and worry didn't sit well with long, sunny days. But cataclysm doesn't adhere to the climate's schedule any more than it does to yours or mine.

The world ends how it will.

Chapter One

In all honesty, it didn't feel real until that arm turned up.

It felt big, it felt all-encompassing, it felt irrevocable. But it didn't feel real.

To Sarah, it didn't feel real.

Something massive had happened, she knew. Something was wrong, badly wrong, somewhere. Close by. Something bigger than she could imagine. But there was a distance to it. It was the arm that turned it into something that could touch her. Something that would change her life, rather than just the world. Her present, rather than just her future. Her tangible reality, rather than just her hypothetical life.

It was easy to forget sometimes that there was a world out there at all. It was one of the nice things about living in Black Crag. There were no traffic jams, no loud sirens speeding past your windows, no crowded streets. You could live your life with space around you.

Even before it started, it was easy to feel like there was no one else in the world. It was easy to feel like there was no world at all, that it began and ended with the slate-coloured waves outside the front door.

Sometimes, Sarah preferred it like that. If she was going to be kept so far away from the world, then she wanted to be able to forget it had ever been there at all.

And then it seemed that maybe it was gone. Which also felt unreal.

No one seemed to know what to say or how to act after it started, so for the most part, they acted the same. Everyone got out of bed in the morning and went about their days.

Those with farmland continued to tend to it. Greta, who owed the village's general store, and Malcolm, who ran its one small pub, continued to open their doors every day and welcome the rest of the village as customers.

And when, after a couple of weeks, they stopped asking for money in exchange, no one talked about it. And when, after not very much time at all, the shelves began to empty without being replenished, no one talked about that either.

They talked about the weather, they talked about their aches and pains, they talked about their dogs and chickens and sheep.

They didn't talk about what was on the radio, because the radio now only held static. And they didn't talk about that, either. They didn't talk about the strange green tint in the sky.

It felt to Sarah that no one wanted to acknowledge the apparent cataclysm. Like they were deliberately ignoring what had happened. She both dreaded the mention of it and chafed at the avoidance.

The quiet life she had on the edge of the world felt like a dream. Too cloying, too simple, too much like a lie. Not that she wanted the truth.

She started going for long walks almost every day.

There was nothing else to do, anyway, nothing that could

hold her attention enough. She'd been doing some correspond-ence college courses, but there didn't seem much point to them anymore. She knew she could still learn from them, even if she couldn't send her work back, but why bother? Even when she did try and do some of the readings, she found it impossible to focus on the words in front of her. She'd read a sentence but forget what it said before the she could start reading the next one.

Even novels had stopped being the escape they used to be. The thrillers she used to love suddenly seemed petty and dry. Walking for hours at a time had become her only source of occu-pation. Of solace. In the beginning, she took her sketchbook with her, even sometimes her paints. And she did sometimes use them. But the problem with painting a landscape was that it made her really look at things. At the sea that connected them to whatever it was that had happened over there. And the spot where they'd seen a plane career wildly towards the horizon. At the sky in the east that was the wrong colour.

So when she took out her pencils and papers, more often than not, she ended up just letting her hand trail idly across the page. And eventually she stopped bringing them at all.

Sometimes she walked up into the hills, walking up rocky little paths, in the steeper places grabbing on to brush to pull herself up. She would hike faster than she needed to, pushing herself until she was out of breath, until her legs ached.

It was almost a three-hour hike to the top of the lowest of the hills, and she would stay up there for a while. The far side descended steeply down before dropping straight into the sea, and something about the view was comforting to Sarah.

Looking across the water from home felt stressful somehow. She couldn't see the mainland, but she knew it was there, just a boat ride away. She could picture the village the ferry used to dock in, the towns further in, and beyond them, the city, and she couldn't stop herself speculating about what had happened there. About what might still be happening there.

But from the hills there was nothing, just water for miles and miles. Looking out over an ocean that was untouched and unchanged was soothing in a way that nothing else was.

Sometimes she walked out across the farmland. The small vegetable farms that served local farmers; markets; the vast fields of wheat, with their golden fronds swaying in the breeze; Helen's little experimental vineyard. Sarah walked through the fields of sheep slowly, greeting them as she went. Sometimes she sat with them for a while, listening to their quiet, undemanding bleats. The sheep had been the village's biggest connection with the wider world; their wool was sent further afield than any of the produce or wheat. But the sheep themselves were, of course, unaware of that and unaware now that their wool was going nowhere. Their lives were unchanged, and somehow they made Sarah feel less alone than her family and neighbours did.

Whichever direction she was planning on heading, she always left the house as early as she could, taking whatever food she could grab on the way out, not telling anyone where she was going. It was important to her to be able to feel like no one knew where she was.

She would have stayed out for days if she could, but she knew that would be cruel. Her mothers would be terrified, and things were hard enough for them as it was.

The day she found the arm, she walked south along the beach, as far as she could go.

The mood in those early days was exhausting. Everyone on edge. Everyone tired and scared and fractious, one bad mood rubbing up against another and spreading throughout the village.

Her mam had snapped at the neighbour that morning, and even though it wasn't directed at her, it had pulled at Sarah's already strained mood. She'd turned and walked off.

'Sarah,' she'd heard her mam call after her, and she lazily waved a hand in acknowledgement without turning around. The call only came once.

She walked on into the morning, trudging through the low morning mist until all she could hear were the waves and her own feet crunching into the sand.

It had been nine weeks since everything changed.

She didn't often go along the coast. She didn't like to; she preferred the wild exhaustion of the hills or the peaceful companionship of the farmland.

The coast felt painful. It was like looking at a wound. The mainland wasn't visible from the shore, but she knew it was there. If she let herself think about it for too long, she could almost feel the movement of the ferry under her feet. See the water stretching out around her. Watch the jetty on the mainland come closer. It was only six months or so since the last time she'd been over there. She'd gone over with her mam to do some shopping for winter clothes. She didn't want to picture it.

The thought of what was over there now, the fear of it, was too much to take.

But somehow, for reasons she couldn't articulate, on this day she wanted the pain. It felt like a bruise she couldn't resist pushing on, to see if it would still hurt.

She set off walking close to the water, watching her boots plunge into the damp sand. She looked at the scuffs on her toes and idly wondered how much longer the boots would last, and what she'd do if they fell apart.

She began to think through her clothes, mentally cataloguing what was likely to last for a while longer and which wouldn't. And then there was the house. The bathroom window had a crack across it that now wouldn't be fixed. The hot water cylinder had been replaced a couple of years ago, so that should be fine for years. Would it need to hold up for years? The village was powered by offshore turbines, so electricity was fine as long as they didn't get damaged. But what if they did?

Food wasn't a problem. There were plenty of vegetables, and the chickens were still laying well. They hadn't had meat in a while, but Sarah didn't miss it. She wondered if someone would suggest butchering one of the sheep, and it was this thought that brought her up short. It crashed into her like a wave and she bit her lip hard, fighting back sudden tears.

She'd never been that fussed about animals, never wanted a cat or a dog. But over the last few weeks, the sheep had become important somehow. She didn't want to face them being butchered. Five hundred or so sheep, and she couldn't face losing one.

Sarah stopped for a while, crouching in the sand, watching the water gently crest closer and closer to her feet. She stayed completely still, until a small wave ran up and pooled against the rubber soles of her boots. She closed her eyes for a moment and then pushed herself back up, turning away from the grey water and trudging onwards.

*   *   *

She found the arm on her way home.

She'd walked for two or three hours before turning back, listening to the rushing of the waves over sand, eyes turned down and towards the water, trying to avoid thinking of anything much at all.

She must have walked straight past it.

On her way home, the tide was higher, and the wind had picked up. The waves, bigger now, with spray flying off them, pushed her towards the long grass at the edge of the beach. She walked the narrow path between the water and the brush, betting with herself that she could keep her feet dry.

She noted the landmarks on her return journey.

The old rotted-out fishing hut with a fallen-in roof. No one seemed to know who it belonged to or how long ago it had been built. It had been derelict for years before Sarah and her family had come to live in the village. She and her brother had told each other stories about it when they were younger. It was the home of a witch, or maybe a pirate. Or maybe it was built by an ordinary man, someone who lived in the village, and who'd fallen in love with a selkie or a mermaid and built her a home near to the sea.

The tree that had been struck by lightning five or six years earlier, one massive branch hewn almost off, hanging by a couple of inches of splintered wood. Sarah loved that it had been left like that – in the city, it would have been tidied up, maybe even cut down entirely.

She walked past the tree and turned to look back at it. And that's where she saw it. The hand poking out from the grass, palm facing up, with the fingers lightly curled, as if it was waiting for Sarah to pass it something.

Her breath caught in her throat and she stood still, the wind whipping her hair around her face. She didn't want to go near it.

But she was curious. Repulsed, yes, but curious too. Slowly, she crept towards it, as if it was a living thing that would be startled and flee if it knew she was there. She picked up a branch and stretched it out, using it to pull the long grass back so she could get a better look.

The arm was wrong, somehow. Finding a severed arm on the beach near your home is never going to be right, of course, but it was more than that. The colour of it was wrong. The dark skin was mottled, a weird pink hue dappled across it, brighter on the palm of the hand and fading over the wrist. The nails looked strange, too. Rougher, somehow, than normal fingernails, thick and coarse and strangely curved.

It could have been the water, she reasoned to herself, but she wasn't sure it had come from the ocean at all. It was lying too far above the high-tide line, and the weather hadn't been rough enough recently to throw anything that far up the shore. And the arm didn't look damaged at all, apart from the fact that it wasn't attached to a person. The skin wasn't broken, it was just the wrong colour.

Sarah knew what salt water did to dead animals – one of the pigs had drowned a few years back – and this wasn't it. If it had been in the water, it would have been in much worse condition, degraded and waterlogged, nibbled on by fish, broken by the movement of the waves.

But where else could it have come from? There were no other people on this side of the bay, and everyone in the village was accounted for.

Could it have fallen from a plane?

Sarah looked around the area, but there was nothing else. No other body parts, no bags or clothes or anything.

And there had been no sign of any aircraft for weeks. Not since the one they'd all watched go down that first, awful morning. And any normal arm that had been there that long would have started to rot by now.

She wondered if she should bring it back with her. People would want to know about it, and if she left it here it could be eaten by a fox or by birds. But what would they learn from it, really? It's not like they had a lab they could use to analyse the tissue. And what if there was something wrong with it, something infectious? What if bringing it back to the village made everyone sick?

For the first time, Sarah wished she hadn't come out by herself. That the decision wasn't hers to make alone.

She wished she had some way of calling someone. In the city there would be a payphone somewhere; she could call and ask her mam what to do. In the city, it wouldn't be her problem at all, there would be a police officer to take care of it.

She was still at least an hour's walk from home. If she took the arm back, she would have to carry it. She would have to walk alone, holding the severed arm of a stranger as the day grew dark around her.

She sat there for a while as dusk began to settle in. Eventually, she made a decision. Or rather, she acknowledged that there was no decision to make. She simply had to face what she was always going to do.

She took off her jacket and wrapped up the arm, tying her sleeves together to make a handle. Gritting her teeth, she picked it up. At first she held it out, away from her body, but it was awkward and uncomfortable, and the walk back was too long.

She carried the arm back along the beach, trying to ignore the reality of it.

When she got to the outskirts of the village, she left it on a fencepost. She had faced carrying it back; it could be someone else's job to decide what to do with it. She walked home and told her mother where it was.

Then she went to her room and stayed there all night.

The arm was the focus of conversation for the next few days. Did it mean there was an outbreak of some strange disease somewhere? Or maybe it was damaged by chemicals. Maybe it had been burned, in some accident, maybe on board a plane that had burst into flames. Or it could have just been the force of the drop, the velocity of its fall, that had caused the strange discolouration, the warped fingernails.

Eventually, though, the debates stopped. What was the point?

It was just the latest in a string of things for which there were no explanations, and then it faded to the background as everything else had.

But for Sarah, the arm was when everything changed.

It wasn't a dream. It wasn't temporary. There was no going back.

The entire world had shrunk to the size of the village she lived in. What happened here was the only thing that mattered now.

The Beginning

It started with a series of inexplicable events that took place at a distance but within sight over the course of a few days. Afterwards, the events were difficult to put into context. No one agreed on what had happened when, on how closely one had followed the other, on which was the first sign and which the last. In the end, it didn't matter. They happened, and then they stopped happening.

And after they were over, there was silence. The radios gave out only static. Phones that were dialled, rang but were never answered. The miles of cable that spread from the village of Black Crag, stretching under the ocean to forge a connection with the world, ended in blank nothingness.

The village that felt like it sat alone at the edge of the world suddenly felt like there was no world for it to sit at the edge of. There was no one to tell them what had happened. No one to tell them when help would come. No way to be sure help was coming at all.

Amid the fear and confusion in Black Crag, there arose speculation and division. The village split into camps of dissent, which shifted and changed and mutated with every new panicked exchange and vitriolic argument.

Fear of danger reaching the island competed with fear that

those on the mainland needed help. Worry that the village was indefinitely cut off from the rest of civilisation clashed with speculation that the rest of civilisation had become too dangerous to approach.

The question that rang through the hearts of the villagers was the same: were they truly alone? And how could they find out for sure?

While no one could agree on what had happened, it seemed certain that it had been catastrophic. That the towns and cities on the other side of the water were now empty.

After days of bitter debate, the village woke to find two of the fishing boats were missing. The owners of the boats were gone, along with five or six others. For a while, the departure of the boats brought a sliver of hope to the people of Black Crag. Surely now, surely soon, they would have some answers. The boats would return in a matter of hours and they would bring news.

The day passed and drifted into night, and the boats didn't return. A new day dawned and died, and still there were no boats. And their absence now served for some as proof that the danger had not passed. That anyone foolish enough to cross the water would also fall victim to whatever had silenced the world.

That perhaps it was for the best that they had failed to return. Perhaps there was some infectious disease that they would have brought back to the island – if they'd survived long enough to make the journey home.

But of course, this view was not shared by everyone. For some, the departure of their friends, their family, made reaching the mainland all the more important. The need to know what had happened to those who had crossed became all-consuming, and after four days, another boat disappeared from the dock.

And then someone made sure that no more boats could leave.

Chapter Two

When the world ends, you'd like to think those who are left pull together, suddenly united in the face of unprecedented hardship, suddenly bound, suddenly made kindred. But it seemed to Sarah that the world had ended not once, not in one simple manner, but over and over again, slightly differently for everyone.

And those differences led to misunderstandings. To arguments. To struggles that seemed pointless, that sucked up the energy around them.

At one point – afterwards, she could never quite remember if it was before the arm, or after it – Sarah's friend Ana said to her, 'Do you kind of feel like nothing's really changed?', and she was so shocked that for a full minute she couldn't respond.

'What do you mean?' she said eventually.

'Well, you know, we're all doing the same stuff every day we were doing before. Whatever happened out there – it just feels like it's nothing to do with us.'

Sarah wasn't sure what to say to that. She didn't know how to explain how far it was from her own feelings.

To her, it felt like the very earth beneath her feet had changed. And the more people walked on it as if it was the same, the more precarious it all felt.

Or it was like she had woken up in a parallel world, exactly like her own except for one thing she couldn't quite put her finger on. Like none of the people she knew were *her* people, like they were wearing the faces of her family, of her friends, but underneath they were something different altogether.

She felt like Alice. If she could only find the Red Queen and shake her, she'd wake up in her own home, in her real home, holding a kitten and wondering if she was only a character in someone else's dream.

The day after she found the arm, Sarah woke up to the sound of her mothers talking about it in the corridor outside her room. Arguing about it.

'I have to at least examine it, Seonaid,' her mam – Billie, the town's doctor – was saying. 'We have to figure out if there's something wrong with it, some kind of infection.'

'That's what I'm afraid of,' Seonaid – whom Sarah and Elliot called Moth –said. 'It's not like you have a hazmat suit. How are you supposed to examine it without being infected by whatever it's carrying?'

'We don't know that it's carrying anything – and if it is, we don't know if it's airborne.'

'Why would you take that risk? What is there to gain? Even if you do learn something from it, what are any of us supposed to do with that knowledge?'

Sarah's mam gave a sigh. She sounded impatient. 'For one thing, it might tell us something about what's going on out there. For another, Sarah was exposed to it for god knows how long after she found it, and if she could have caught something from it, then I will need to know what that is.'

There was a moment of silence.

'Right,' said Sarah's moth eventually. 'You're right. I guess I was trying not to think about it.'

'I know, love. But we have to.'

Their voices moved away, towards the kitchen, and after a moment Sarah heard her bedroom door open. Her younger brother stepped into the room and looked down at her.

'Just so you know,' he said, 'you're not allowed to die.'

Sarah smirked reflexively, and sat up. 'Why?' she said. 'Would you miss me? Would you be heartbroken? Would you be lost without me?'

'Shut up,' Elliot said.

'You don't need to say anything more,' Sarah said. 'I know that you adore nothing so much as me. That without me, your life would wither into pale nothingness.'

'I don't know why I talk to you.'

'Because you love me.'

'You are the most annoying person in the world.'

'I guess the odds on that being true are a lot higher than they used to be,' said Sarah. She was silent for a moment, stricken. 'That was a bad joke. I shouldn't have said that.'

Elliot didn't reply for a moment. He was chewing his lip. 'Do you think Mam's right, though?' he said. 'Did you get sick off that thing?'

Sarah pushed back her covers and stood up. 'I don't know. I don't feel sick.'

'OK,' said Elliot. 'Good.'

'Don't worry, El,' she replied. 'If I am sick, I've probably already given it to you, so you won't be alone for long before you follow me to the grave.'

'You are not as funny as you think you are.'

'I am exactly as funny as I think I am, thank you,' said Sarah.

But after Elliot had left the room, Sarah took a few moments with herself. She peered in the mirror at her face. Were her eyes a bit yellow, or was that just the morning light? She closed her eyes and tried to take stock of her body. Was her skin tingling, or was she imagining it?

Did she feel weird, or was it just that she'd never really thought about how she felt at all?

It was clear as soon as Sarah went outside that her mothers weren't the only ones arguing about the arm. Everyone seemed to be talking about it, and everyone seemed to disagree on what to do with it.

But as debate raged throughout the village, inside the house it was over. Billie gave Sarah a check-up, while Seonaid looked on with worried eyes.

'Everything looks normal for now,' Billie said, 'but I'm going to keep an eye on you. No big walks for a few days, just in case.'

Sarah rolled her eyes.

'It's for your own good, love,' said Seonaid.

'I'm fine, Moth. There's nothing wrong with me.'

'We just want to be sure,' said Billie. 'I'm going to try and learn what I can from that arm.'

She stocked herself up with surgical masks and gloves, and took herself off to the edge of Black Crag, where Sarah had left the arm.

Barred from walking too far afield, Sarah went out to wander around the village. But it was clear that other people shared Billie's concerns about the arm. A few people looked askance at her, a couple whispered to each other when she walked by, one or two skirted around her as they passed by.

Ana waved at her from across the way, but yelled, 'I can't come near you! I'm sorry, I promised my dad!'

Sarah waved back and tried to smile. She was starting to question whether she should have come out at all. Maybe Ana's dad was right to be worried. Maybe she should be quarantined. What if there was an infection in the arm? What if she'd caught something? She might have already spread it to Elliot and her mums.

Suddenly, the prospect of being around people at all seemed horrifying. Reckless in the extreme.

What had she been thinking? She should have left the arm where she found it, should have run as soon as she'd seen it. She should have recognised that she could already be carrying something and stayed away until she was sure she was safe to be around. Or live alone, some miles from home, waiting for whatever it was to take her, like it had taken everyone on the mainland.

Well, she might have done the wrong thing yesterday, but maybe there was still time to make it right. She turned on her heel and headed away from the centre of Black Crag. Too risky to go home for supplies; she'd spent too much time around her family as it was.

She was almost at the edge of the village when she heard her name being called insistently. 'Jesus, Sarah, open your ears.'

She turned and recognised the tall redhead immediately. 'Oh, Beth,' she said. 'You'd better not—'

'Do you know how long I've been calling your name?' said Beth, laughing. 'I honestly started to worry you were ignoring me on purpose.'

Sarah felt herself instinctively backing away as Beth walked towards her. They'd only recently become friends. Beth was the nurse in her Mam's clinic. She was a few years older than Sarah, which, until the last year or so, had felt like too big an age gap for real friendship.

Beth noticed her backing away and, for a moment, she looked hurt.

'You should probably stay away from me,' said Sarah. 'I don't know if you've heard—'

A sudden smile flashed across Beth's face. 'Ah,' she said. 'Yes, of course. I should cross myself at your approach, or throw salt over my shoulder, for thou hast been corrupted by the Arm of Death.'

Sarah couldn't help laughing a little, but she didn't come any closer. 'You make it sound like this is all superstition,' she said.

'Isn't it?'

'No. Maybe not. I could really be infected with something.'

'You could,' Beth acknowledged with a small, sympathetic smile. 'But we don't know that you are. We don't have any real reason to suspect it. And if we all jump to being afraid of each other the moment anything unusual happens, then this little community at the end of the world isn't going to last very long.'

'If we always assume everything is safe and fine, we won't last long either.'

'And what's the point in lasting if we've torn each other apart? Don't borrow trouble. If you're sick, we'll deal with that when we have to.'

Sarah was silent for a moment.

'You OK?' said Beth.

'Yeah. I don't know if I'm listening to you because I think

you're right or because I just want you to be. Because it's comforting.'

'Hard to know,' said Beth briskly. 'Best to assume the former.'

'Well. Maybe,' said Sarah. 'Anyway, is that what you were yelling at me for? To tell me not to worry?'

'Oh, no,' said Beth. 'That was a bonus. I wanted to ask you if you could send your mum over when she has a moment. My dad's having some trouble with bedsores. I need her to have a look at them.'

Beth's dad had been dying by inches for ten years, but had insisted on staying at home rather than moving to a care home on the mainland. Sarah had always thought it was unfair – his decision tethered Beth to her home, as she was his only support. But Beth never seemed to mind.

'Yeah,' said Sarah. 'I'll let her know. She's gone out to look at the arm, though. I don't know how long she'll be.'

Sarah felt better after talking to Beth, but she still couldn't quite be comfortable. She was on edge, pacing around the field behind her house, waiting for something to happen, something that would make it clear whether she was in danger. Whether she was a danger to others.

Just before midday, Elliot came to find her.

'We have to go to the hall,' he said. 'Moth and Mam have called a meeting about whether you're going to die and kill us all.'

'Right,' said Sarah, smiling grimly at the joke. 'Grand. Can't wait.'

'And I am willing to walk bravely beside you,' said her brother. 'As a show of support.'

'My hero.'

But when the two of them entered the Black Crag Hall a few minutes later, Elliot immediately abandoned Sarah for his friends. Sarah noticed a few people glancing at her, and some muttering to each other. She turned to leave, but a hand grabbed her arm.

'No, love,' said Seonaid. 'Stay. It'll be all right.'

'Hey, Moth,' said Sarah. 'What's going on?'

'It's not a big deal, but your mam thought we should talk this arm thing through as a community, you know. Get it all out into the open. It's no good having people spread rumours and nonsense just because they're a little nervous.'

Sarah thought this was rather understating things, but she didn't say anything. She didn't get much of a chance to, even if she'd wanted to. Graeme, a farmer who lived on the other side of the village, had walked out in front of the crowd and was trying to get their attention.

'OK,' he said, when everyone had quietened down. 'All right. Ah, I know this all seems a trifle formal, but I'm assured there's no cause for alarm. Dr Harrison asked us all to collect here as she knows there are some concerns floating around about an incident that occurred yesterday. So let's all give her our attention and she can address, well, those concerns.'

'Yeah, thanks Graeme,' said Billie as she stood. 'There's no reason to be coy, I don't think, so I won't be. I've heard a lot of talk about the arm my daughter found – and to be honest, most of it is rank nonsense. I've heard people claiming that the arm has black goo oozing from it, that it looks like something is growing inside it. That Sarah hasn't stopped vomiting since she found it – which, you can see for yourselves, is not true.' She waved a hand to the back of the hall, where Sarah stood with Seonaid.

'I've examined my daughter and she shows no sign of infection. And I've examined the arm, and I don't think it poses too great a risk right now. However—'

'How do you know that?' someone yelled from the front of the hall.

'Most infections that can be passed from dead bodies only pose a risk to people who handle those bodies in certain ways, such as performing autopsies. Sawing a body open can, for example, realise particles into the air that may be harmful.'

'Jesus, Billie,' said Graeme with a grimace.

'You butchered a pig two weeks ago, Graeme,' Billie replied.

'Even so,' he said, but waved for her to continue.

'Just being near an infected body, or part of one, is usually insufficient to pass on infection. There are a very small number of diseases that are exceptions to this, and the odds of them being present in this arm are extremely low. Also, without lab testing, I can't even confirm that the person this arm belonged to was carrying *anything*, let alone a communicable disease that is able to be passed on post-mortem.'

'You can't confirm that they weren't either,' said another voice from the crowd.

'That's true,' Billie acknowledged cheerfully. 'But even if they were, there is a very low chance that mere exposure to the arm would pass it on. What does concern me – mainly because I can't have proper tests run – are the gases that will be released as the arm begins to decompose.'

'So there is a risk?' said Graeme, in a gentle, worried voice.

'I don't know,' said Billie, 'and I have no way of finding out. So I have decided to burn the arm.'

Graeme nodded, looking relieved. 'Good,' he said, 'excellent. Thank you, Dr Harrison, for your speedy response. And is there anything—'

A voice interrupted from the front row. 'Excuse me,' it said. '*You've* decided? Are you sure you have the right to decide for all of us?'

Sarah couldn't see who was speaking, but she didn't recognise the voice.

'Well, Thomas,' said Billie, 'as far as I'm aware, Beth and myself are the only people with medical knowledge in Black Crag. Human medical knowledge, that is,' she added. 'Sorry, Dan.'

'S'all right, Bill.' The local vet waved a dismissive hand.

'And that means you get to make decisions on behalf of the rest of us?' said Thomas, his voice still floating out to Sarah from the front.

Who was this guy? She was sure she didn't know anyone named Thomas.

'You're not in charge just because you're a doctor,' he went on.

'I didn't think I was,' said Billie. 'I just didn't think anyone would want to keep it. I can't think of any reason why they would.'

'You can't think of any reason?' said Thomas, standing up and turning to the crowd. Sarah finally got a look at his face, and it was familiar. Someone she'd seen around the village but never really thought about or spoken to. 'This is the only piece of evidence we have, and you want to burn it?' he was saying. 'Think of what we could find out.'

'We can't find out anything,' said Billie, 'except whether the gases it will emit over the next few weeks could kill us.'

'Well, maybe some of us are willing to take that risk. What, are we just not going to try and find out what's happened over there? Just keep pottering away on our little island as if everything was normal? What's the matter with you?'

Graeme moved back towards the front. 'Well, OK, Thomas. That is a fair point. But I suppose we have to weigh up what we might discover from the arm, with the potential it has to do us harm. You don't want the doctor making decisions for all of us, and that's fine. We can put it to the vote.'

Thomas looked a bit mulish but didn't reply.

Graeme turned back to the collected villagers. 'OK, all. Dr Harrison has recommended burning the arm, and I have to say I think that's best. But Thomas would like to keep it for further unspecified study. So we'll take a quick vote: aye to burning the arm, nay to keeping it.'

Sarah didn't realise how tense she was until the loud chorus of 'ayes' filled the hall. She just wanted the situation to end. Surely no one would want to keep the arm around now that her mam had examined it? Billie was the only one who could have learned anything from it, after all.

But it seemed that Thomas wasn't the only one who wanted more. Around a dozen people joined him in voting nay, and Sarah saw a few of them approach him afterwards, all muttering together.

The Birds

Seonaid would always swear afterwards that the birds were the first sign, but no one would believe her. After a while, she wasn't even convinced herself. She wasn't even sure if she'd seen it, or if it was merely a dream she'd cemented in her own mind with frequent retellings.

It had been a hot day and she'd had to stay late at school. In the heat, and in the fractious mood of a nearly ended term, the kids had been difficult to control. There had been a fight and she'd kept those at the centre of it behind.

She was exhausted as she walked home. Not wanting to bring her bitter mood back to her family, she took a few minutes to sit alone out on the pier, letting the sea breeze cool her body, and the sound of the waves soothe her mind.

The sun was beginning to sink in the sky, but the day was still hot. It had been like that for weeks, temperatures reaching their peak in the middle of the afternoon and hovering there until long after dark.

Seonaid wasn't sure how long she sat there, waiting to feel refreshed, waiting to feel more comfortable with the day.

The birds were there for a while before she noticed them.

They were a way out to sea, far enough that she couldn't be sure what varieties they were, although a couple looked big enough to be albatrosses. But there were others that were smaller, which must have been gulls or terns or petrels.

There were about twenty of them, clustered together. They were barely moving. Doing just enough to keep as still in the air as possible. There must have been some kind of updraft, Seonaid thought to herself, keeping the birds aloft. She'd never seen birds behave like that.

As she stood and turned to walk home, she started wondering if she could find some research on that kind of thing, some ornithological studies. It might make a good lesson for some of the kids; they could do a project, spend time observing and reporting on the birdlife in the area. Maybe she could tie it into conservation.

By the time she reached the house, the eeriness of the sight, the strangeness, had left her, and all that remained were practical questions on building a lesson plan. When she walked through the door, she was hit by a strong, acrid smell coming from the kitchen. She walked through to find her daughter Sarah dumping a pan into the sink and flooding it with water.

Sarah turned as she walked in, looking shamefaced. 'Sorry, Moth,' she said. 'I'm starting again.'

Seonaid had laughed wryly about it then, and again later with her wife after the kids were in bed, but there was an overwhelming sadness as well. Sarah had been exuberant over the past couple of weeks, elated. She'd always been expected to help around the house – she and Elliot both had regular jobs to do, and each of them cooked once or twice a week – but recently Sarah had been bending over backwards to do as much as she could.

To Seonaid, it was oppressive.

She knew the reason for Sarah's happiness and, while she understood it, while she'd felt it herself once, it was breaking her heart.

Sarah was leaving. At the end of the summer, she would be moving to the city for university, and the thought of it was making her happier than she had been in a long time.

And she deserved to be happy; she was right to be. She'd be studying with some of her old school friends from before Seonaid had dragged the family back to the village she'd fled herself thirty years earlier. She'd be doing what she loved – painting. Finally getting the education in art the tiny village school couldn't begin to give her.

Seonaid knew that Sarah missed the city. It was easier for Elliot; he'd only been four when they'd moved. He hadn't started school yet; his world had still been confined mostly to his family. But Sarah had been old enough to feel the loss.

So Seonaid didn't blame her for being so excited to leave. But it hurt, too, to see it. To have to see, every day, how happy her daughter was to be leaving her.

As she fell asleep that night, her wife in her arms, those were the thoughts that occupied Seonaid's mind. The birds and their strange behaviour were all but forgotten.

When, a week or so later, the strange thunder shook the world, she didn't think of the birds. When the radios fell silent, she didn't think of the birds. When Arthur, the ferryman, arrived, traumatised and silent, she didn't think of the birds.

But some time later, when she saw a gull hovering over the ocean for a moment before flapping its wings and soaring away, she remembered. And in remembering, in considering all that had come after, the sight of the birds that day took on new significance. What had seemed at the time to be odd behaviour, something that could perhaps be explained by someone with more expertise than Seonaid, suddenly became a portent. The first indication that something fundamental had shifted and broken.

That the world was dying.

Chapter Three

Sarah didn't sleep the night of the meeting.

She didn't sleep much for the next few nights either. Her mam asked her not to venture too far away from home for a few days, just to be on the safe side. Every morning and evening, she took Sarah's temperature, checked her blood pressure, and peered into her eyes just to make sure nothing was developing.

'I'm not worried,' she told Sarah. 'This is just to be safe. It's extremely unlikely that you'd've contracted anything.'

Sarah wasn't worried either, and the repeated examinations were beginning to chafe. 'For Christ's sake, Mam,' she said after the tenth blood-pressure reading was normal. 'Can I not just tell you if I start feeling off?'

'I think I should keep checking for at least another week, just to—'

'I know, just to be safe. But what point is there anyway? Even if I had got infected with something, what would you be able to do except give me whatever antibiotics you have?'

'I—'

'And we wouldn't even be able to tell if it was a bacteria, so you wouldn't want to give them to me, so you'd probably just put me to bed and give me lots of fluids.'

'Sarah, I—'

'So what's the point? Every time you do a check-up, we're all thinking "What if?", and it's scary and stressful, and finding out that "yes if" would be useless anyway, because what could we even do?'

'Well for one thing . . .' Billie trailed off.

'Yeah,' said Sarah. 'For one thing, we'd all have to isolate ourselves until we got better or died. Wouldn't we? Except we'd probably already have spread it around. This infection that probably doesn't exist.'

Her mam didn't answer.

'I'm going for a walk,' said Sarah, and Billie didn't try to stop her as she stormed out of the house.

Sarah stalked off towards the cliffs to the north. She needed to feel some space around her, needed to feel small. Or to feel that the world she was in was big.

She felt constrained, trapped. Desperate to get out. Her mothers' caution had kept her tied to her home, tied to Black Crag, and she needed to get away.

She found herself out of breath after a few minutes and forced herself to slow down. It went against her instincts – she wanted to run – but the faster she moved, the quicker she'd be too tired to continue. And she wanted to walk for a long time.

The wind whipped her dark hair around her face and stung life into her cheeks, but she still felt like she was static somehow. Motionless. The exercise sent blood rushing through her veins, heat spreading through her limbs, sweat dripping down her face, but she still felt cold.

The sun was high in the sky, blazing down on the scrubby grass and heather that stretched ahead of her and up into the hills. She set her face ahead and tried to forget the small crowd of civilisation at her back.

It took her more than two hours to reach the hill top. The mottled green of the hills stretched out behind her, spotted with patches of brush and trees, gently thrumming with the small lives of field mice and hares, with grubs and worms.

Ahead of her, the ground sloped away briefly before disappearing, cut off into sharp, glittering cliffs. It was a windy day and the ocean below was crashing against the cliffs, sending white spray cascading up them. The water stretched away in undulating shades of indigo and cobalt, glistening in the sun. Sea birds soared above the waves, every so often plunging down to meet them, before rising again.

Sarah stood at the top of the cliff, looking out on an ocean that stretched for miles, and waited to feel the vastness of it flood into her, waited for the feeling that she was just a speck in a world that was immense and immensely varied.

The feeling that if she squinted just right, she would figure out how to grow wings, she could leap from the cliff and soar out towards the horizon.

It didn't come.

Instead of feeling infinity in front of her, she felt a wall. Like she was standing on a cliff inside a snow globe. Like if she grew wings and leapt from the cliff, she would end up flapping uselessly against an invisible barrier, like a bee trapped on the wrong side of a window.

She felt bile rising in the back of her throat. The wind whipped the breath from her lungs, and she couldn't get it back again.

The force of her panic beat against the inside of her chest like it was going to crack her wide open.

I should scream, she thought. *This is the point in the movie where someone screams into the void.*

But she didn't. It didn't feel like it would be enough. She would scream and the scream would make her feel even more trapped, like everything around her was even smaller than it was. And somehow, she felt like if she moved at all, she would do something dangerous. Irrevocable.

So she didn't move and she didn't scream. She stood very still, looking out at the ocean but not really seeing it, and waited for her body to feel like it was her own again. She didn't know how long she stood there. She didn't notice the time passing, she didn't notice the feel of the wind on her skin, she didn't notice her jagged, shallow breaths.

But slowly her breathing became steadier. Her face was warmed by the sun, beating back the north wind, which remained chilly, even in the height of summer. The panic was gone, but in its place was a dull heaviness – petty and prosaic.

With nothing else to find there, at the top of the cliffs, with no release or epiphany to be reached, Sarah turned away from the sky and began the slow walk home.

By the time she reached the outskirts of Black Crag, she was calmer if not more cheerful. Resigned, perhaps. She didn't want to go home, didn't want to talk to anyone, but there was nowhere else to go. Nothing else to do.

Still, when someone called hello to her as she walked past the first few houses, she couldn't bring herself to do more than wave a hand in acknowledgement, without even looking to see who it was.

When they called out to her again, though, she spun on her heel and glared. She felt a twinge of guilt at the startled gaze she met in return.

'Hi, Nathaniel,' she said, trying to be polite but not quite managing to keep the impatience out of her voice. 'Did you want something?'

She didn't know Nathaniel very well. He was two or three years older than her and worked on his parents' farm, but he seemed nice, and always made a point of saying hi.

'Oh,' he said, 'I'm sorry. Nothing. I just wanted to see if you're OK. After the whole meeting thing.'

Somehow, his kindness grated. She knew it was unjust, but suddenly she wanted to wound him. And she felt like she could.

'Seems like that would be none of your business,' she said.

Nathaniel stared her, his cheeks growing red. 'Jeez,' he said. 'Sorry I asked.'

'Yeah, me too,' Sarah said, and walked away, bitter defensiveness curling in her stomach. Why should he ask if she was OK? They barely knew each other. Why should anyone be looking at her and wondering how she was? The weight of other people's concern felt like an imposition. Like something to be answered, something to live up to.

By the time she got home, she'd talked herself into a stew, resentment twisting through her like ivy.

Elliot was the first person she saw when she walked into the house.

'Sarah, guess what?' he said, his eyes lighting up at the sight of her. 'Ewan's cat is having kittens, and Moth and Mam say we can have one when they're born.'

'So what?' said Sarah. 'There are cats bloody everywhere.'

She walked passed Elliot without looking at his face, wanting to avoid the hurt look she knew was in his eyes. She moved towards her bedroom, but her parents had heard her come in.

'Sarah, you're home, excellent. Come here and I'll give you a check-up,' said her mam, just as Moth said, 'Where have you been? I couldn't find you anywhere. You didn't go for one of your big walks, did you?'

'Mam! Moth!' Sarah yelled. 'Leave me alone! I'm fine, I've been fine this whole time. Why won't everyone stop bothering me? There's nothing wrong with me.'

She stormed into her room and paced the floor. She wished she hadn't come back home. But she didn't want to go back outside. She couldn't think of anywhere she wanted to be. She felt uncomfortable, itchy, like there wasn't enough room for her inside her own body.

After a while, her mam knocked on the door.

'What?' Sarah said sharply.

'Dinner's on the table,' said her mam, through the door. 'I'm not going to do another check-up, but you need to put some nutrients in your body. Come and eat. At the table. With all of us.'

Moth and Mam kept up a steady stream of conversation at the dinner table, but the meal still felt interminable to Sarah. The normality felt insufferable; it was as if she was in a play and the theatre was on fire, and all the other actors were just carrying on with the scene, and she didn't know how to make them stop.

*   *   *

Sarah's mood hadn't changed by the next morning, but it had shifted slightly. It wasn't crawling over her skin anymore; it was sitting leaden in her gut.

She submitted in silence to yet another check-up, and ate the overlarge plate of eggs her mam put in front of her without complaint. Then she walked out the door, and immediately came to a stop.

She didn't know what to do with herself. She didn't want to stay in the village, but she didn't want to leave it only to feel even more trapped again. She didn't want to run into any of her friends, but the only way to avoid them was to stay in the house – and she didn't want to do that.

After a few minutes, her mam poked her head out of the window.

'Can you do me a favour and go and see if Graeme has any sausages for us? He was planning on butchering a couple of pigs the other day and said he'd keep some for me. And can you drop past Helen and pick up a dozen eggs and check what veggies are in the shop today? Oh, and Mel needed a refill of her prescription – can you drop these off to her?' She passed a small paper bag through the window. 'Tell her I've enough in store for the next few months, so not to worry for now. Thanks, love.'

She pulled her head back inside and left Sarah on the doorstep.

This set the pattern for the next few days. Every morning, either Moth or Mam would give Sarah a list of jobs to do, and she'd slowly work her way through them. Then she'd go home. By the end of the week, she'd reorganised her mam's filing system, laminated exercise books for all Moth's students, cleared out the shed, and wound up dozens of skeins of wool into balls. It was clear that her parents were trying to distract her, but she was grateful for the distraction. She didn't know what else to do.

She was walking back from dropping off homework to a student of Moth's who was home with a bad cold when she ran into Ana. She hadn't seen her since the night of the meeting, and part of her wondered if her best friend had been avoiding her on purpose.

'Hey,' said Ana. 'Sorry I haven't been around. I've been really busy with . . .' She trailed off, not bothering to come up with a specific excuse.

'Yeah,' said Sarah. 'Me too.'

'My dad's calmed down, you know. He doesn't think you might be infected with anything anymore.'

'Oh,' Sarah said. 'Great.'

They walked together in silence for a while, and it stopped feeling quite so awkward. Sarah felt calmer than she had all week. She'd been so afraid of running into Ana, of having to talk to her, but now she couldn't remember why. Ana was her best friend; there wasn't anything they couldn't talk to each other about. And there was never any pressure with her to talk at all.

'Have you been doing OK?' Ana asked, after a while. 'That must have been awful for you, that meeting.'

Sarah took a minute to respond. 'It's not the meeting,' she said eventually. 'I mean, it was horrible, but I get it, people are scared. It's no big deal. It's more, I don't know, like I've just realised I'm not waking up from this, you know?'

'Yeah,' Ana said. 'Totally. It's weird how normal everything is when all this is going on.'

'Yeah, I guess,' said Sarah. 'But also there are just so many things that aren't going to happen now. And no one's talking about it. About them. Everything that was supposed to happen and that's now just . . . gone.'

'It is weird,' said Ana. 'But I guess it's normal too. Like, you know, that's just what happens when there's some big catastrophe. Everyone just immediately knows that it's all different now.' She gave a small laugh. 'And I know this is selfish, but I'm not sorry that my mum has stopped harping on at me to decide what to do with my life.'

They were almost at Ana's house now.

'How are you doing this?' Sarah asked. 'How are you so calm and OK? So philosophical?'

Ana thought for a moment. 'There's just nothing I can do. I have no control over anything.'

'So you're just giving up? And that makes you OK with everything?'

'I don't even know what "everything" is. No one does. There's nothing to give up on, because there's nothing to do. I'm just trying to get through the day, I guess.'

'Yeah,' said Sarah. 'I guess.'

She said goodbye to Ana and walked home slowly. She picked at her food at the dinner table, until she caught her mam giving her a look, and forced herself to eat it all. But later, when the rest of her family was getting ready for bed, she went out into the backyard. She went to the old swing set and sat down, looking at the stars, swinging herself gently back and forth with her foot.

It was almost midnight when Moth came out to sit with Sarah. For a while, she didn't say anything, just stared up at the stars.

Eventually, she said, 'Did I ever tell you how your great-uncle Douglas died?'

Sarah shook her head. She didn't think she'd ever heard Moth talk about a great-uncle.

'He was my dad's twin. Identical. My grandma once told me she used to get scared about how close they were. They always seemed to know what each other was thinking. They could go for days without any company other than each other. When they were twelve, my dad had appendicitis and had to spend a couple of weeks in hospital on the mainland, and Douglas was so distraught at being separated from him, he stopped eating until he was home.

'They loved going camping – whenever my granddad could spare them from the farm, they'd go off for a few days, often without telling anyone where they were going, although they usually brought home fish they'd caught or rabbits they'd hunted.

'Douglas wanted to be a vet, so when he was just about your age, he decided to go away to study, while my dad stayed here to help on the farm. Before he was due to leave, they went on one last camping trip together. They were supposed to be gone for three days, but it was almost a week before my dad came home, carrying his brother's body on his back.

'My dad didn't tell me about it until after we all moved back here. Do you remember, he was so sick but he seemed so happy? Partly I think because he loved to have you and Elliot around, but also because I think part of him had been waiting to die ever since that weekend.

'He told me that they'd found a cave system in one of the cliffs. When they tried to explore it, a section of the floor fell away and Douglas fell through. It took my dad a couple of hours to find a way to get safely down to him, and when he did, Douglas was already dead. My dad said he never knew how long he sat there beside him. He remembered thinking that he could just stay there forever. Until he died as well. He couldn't imagine life without his brother in it.

'But at some point, he stood up. He found another exit from the caves, on the level they'd fallen through to. And he carried his brother back home.

'He told me he'd been confused about that decision his entire life. He didn't want to get up. He didn't feel compelled to. He didn't exert himself over his pain in a triumph of the human spirit. He just moved. He just moved in the direction he needed to go in until he got there.

'He took his brother home and then, for a while, that's all his life was. Moving in the direction he needed to go in, without wanting to or feeling driven to. And after a while, he started to move because he wanted to, and he started to do things because he felt driven to do them. And he fell in love with my mother and had me, and his life grew into something big and full again.'

Moth fell silent, and she and Sarah sat looking at the stars for a few minutes, silent and still.

'But he still wanted to die,' Sarah said, after a while. 'In the end.'

'Being ready for death, reaching the end of your life with an element of joy – that's not the same as wanting to die,' said Moth. 'My father's world was irrevocably broken, and he had to learn to survive in it.'

Sarah felt her throat tighten and her eyes get hot. She swallowed and said brusquely, 'Fine. I get it.'

Moth turned and looked at her. She looked like she wanted to say something more, but she just nodded, before standing up and walking back into the house, leaving Sarah alone again.

The Storm

Graeme had called a village meeting on the second day of the storm, but hardly anyone had turned up.

It's just weather, they were saying. *What's the big deal about a storm?*

Graeme didn't think they were wrong, necessarily, but it was undeniably strange weather. And, Graeme reasoned, it was never a bad idea to get ahead of a potential problem. That way, you wouldn't be caught unawares, and if there ended up being no problem at all, well, you're better off over-prepared and embarrassed than unprepared and dead.

Not that he thought anyone would die.

He had to admit, though, that for the few who did turn up to the meeting, it did feel a bit like a waste of time. They might all agree that the storm was unusual, that it was eerie – frightening, even – but it was hard to see what impact a meeting would have. Sure, they could all agree to shore up their food supplies, they could cooperate to protect the animals, they could review what medical supplies were readily available and what was lacking.

What they couldn't do was determine how long the storm would last, or whether it would get more violent. They couldn't discover why the clouds had that sickening yellow shade to them, or why there was so much thunder but no lightning at all. Why rain pelted down on to the ocean but the village itself stayed dry. With all their combined meteorological knowledge, they could not between them understand why a storm of such violence hadn't blown itself out within a few hours.

On the third day of the storm, Graeme wondered if he wouldn't have been better off waiting till now to call for a meeting. Maybe more people would have shown up, taken it more seriously. A two-day storm might be nothing, but a three-day storm deserved attention.

On the fourth day, he wondered if he should call a second meeting. But he couldn't think of what he'd say at it, other than, 'This has been going on for four days,' which, naturally, everyone would already be aware of.

On the evening of the fifth day, the winds finally began to die down. The strange yellowish clouds cleared and the skies quietened.

Graeme took a walk through the village to see how people were feeling. He expected concern, even fear, but what he found was relief. Everyone simply seemed glad that the storm was over. No one wanted to question it. And they weren't alone in this. The news on the radio was dismissive – a once-in-a-generation storm, they said, but it was over now and not likely to be repeated.

So Graeme let it go. He was being fanciful, he supposed. Paranoid.

The storm would be spoken about in the same way as the record-breaking blizzard some forty years previously.

Everything would just go back to normal.

Chapter Four

It shouldn't be this boring, Sarah found herself thinking. *Something this massive, this world-changing shouldn't be so boring.*

Everything always the same, the great happening over on the mainland, which seemed like the most important thing that had ever happened, rendering everything here on the island irrelevant.

She was supposed to be used to it by now. Ana was used to it. Moth and Mam were used to it. Elliot seemed fine. They were all prepared to keep putting one foot in front of the other, to keep doing what was in front of them to do.

Well. Sarah didn't have anything in front of her to do. That was supposed to have been the point of this summer. One long, lazy summer with nothing to do but rest and relax. One last summer of irresponsible teenage life before she grew up.

That was the plan, and it was hard to let go of, even though it was essentially still happening. Surely the radio on the kitchen counter would spark to life with news of the outside. Surely a boat would appear on the horizon. It had been bearable for as long as she was waiting for that. But now she'd stopped waiting. The arm had been the message, and it had said that there would be no news.

So she was doing nothing, or nothing important, and it wasn't a summer of rest at all.

And, oh! How she wanted that summer of rest.

The lists of tasks from her parents helped a bit; the semblance of routine kept Sarah going, more or less, most days. But there was still a part of her that just couldn't bear to be around people at all.

That part won out on a blisteringly hot day a couple of weeks later.

Sarah left the house as Moth and Mam were sitting down to breakfast and set the sea to her back. She'd grabbed some toast on her way out the door and ate it as she walked. Farmers were out working already, but the rest of the village hadn't properly started humming yet, so she wasn't worried about running into someone and having to make polite conversation.

She walked slowly through the fields, feeling the early morning sun warm her back, watching its rays spill out across the land around her.

Wheat waved gently in the breeze, waiting to be harvested in a few weeks. She walked past the remnants of Helen's optimistic vineyard, the vines now black and dead.

She stopped for a while in a field of sheep, sitting cross-legged and chatting to the ones that trotted over to her.

It was while she was talking to the sheep that she first heard something. A low, rough sound, like someone clearing their throat. She looked around and couldn't see anyone, but she decided to move on anyway, worried that whichever of her neighbours owned this field would be unhappy about her bothering his sheep.

The sun was higher in the sky by this point and beating down on her head. She kept walking.

She headed through a field that was lying fallow, one that she knew eventually gave way to a cool fen. When she was halfway across the field, she heard a scuffling sound from behind her, and spun on her heel.

There was someone climbing over the fence she'd climbed over a few minutes earlier. She turned away and picked up her pace, hoping whoever it was would give up. She snuck a look back as she climbed the fence on the opposite side, but there was still someone there, although they were lagging behind.

Sarah sped off across the ground, stepping carefully as it became wetter and mossier. There were a few scrubby trees; she ducked around them, moving away to the right. Her favourite spot in this area was to the left, where a large willow grew in the middle of the fen, with roots you could sit on spilling out from the trunk.

Sarah didn't want whoever was following her to find the willow, so she went to the right, which led only to a small grove of birches. It was nice, but it wasn't special. As she reached the birches, she looked around again. For a moment she thought she was finally alone, but then he finally stepped into view.

It was Nathaniel.

Sarah exploded. 'What? What do you want?' she yelled. 'Why are you following me? Why do you think you have the right to follow me?'

Nathaniel didn't seem surprised by her shouts. He blinked and smiled a little, but didn't say anything.

'Well?' Sarah said. 'What is it? Are you just going to stand there and smirk at me? Did you think that I walked this far from home because I wanted some asshole I barely even know to come here and smirk at me?'

Still nothing.

Sarah dumped her bag on the ground and stalked up to him. 'You tell me right now why you're following me,' she said.

'Do you feel better?' Nathaniel asked.

'No, I don't feel better,' Sarah said. 'Better than what? Why would I feel better?'

'I don't know,' he said. 'Seems like you needed to yell. It's seemed like you've needed to yell for a while.'

'What the hell do you know about what I need?'

'Everyone needs to yell sometimes.'

'So you've been stalking me all morning because you thought I needed to vent? You wanted to goad me into screaming at you so I'd feel better?'

Nathaniel grinned. 'Not specifically. I didn't have a plan. I just wanted to see if you were OK. I wondered where you go, when you leave the village for a whole day. Worried it was somehwere . . . I don't know . . . dangerous.'

'What are you talking about?' Sarah spat. 'We are not friends. I'm not yours to worry about.'

Nathaniel's eyes widened in mock dismay. 'Oh god,' he said, 'I'm so sorry. I must have misread the newsletter on "people I have been assigned to worry about". Honestly, I've never been so embarrassed.'

Sarah stared at him for a moment. She couldn't remember the last time she'd even talked to Nathaniel, other than to say hi if they passed each other in the street. Not since he'd finished school, a couple of years before she did, and it wasn't like they'd really been friends there anyway. The school was small enough that everyone hung out a bit, but Sarah couldn't remember ever having a conversation with Nathaniel alone.

She didn't know how to talk to him. She'd been so sure that as soon as she lashed out, he'd back off. That he'd be hurt or offended, that he'd rush away from her. But he didn't seem to care that she was angry. He seemed satisfied. Happy about it.

'Worry about who you want, but don't make it my problem. You don't get to check up on me.'

'Right,' he said. 'Noted. Fine. You're clearly doing fine, and are obviously talking through your issues with your loved ones and have no need of further help from any quarter.'

Sarah had never been in an argument so infuriating. 'Why do I need to be fine for you to leave me alone? Why should I be fine? Why should any of us be fine? Aren't I allowed to do whatever it is I'm doing – which, by the way, is none of your business – in peace? We're in the middle of god knows what disaster and you're worried about me taking long walks?'

Nathaniel sat down on a rock and pulled a sandwich wrapped in wax paper out of his bag. 'Well, yeah,' he said, unwrapping the sandwich and taking a bite. 'Most people in a disaster get to work, you know. They help out.'

'Help out with what? We don't even know what the disaster is.'

'We know we have to survive on our own, at least for a while.'

Sarah gaped for a moment, flailing for something to say. Anything to say. Eventually, she decided it was too awkward to yell at him while he was sitting down, so, in frustration more than anything else, she plopped herself down onto an old tree stump.

'Did you bring lunch?' Nathaniel asked. He pulled another sandwich out of his bag and held it out to her.

'Yes, I brought lunch,' Sarah said. 'I'm not hungry.' She sat in silence for a few minutes, and then added, 'You can go back when you've finished eating. I'm fine, so you can go back and leave me alone.'

Nathaniel chewed thoughtfully. 'No,' he said. 'I don't think I will.'

'Oh, for Christ's sake,' said Sarah. 'What do I have to do to get you to leave me alone?'

'You have to tell me what's really going on.'

'You know what's really going on. The same thing as for everyone else.'

Nathaniel raised an eyebrow at her and kept eating.

'Do you honestly need me to spell it out?' said Sarah.

'I'd love that, actually,' Nathaniel said, pulling a water bottle out of his bag and offering it to Sarah before taking a sip.

'Are you serious?' said Sarah. 'Something has happened over on the mainland, maybe all over the entire world, and we don't know what it is. Something massive. Something unimaginable. Something that has cut off all contact. Something that means no one from the mainland, none of our friends and family, can get to us at all. They might all be dead.

'We are here, alone, and we don't know how long for. Maybe forever. *That's* what's going on.'

Nathaniel opened the second sandwich and took a bite. 'And?' he said.

'And what?'

'What else?'

Sarah sat staring at him for a minute. 'There isn't anything else,' she said, but as she said it, she could hear how unconvincing she sounded. She stood up. 'And if there was, why would I talk about it with you? When I could talk about it with my parents or my friends. People who actually know me?'

'I don't know,' said Nathaniel. 'You probably should.' He looked up at her, a bland smile on his face. 'But I don't think you are. So if you don't want to talk about it to your family or to your existing friends, I thought you might want to talk about it to someone you barely know. Someone who you don't care if they hate you for it.'

Sarah felt a sudden stillness descend on her. How did he know? How did he know how much everyone would hate her if they knew what she was thinking? She pressed her lips together and swallowed.

'Don't be ridiculous,' she said. 'It doesn't matter. There's nothing else that matters. Everyone is in exactly the same situation as I am; there's no point acting like I'm affected in some different way. Everyone else is just as – stop looking at me like that!'

He didn't stop looking at her like that.

'Fine,' she said. 'Fine. You want to know what else is wrong? You want to know just how much of a selfish asshole I am? I was supposed to get out. This was my last summer on this fucking island, and then I was going away to university and I was never coming back. I was going to study art; I was going to learn how to paint, really paint, from real artists. I was going to travel the world. See everything.

'I had a whole life, a bigger, broader life about to start and now it's gone. Maybe forever. Now I'm stuck here. I'm stuck here, maybe forever, and I hate it and I shouldn't hate it! I should be grateful that whatever happened hasn't reached us. That Moth and Mam and Elliot are all fine, and that I'm with them.

'But the truth is that this place was only bearable because I was going to leave it.' She was staring down at him now, breathing hard, her hands in fists. 'So there,' she said. 'That's it. That's what else. Are you happy now?'

Nathaniel folded up the empty pieces of wax paper from his sandwiches and tucked them into his bag. He nodded a couple of times. 'Yeah,' he said. 'I think it's great that you've got all that out. Well, I've finished eating, so I guess I'll head back.'

He stood up, shouldered his bag and walked off the way he'd come, leaving Sarah standing there alone.

After he left, Sarah sat down again. She felt deflated and exhausted.

The hot sun pricked through the leaves above her as she sat. She wondered idly how hard it would be to build a hut here. She could live on the mushrooms that grew in the fen, or venture to the shore to the west for oysters. If she needed anything else, she could sneak back to the village at night, taking what she needed and leaving charms made from bracken and driftwood as payment. She could live out here for years, completely alone, never to be seen again. Sometimes someone would catch a glimpse of her, but only a glimpse. Not enough to feel sure she was real.

She would slowly develop into an urban legend: the hedge witch living on the edges of the farmland. There would be dark rumours about who she was and what she wanted. Children would bring home stories of her enchanting animals to do her bidding, and their parents would use her as a threat. 'Don't stay out past nine, or the witch will catch you and eat you.'

Sarah laughed for a moment at the idea of her own parents

saying something like that. Moth and Mam would be more likely to say she was just a poor old woman who wanted to be left alone, and everyone should let her be.

Kids would start daring themselves to try and find her – perhaps it would even become a rite of passage. The night before your fifteenth birthday, say, you would be tasked with venturing into the fen to find the witch's hut, and carving a sliver of wood from the wall to prove you were there.

That would be Elliot in a few months' time. Sarah smiled as she pictured him venturing out in the dead of night to find the witch, only to discover it was his big sister after all. She would have a hot chocolate waiting for him. Well. There probably wasn't enough time to become a local legend before Elliot's birthday.

Sarah sighed and stood up. She began the long walk home.

Her parents, Ana, Elliot and now Nathaniel – they had all tried to help her feel better. To help inspire her to be better. All while she was sitting here resenting the fact that she was trapped with them.

She walked slowly, but steadily. She didn't stop to commune with the sheep, she didn't check on the progress of the grapes, she didn't pause to appreciate the evening light glinting off the golden fields of wheat.

She made it home just as Moth was setting dinner on the table, and she sat with her family and tried hard to be kinder to them.

The Radio

It was Billie who always wanted to turn the radio on in the mornings.

She'd never really used to like the radio, back when she'd lived in the city – it just felt like more noise. She'd loved living in the city to the extent that she'd ever thought about it. She was born there, she grew up there, an only child in a penthouse apartment. Her parents were both doctors, and she'd gone to medical school primarily because she didn't have any strong ideas of what else she might do with herself.

She was relieved to find that she loved being a doctor – although there was a small, secret part of her that wished she didn't. A small part of her that wanted to be different from her parents.

When she'd met Seonaid, she'd been fascinated and horrified by her accounts of growing up in Black Crag. She couldn't imagine living somewhere so quiet. But when she'd come to visit for the first time, she'd found it wasn't quiet at all.

The sound of the waves was constant, and so much louder than she'd thought it would be. And on top of that were the birds – gulls cawing, owls hooting, all manner of sounds Billie was completely unfamiliar with. It was eerie and overwhelming, and she'd been extremely glad when the visit ended and she and Seonaid could go back to the safe and familiar soundscape of the city: the hum of traffic, the sounds of the neighbours' television sets.

She'd become more comfortable with Black Crag over the years. They'd tried to visit more after Sarah and Elliot were born, and the disquiet lessened with each trip. And then she'd found herself dreading going home.

She'd fallen in love with the slow mornings, being woken by her children. With the ease of strolling down into the village centre to pick up groceries, rather than having to fight through traffic and crowds just to get the necessities of life.

At home, her practice was constantly understaffed, always stretched to the limits. It was rewarding work but exhausting, and she was beginning to think that she needed something calmer. Something that demanded less than twelve hours a day from her, something that left her something of herself to bring home to her family.

When Black Crag's previous doctor had started to talk about retiring, Billie had suggested that she could take over his practice. Seonaid had said a flat no. She'd left for a reason, and she'd never go back.

And then her father had got sick.

It wasn't deliberate, at first, moving back. They came to help look after him, to help Seonaid's mother cope, as he died slowly.

At first they didn't even enrol the kids in school. It was only supposed to be a couple of months, after all. But nothing goes how it's supposed to.

Seonaid's father took eight months to die, and after he did, it was immediately clear that they couldn't leave. Her mother wouldn't cope. So they stayed for a while longer. They fell into a rhythm.

After another four months, Billie suggested they stay.

'I know you never wanted to come back,' she'd said, 'but isn't it nice here? Isn't it nice to have time with the kids, to have space around us? To live slowly and gently for a change?'

'For a change,' Seonaid had said. 'Not for good.'

'It doesn't have to be for good. We can move back at any time. We can go anywhere we want.'

Seonaid hadn't been convinced, but her mother was leaning on her more and more with each passing month. The longer they stayed, the harder it became to leave.

The years passed and they became settled. Established. And Billie began to feel the quiet a bit too much. She was happy to be living in Black Crag, happy to have more time, more space. But sometimes the birdsong and the waves made her feel a little overwhelmed. So she started turning on the radio as soon as she was awake. It was a way of feeling like she was still connected to the wider world. Just having a constant flow of stories from further afield at a low volume.

Sarah would often turn it over to a music station, which was fine, but Billie would always turn it back to talk radio as soon as the kids were away. She didn't pay close attention to it – it might as well have been music, really – but something about the constant flow of human conversation was what she needed. It filled the world around her when it started to feel too empty.

It was better, she thought, than having to live amongst the noise. Just letting the hum of other people's lives into yours when you wanted to, rather than having it surround you constantly.

They'd been there for eight years when Seonaid's mother had died too. Billie had wondered if Seonaid would want to leave again, now there was no one keeping them there, but she had just said that it was the middle of the school year, it wouldn't be fair on the kids to disrupt them – both their own two and those Seonaid taught.

And Billie was the village's only doctor; it might be difficult to find someone to replace her.

So they stayed again. And Billie was happy, Seonaid was happy, Elliot was happy. And if Sarah looked forward a little too eagerly to finishing high school and moving away for university, then that was only to be expected. After all, Seonaid had been the same way.

They stayed in this remote village, in the quiet, with the radio to keep them a little more tethered to the big world that was still out there, even if no one really paid attention to what it was saying.

And then it stopped saying anything.

It happened over night. Billie came downstairs and flicked on the radio, and heard only static. She spun the dial around and found nothing. She flipped between AM and FM, and there was only white noise.

She was annoyed, a bit confused, but not overly worried. It could be that something was wrong with the set, or perhaps that there was interference from the weather. The storm had blown itself out the day before, that wild and chaotic storm that had seemed like it would never end. She wondered if it had knocked out some of the broadcasting systems, and how long it would take to fix it.

She turned the volume down but left the radio on, tuned to her favourite talk radio station. She had her breakfast, walked the ten minutes to the doctor's office, and turned on the radio there to find that it too was only giving static. Again, she kept it on with the volume down low enough so that the sound wouldn't grate, but high enough that she'd notice if they fixed the issue and began broadcasting again.

Her nurse Beth came in and said that it seemed to be everyone. She usually left the radio on for her father, who was confined to the house; she was worried about him being bored without anything to listen to. When her radio had played only static, she'd asked her next-door neighbours about theirs. And then on her way to work, she'd asked everyone she'd seen.

'They all said the same thing,' she told Billie. 'Just static, on every station.'

And it stayed like that. Billie knew she wasn't the only one keeping the radio on just in case. Across the village, on kitchen counters and office bookshelves, radios sat sending out a constant stream of white noise, waiting for the world to wake up again.

Hoping that one day it would.

Chapter Five

A strange thing about a disaster is that we all experience them together and alone at the same time. Human nature contains such variety that the same blow dealt at the same time to all of us leaves a unique mark on each. We are wounded by the same weapon but none of our wounds are alike. Even those we know the best, even those we love the most, may surprise and upset us with how different their feelings are from our own.

Not everyone in Black Crag felt robbed of their future. Not everyone felt like they had lost something crucial to their survival, to their happiness. Sarah's best friend was in a completely different situation.

Ana didn't want to admit it, but she was enjoying the cataclysm.

She'd grown up on a farm with parents who barely spoke to each other. It had never been a comfortable home, and things had become even more strained when her father had had an accident four years earlier. He'd fallen under the wheel of a tractor and lost the use of his legs. The farm had to be sold, and Ana and her parents moved into the centre of the village.

Now Ana's mother worked on a couple of the farms on an ad hoc basis and did clothing repair for the village, and her father sat in his chair in the front room, watching people pass by the window.

Ana knew her mother meant well, but from the moment of the accident, something between them had changed. Somehow Ana felt like her mother expected her to suddenly be an adult. To be an equal. To be able to support her, to feel the same feelings about their situation as she did. And as soon as Ana had finished school, her mother expected her to contribute to the household as her father had used to.

Ana picked up odd jobs around the village, helped out during the harvest, but the work was inconsistent, and she wasn't particularly motivated. There had been arguments. Her mother had accused her of laziness, a lack of ambition. And to some extent, Ana agreed. She wasn't ambitious.

She wasn't like Sarah, who had been talking for years about leaving. Going to university. She wanted to study fine art, to do a master's, even. Ana knew Sarah had always loved to paint, but secretly thought that what she really wanted was to live in some big city in the centre of things. To feel the world rushing by around her, with endless possibilities for how to spend her days. For how to live.

Ana wasn't that bothered by any of it. She loved Black Crag. The quiet of it, the beauty. The small community of people who all felt like family. People who'd known her from the day she was born. All she wanted was a quiet, beautiful life. A little house with a little garden. A husband and some babies. Slow mornings baking scones for lunch.

But her mum thought she just wanted to mooch around, living off someone else.

In the months before the radios went silent, Ana's mum had decided that she needed to go to the mainland and find an apprenticeship somewhere, or find some diploma to do. To have that all taken off the table was something of a relief.

Ana had never been to the mainland. She'd never really wanted to go. So while she knew something horrific had happened over there, it was hard to feel that it was really real. She knew that it was a horrible thing to be at all happy about something that had obviously devastated everyone nearby, possible everyone everywhere, but that thought was purely academic. Her life now was real.

Her mother had stopped twitting at her to become a more productive person, the weather was beautiful, and there was a boy she'd suddenly noticed, as if she hadn't known him all her life. Someone who seemed ripe for a flirtation. It was promising to be, for her if for no one else, a perfect summer.

The one cloud in Ana's sunny apocalypse was the lack of parties. In a normal summer, there were socials and beach days and movie nights. Endless opportunities to break up the weeks. But now, no one was throwing any parties at all. It's not like the mood was all sombre all the time, people were getting on with their lives, but the disaster over the sea hung in the background. The ominous green sky hadn't reached them yet, and they still had to make breakfast every day.

Because what more could you do, Ana reasoned with herself. The most important parts of life were the ones right in front of you.

She decided that she would have to be the one to break the seal. She would bring it up with Sarah, even though her friend had been in such a weird mood recently. Her motives were in part altruistic, although there was selfishness in them as well.

Sarah was always the one who heard Ana's ideas first; talking them through with her always helped them become more real in Ana's mind. But Ana was also genuinely worried about her friend; she thought that maybe having a distraction would break her out of her extended tantrum.

'I think we should have a bonfire,' she said, as the two of them sat on the dock, having both escaped their mothers. 'This weekend. On the beach just outside the village.'

Sarah stared. She hadn't really thought about how Ana was feeling about things – she seemed to be her normal, gently cheerful self. Now she wondered if her friend had been secretly losing her mind.

'Do you really think people want a bonfire?' she said slowly. 'It's not really the time for it right now.'

Ana shrugged. 'I think people are desperate for it,' she said. 'But no one wants to say so. Or maybe they don't even realise. We're just getting on with our lives in every other area, but it's like we're afraid to have fun in case it seems disrespectful. To whatever happened over there, to all the people who are, well . . . presumably dead.'

Sarah's face clouded over at that. Her mind flashed back to her last day of school before she moved. Her childhood best friend – a quiet, serious-minded boy called Rahul – had brought in cakes for the whole class. He'd cried at the end of the day and begged her to write him letters. She had, for a while, and he'd written back. But the letters had slowed over time. It had been four or five years since they'd stopped. Sarah found herself wondering who had been the last to write. Which one of them had been the one to fail to reply? Her mind started to drift into dangerous territory, wondering what he'd been doing when disaster struck. Wondering if there was any chance he was still alive. Wondering how he'd died.

She gulped and tried to wrest herself away from the thought.

'Sorry,' said Ana. 'I know I'm too . . .'

'Flippant?' said Sarah.

'Yeah, I guess. I know you have friends and stuff over there. Sorry.'

'It's OK.' She'd said it as a reflex. Manners winning out over truth. 'I mean. It's not OK. But I know it's hard to make it feel real. When everything here is so normal.'

'Yeah,' said Ana. She chewed her lip for a minute. It suddenly struck her that she and Sarah had been friends for years without Sarah ever needing anything from her. She'd always been the one that was OK. When Ana had been left reeling after her dad's accident, when she'd been frustrated by her mum, Sarah had been calm and stable. Ana didn't know how to navigate things the other way around.

'So, anyway,' she said awkwardly. Insufficiently. 'I think people need something. Something fun. Something with drinking and music and dancing and kissing. A night where we get to stop pretending we're not happy to be alive. That we're not glad to have avoided whatever happened to everyone else.'

'I don't know,' said Sarah. 'It seems a little weird. To have a party after . . .'

'After the world has disappeared?'

'Yeah.'

'Not that we *know* the world has ended. Not that we know anything.'

'That's the thing, I think,' says Sarah. 'It feels like we would be choosing to act like, because we don't know *what's* happened, we don't know that anything's happened at all. But we do. We know something terrible has happened.'

Ana screwed up her face. 'But I don't think that's what it is. That's not what it feels like to me. Just, I think we're all . . . you know . . . holding ourselves in too much. We're all pent-up emotion and stress. We need to snap the rubber band.'

'Maybe,' was all Sarah would say. She didn't know how to tell her friend that she found the whole idea repellent.

'Come on,' said Ana. 'Say you'll come.'

'I don't know. You have fun, though.'

'Come on,' Ana said again. 'It'll give you something to do other than snapping at your mums for trying to take care of you.'

'I haven't been snapping—'

'You have,' Ana said. 'And it's making you even moodier. We're nineteen, Sarah. We're supposed to have aged out of our teenage angst. You're sulkier than you were when we were fourteen. You need a chance to let it out.'

'Will everyone stop having a go at me, for the love of god! I can't have a conversation with anyone without it turning to, "By Christ, Sarah, you're a moody one lately, are you not?" Like it's normal to not be a bit turned around by the fucking apocalypse.'

'See, this is exactly what I mean,' said Ana, calmly. 'You're on a hair trigger. You need this.'

'I don't need this,' said Sarah. 'I need . . . I don't know what I need, but it's not a night of drinking on the beach with a bunch of people desperate to party on a grave.'

Ana sighed. She felt sure that she was right, that everyone needed to blow off some steam, Sarah more than most. But she didn't know how to convince her. And she didn't know how else to help.

'OK, love,' she said simply. 'I hope you change your mind.'

Sarah shook her head at Ana and walked away. But despite her friend's reaction, Ana felt pretty cheerful. She felt committed now. Telling someone, even someone who thought it was a bad idea, had solidified things in her mind. Before, it had been a vague plan, but now it was solid. She knew the exact place for the bonfire, she knew who to put in charge of the music, and she knew who she was going to try and make out with by the end of the night.

She'd enjoyed the last few pressure-free, focus-free weeks, but having a new goal ahead of her was invigorating. She was determined to make it the best party the village had ever seen.

Ana made some careful, calculated decisions about who to bring in on her plan. She didn't mention it to her mum, or to anyone who talked to her mum regularly. She was hoping that when the time came, she could pass it off as a party she was going to, rather than one she had organised from the ground up.

And she didn't tell Marcus. She had a plan for Marcus.

Marcus, whom she'd known all her life and barely noticed. Who had sat at the back of the class, moody and silent, head down. Whom Ana had caught sight of a couple of weeks ago, and suddenly seemed a foot taller. Who suddenly had broad shoulders. Whose hair flopped in his eyes in a way that gave him an air or fascinating inscrutability, where it had once made him look like a bashful child.

She'd laid some groundwork since then. When he'd caught her blatantly staring at him, she'd grinned saucily and flipped her hair. Once, she'd looked at him over the top of her sunglasses while she ate an ice cream. And just the other day, she'd winked at him while he was carrying home a load of shopping.

Ana was fairly confident that she'd done enough work in that direction for the time being, and she much preferred to leave some part of the dance to her partner.

With this in mind, she kept out of his way as she got busy planning. She talked to Scott, who was great with a playlist and whose dad had a massive outdoor sound system, and he was immediately on board.

She roped a couple of guys into building the actual bonfire, which she made sound like the most fun part of the plan, because it involved setting something alight, but which she knew would mainly involve hauling a large quantity of wood to the desired spot.

She got a deal with Malcolm, who ran the pub – in fairness, he was her uncle – to provide a couple of kegs and a few pizzas, and she told one or two of her most excitable friends that Saturday night on the beach was going to go off.

Then all that was left to do was wait. By Thursday, she was sure, Marcus would sidle up to her and ask what she knew about the weekend's big party. She'd play coy, look up at him from under her eyelashes and heavily imply that she'd be there – that is, if she knew for sure that he was coming.

But Thursday came and went, and Marcus didn't talk to her at all.

By Friday afternoon, Marcus still hadn't come anywhere near Ana, even though she'd happened to walk past his house wearing a very short skirt while he was working in the front garden.

Maybe this was going to take more work than she'd thought.

She grimaced and stomped down the street, wondering if she needed to rethink her party outfit. She'd been planning on dressing casually – it was a beach party, after all, and she didn't want to overdo it. But maybe she'd need something more daring to get Marcus's attention.

Overall, however, she was still excited. Loads of people had caught on, and she was pretty sure she was about to throw the best party this island had seen in a generation.

So all in all, she was feeling pretty at peace with the world when she ran into Sarah.

'You're around a lot,' Ana said. 'I thought your mam was letting you go for your walks again. Thought you'd be off wandering the moors all disconsolate and whatever.'

'Well, I'm not,' said Sarah. 'I'm here.' She tried not to sound too petulant. She was still feeling suffocated, still feeling so trapped, and she didn't know how to get rid of the feeling. She knew it wasn't anyone's fault, but it was there, and it seemed like all she could do was try to stifle it.

'That's excellent news,' Ana was saying, 'because I need you to come to this party tomorrow. It'll be so boring without you.'

'If you think it'll be boring, then don't go.'

'I have to go! I arranged it all, and it's going to be the greatest party ever.'

'Then go! You don't need me to come.'

'I do, I do need you to come, because what if Marcus doesn't realise I want to flirt with him and I look like an idiot?'

For a moment, Sarah was distracted from her own sense of claustrophobia. She stared at Ana. 'You want to flirt with Marcus?' she said.

'Yeah, have you not seen him? He's really grown up well, it's astonishing.'

'I'm not sure you'll have much in common. All he ever talks about is fishing.'

'I'm not looking for a husband, Sarah. I'm looking for fun.'

Sarah smirked a little. 'Well, I hope you find it. I'm not optimistic, but maybe I'm wrong.'

'I'm sure you are. But come, please. It will be so much more fun with you there.'

Sarah sighed. 'No, I don't know, it feels weird. And if you're going to abandon me for a guy all night—'

'I won't abandon you all night.'

'It just feels wrong.'

Ana rolled her eyes, but didn't push it. 'Well,' she said. 'Maybe you should come over some night next week. We can have a sleepover, like we used to. You should do something fun. Every so often.'

Sarah gave a small smile. She knew Ana was trying to help, even if it did feel like the wrong tactic to adopt. 'Maybe. I don't know.'

'I'm telling you,' said Ana. 'This angst is unsustainable. You must be exhausted.'

Sarah actually laughed at that, and Ana beamed in triumph. Maybe she was getting somewhere, after all.

Elliot came out of a house in front of them as they walked. He looked excited, but he approached them a bit warily. Sarah noticed how furtively he glanced up at her, and felt a drop of guilt in the pit of her stomach. Was he scared of her?

'Ewan's cat had her kittens,' he said. 'I picked one out, but it's too young to leave its mother yet.'

'Oh,' said Sarah. 'That's nice.'

'I haven't thought of a name yet, though.'

'Well, I guess you have time.'

Elliot smiled a little. 'Yeah.' There was a brief silence and then he said, 'Well. See you later.'

Ana stood there staring from Sarah to Elliot's retreating back for a moment. 'Oh my god, I thought you liked your brother,' she said.

'I do like my brother.'

'Then why are you talking to him like he's some hated uncle and your mums have told you to mind your manners?'

'For Christ's sake, Ana, I was being nice.'

'You were not being nice; you were being polite.'

'What's the difference?'

'Oh, come on, you know the difference. You're way better at English than I am, and *I* know the difference.'

Sarah let out a groan. 'Ah, leave me alone, Ana. I'm trying.'

'Yes,' said Ana, with a very straight face, 'you clearly are. Great effort. Solid try.'

Sarah looked a little embarrassed and rolled her eyes. 'I'm definitely not coming to your party now,' she said.

'Sure you're not,' said Ana, and she winked at Sarah before walking away.

The Planes

Elliot had seen the first plane, but no one believed him.

After days of the storm battering the house, the strange stillness of a peaceful night unsettled him. He'd had a fitful night of sleep and woken up in the early hours of the morning, as the sun was just starting to rise over the ocean. He'd gone to the kitchen for a glass of water, and as he drank it, gazing out of the window, he saw the plane. It had a plume of smoke trailing behind it as it swept across the sky at the wrong angle.

He stood frozen for a moment as it disappeared over the horizon. His mind struggled to take in what he'd seen. He stared at the now-empty sky, trying to find some proof of what had been there just moments before, but the plane was gone, the smoke had dissipated, and there was no trace left to see.

Elliot realised after a moment that he was breathing hard and his hands were shaking. He swallowed hard and tried to calm himself down. Tears prickled his eyes as he turned towards his parents' bedroom.

Moth and Mam were concerned when he woke them up crying, but they didn't take him seriously. *It was a dream,* they said. *It's OK, you're awake now. It was just a dream.*

But Elliot knew it had been real. He'd really seen it, and now the image wouldn't leave his mind.

Greta was opening the shop for the day when the second plane fell. She felt for a moment as if she wasn't standing on solid ground, as if suddenly, just for a moment, she was being suspended in the air by some unknown force. But it was only for a moment, and then reality snapped back into focus around her. She yelled and pointed, and those villagers who were out on the streets early turned to watch with her, falling silent as they gazed together at the horror in the skies.

The plane twisted in the air, rolling over and over as it carved a path towards the earth. It seemed to last for hours. Greta felt tears streaming down her face as she watched its doomed journey. She was terrified that it would plummet into the sea in front of them, but its arc through the sky was deceptive and it vanished over the horizon instead.

But she knew what it must have looked like when it finally hit the ground.

They saw two others fall out of the sky that day. And then they never saw a plane again.

Chapter Six

Sarah was sure she wasn't going to go to Ana's party, until suddenly it was seven at night as she was walking down the beach towards it. There were already quite a few people around, but it was still pretty low-key. The sun wasn't yet starting to set – it hung above the low hills on the west of the island, throwing shadows across the sand.

The bonfire had been laid but not yet lit, and a few people were hanging around it, suggesting minor adjustments to its structure to better ensure a good blaze. The day had been hot but the ocean breeze was beginning to cut through. Sarah pulled on a flannel shirt over her crop top. She could see Ana chatting to a couple of guys near the trestle that had been put out for food, but she didn't go over to talk to her. She went to get herself something to drink and Tommy Bradford, who was doing the same thing, handed her a beer, before grabbing one for himself. *He's only seventeen,* Sarah thought to herself. *He's too young to be drinking.*

Then it occurred to her that maybe there was no legal drinking age anymore. If there was no state to enforce the laws, then there were no laws. She wondered idly what would happen if she started throwing rocks through people's windows. If she stole something. If she stole a pig. Probably there would be another village meeting, to decide what was to be done with her. Or to her.

She'd been sitting there on her own for around ten minutes when she felt someone sit beside her. It was Ana.

'I didn't think you were going to come,' she said, with a grin.

'Yeah,' said Sarah. 'Neither did I.'

'I'm glad you did.'

Sarah was silent for a moment or two. She took a sip of her beer. 'I still think it's weird,' she said, 'but what else is there to do, I guess.'

Ana laughed a little. 'I should be offended that you've only come to the party I spent all week organising because you couldn't think of anything else to do,' she said. She bit her lip, looking down at the sand. 'I'm not trying to be disrespectful or anything, you know. I just . . . I just think it will be good for everyone to pretend for a night. Pretend that everything is OK, you know? Tomorrow, we'll remember that everything's awful.'

Sarah bit back a reply. She didn't want to keep brushing her jagged edges up against her friends and family. She had to be better. 'Are you having a good time?' she asked.

'Just about,' said Ana. She turned and looked around at the growing crowd and smiled. 'Part of me was convinced no one would actually show up. That it'd just be me, a massive speaker and a giant pile of beer.'

Sarah gave a small laugh. 'Come on,' she said. 'You've always been good at this kind of thing. And I guess you were right. People wanted a chance to blow off some steam.'

As they sat chatting, Sarah slowly felt herself relaxing a little into the atmosphere. She was almost happy to be there. Almost.

She'd missed this, she realised. She hadn't been doing it con-sciously, but she'd been avoiding Ana –she'd been avoiding all her friends – and she didn't really know why. But now, even though she couldn't forget, not the way everyone else seemed to be forgetting, part of her couldn't resist letting herself act a little bit like everything was fine. Maybe if she tried to act like life was normal, it would start feeling normal.

'Well,' said Ana, 'I can't sit here chatting to you all night. I mean, I could, but it won't help me explore Marcus Brown's back teeth.'

'Gross,' said Sarah, while Ana waggled her eyebrows at her. 'Is that your only goal for this party?'

Ana shrugged as she stood up, brushing sand from her jeans. 'Well,' she said, 'one of them. I promise not to leave you alone all night.'

She gave Sarah's head a tousle and walked off towards the group of boys who were starting to light the bonfire.

Sarah did try. She really did. She chatted to a few of her friends, to a few people she didn't know so well.

Beth was there, the nurse from her mam's work.

She'd only recently started to feel like a friend, instead of an adult. And Sarah liked having a friend who was a bit older, who could give her advice without feeling like she was dictating to her.

Beth joined Sarah on the sand and passed her a drink. 'I thought yours might be empty,' she said, as she sat.

'Thanks,' said Sarah.

They sat for a few minutes.

'Seems like some of the kids here are too young to be

79

drinking,' Beth said. 'But I have to say, it's hard to care. I mean, is there even a drinking age anymore?'

Sarah turned to look at her. 'I was just thinking that. Like, who's going to do anything about it?'

'As opposed to all the serious responses to under-age drinking that used to happen here,' Beth said, smiling.

'Sure, but what about other crimes? If someone graffitis the wall of the pub, or steals someone's jewels, or beats a person up – what'll we do?'

'Are you thinking of doing any of those things?'

'No,' said Sarah. 'I mean, yes. I don't think about actually doing them, you know, but I've *thought* about doing them. You know what I mean?'

'Sure,' said Beth. 'A fantasy is not a crime.'

'But what I mean is, are we just not falling into chaos so far because we haven't brushed up against the thing that would make us? If someone did do something, something serious, and the rest of us tried to, I don't know, mete out justice or whatever, what would happen? No one really has any authority. People would protest, you know?'

Beth smiled. 'Are you afraid we'll take a turn for the *Lord of the Flies*?'

'No,' said Sarah. 'I don't think so. But, well . . . we could, I guess.'

'Personally, I don't think human beings are that prone to falling into chaos. It makes for a more entertaining story if we are, of course. But I don't know, I think we crave stability. And we know that, in the end, stability requires cooperation. As long as we can feel like the people around us are looking out for us, we tend to trundle along together pretty well.'

Sarah didn't know how to tell her that it was the trundling along together that was infuriating her. The bland acceptance. She said something noncommittal and got up to walk away. She didn't know if she was walking away to find a different bit of the party or if she was walking away to leave it, but she realised as soon as she stood that she was drunker than she'd realised.

She stumbled a bit as her body got used to being upright, and then she went to get another drink. It felt good, she decided. She felt like things were loosening. She'd been trying to keep her bitterness wrapped up tight within herself – it was a strain. Maybe Ana had been right. Maybe she should embrace the feeling that the strain was easing, at least for a bit.

It felt good to be walking, too. To have the heat of the fire on one side and the cool sea air on the other. Sarah felt more vital than she had in weeks; she could feel the blood moving under her skin.

She walked with no real destination. Her path took her along the beach and back again, the music fading and rising as she went, passing the fire again and again.

People kept trying to talk to her as she walked, a group of younger boys kept pestering her to tell them about the arm she'd found, what it had looked like, what it had felt like to touch. She told them to back off and kept walking.

A couple of her friends came up and started talking about what they were wearing, what they were doing with their hair, and Sarah ignored them, letting them bob around her chattering as she walked and drank.

The music was louder now, and faster. People were dancing, barefoot in the sand, letting their arms wave in the air. There were couples making out dotted around the place – Sarah could see Ana and Marcus together, dancing more slowly than the music demanded.

People were having fun. People were having so much fun. Why couldn't she? She didn't want to be this miserable. She could feel anger curling within her, and she didn't want it to be there. But it was. Maybe if she kept drinking, if she kept loosening up, she'd figure out how to have fun again. But it started to become clear that as she drank more, the resentment she'd been trying to keep buried was clawing its way free. She wasn't having fun. She kept stewing and drinking and walking, and with each passing moment, another tendril of rage broke free.

Sarah had never felt so alone. So separated from the people around her.

The pounding rhythm of the music didn't match the discord flowing in her blood. The sight of her friends dancing felt distant, like it was happening on a screen somewhere, instead of all around her.

She felt like she was slightly out of time and space, like she'd been knocked into a different dimension from everyone else. She walked slowly across the sand, the music getting louder and more discordant in her ears, the bass vibrating against her feet.

She wasn't really aware of where she was going until she got there. And then she was standing in front of the speakers, which were set on a table just where the sand met the grass. She reached out a hand and pressed it to the side, feeling the sound waves ripple up her arm and into her chest. And suddenly she was pushing with all her might, sending one speaker crashing into the other before they both toppled forwards into the sand. There was a great screech, and then silence.

A wave of confusion swept over the dancers, over the couples making out in the dunes, and one by one people turned to stare.

Sarah stood there for a moment, frozen and breathless. Then, out of nowhere, she was yelling. 'What are you all doing? What are you doing? Dancing and kissing and acting like it's normal to be dancing and kissing? Don't you understand? We're all trapped here! I was supposed to be leaving, I was getting out of here, and now I'm just stuck here forever. We're all just stuck here forever until we die. What the fuck is there to dance about?' She took a step forward, lost her balance, and stumbled on to her knees.

And then Beth was beside her, helping her up. 'Come on, kid,' she was saying. 'I'll help you get home.'

Sarah let Beth lead her away from the crowd, tears streaming down her face.

The Sky

It wasn't until mid-afternoon that the residents of Black Crag noticed what was happening to the sky. There was already enough to talk about.

The remnants of the storm were still being swept away. There were still people spinning the dials of their radios, hoping to find a station that was working. The image of planes spinning through the air was still playing in their minds.

And then they noticed the horizon to the east had a strange green blooming above it. It hovered hazily at the edge of the world, and it was several hours before anyone would notice it was growing. Spreading upwards slowly, shimmering slightly as it expanded.

Over the coming weeks and months, Black Crag marked the progress of the green across the sky, wondering but not asking what it meant. Wondering if it would reach their shores and what would happen if it did. Why it didn't hide behind the clouds the way the blue sky did, but instead hovered in front of them.

But eventually its progress slowed and then stopped. People stopped talking about it. They may have even stopped thinking about it. It just became a thing that was, and needed no remarking upon.

It almost became a thing they forgot to see. So it was a while, in the end, before anyone noticed that the green stain in the sky had started shrinking.

Chapter Seven

Sarah woke up slowly and then suddenly. The memory of the previous night seeped into her mind, and she turned over and buried her face in her pillow. Her head was throbbing and a steel ball of shame sank into the pit of her stomach.

There was one place left on earth to live, and she was making it her own personal hell. She turned over and the sun hit her eyes, coming in low through her window. It was still early. She could sleep for another couple of hours. She *should* sleep for another couple of hours.

She got up.

The house was still quiet as she walked through it. She looked into the kitchen, and her mam was sitting there with a cup of coffee and a book. Sarah waved good morning but avoided her eye. She had to have heard Beth deposit Sarah at home in the middle of the night, and Sarah was not ready to find out what either of her parents thought about that. Sarah headed to the drawer under the sink. She pulled out a roll of rubbish bags and headed out of the front door.

The day was already warm as she walked down towards the beach, and too bright for her state of mind. But she kept going. She couldn't think of anything else to do.

The remnants of the bonfire lay black and charred on the sand, with a circle of abandoned bottles and paper cups spreading out around it. She started with the ones lying dangerously close to the high-tide line and began picking them up.

She wondered idly if letting rubbish be swept into the ocean was another of life's rules that didn't need to be obeyed anymore. Surely the quantity wouldn't be high enough to cause significant damage anymore.

It occurred to her then that they didn't actually know if there had been any effect on sea life after the events. There hadn't been any problems with fishing, and there were still plenty of seabirds around. But surely there had to be some impact.

This was the problem with a disaster, Sarah thought to herself. Every train of thought led back to it. It was exhausting. Depressing. You couldn't so much as clean up after a party without your mind wandering back to it. The situation was Rome, and all roads led to it.

After a while, Sarah noticed she wasn't alone. Ana was picking up rubbish on the other side of the circle. Sarah gave her a small wave and kept working. Slowly, they picked their way towards each other, clearing away the dross, leaving plump rubbish bags sitting in their wake, until they both stood beside the pile of black wood and ash.

Sarah took a moment before she spoke. She chewed her lip a bit. 'Hey,' she said, finally. 'I . . .' She trailed off into silence.

Ana was looking at her with an eyebrow raised, but she didn't say anything.

'I'm . . . you know. I'm sorry.'

'OK,' said Ana. 'Good for you.'

'I didn't mean it, Ana. I was just . . . I was drunk.'

'Right. Well, thanks for helping clean up.' Ana turned and walked away, picking up the full bags as she went.

Sarah started after her. 'Ana,' she said. 'Please! I'm sorry.'

'Yeah,' Ana shouted over her shoulder. 'I heard.' She kept walking, leaving Sarah alone on the beach.

'Where have you been?' Moth asked, as Sarah walked back into the house. 'Your mam said you went out first thing.'

Sarah couldn't meet her eyes. 'I just went to help clean up,' she said. 'After the bonfire.'

She wondered how long it would be before her parents found out what had happened at the party. It was one thing to have come home drunk; she knew they'd understand that part. But the things she'd said . . . she knew moth and mam would be disappointed in her. She felt itchy with shame and with the knowledge that she couldn't hide it.

'Ah, that was nice of you, love. I have to say I'd expected you to stay in bed till noon, after a night out like that.' Moth kept talking as she settled into her chair and pulled out her knitting.

Sarah stood, awkward and ashamed, in the doorway.

'I'm glad you went out, though, and spent some time with your friends. It will have done you the world of good, I'm sure. It's natural, of course, to have been knocked a bit off your axis, to have wanted to spend so much time out on your own, but it's not good for you to be alone so much. You used to be such a social butterfly, you know, always with some grand scheme or other with Ana.'

Sarah didn't answer.

'Me and your mam have been worried about you, you know that. We know this is all a lot to adjust to, and we want to give you space, but we also need to know you're OK, you know? That you're getting through it. It's good to see you joining the world again.'

Sarah stared at her. Moth didn't even seem to notice her choice of words. Or maybe it was deliberate. Maybe in her eyes, Black Crag was the whole world now. Maybe it had been easy for her to accept that everything else was gone.

'Right,' she said, and left Moth to her knitting.

Sarah knew that it wouldn't be long before Moth and Mam knew about the scene she'd made. She knew there was nothing she could do to prevent it. Mam had probably heard it all already, in fact. She was at work with Beth, and Beth would surely have told her everything.

She didn't know what else to do, so she made Moth and Elliot lunch. She cleaned up after them, and then she did the laundry. After that was finished, she cleaned the oven and weeded the herb garden.

She wasn't sure why she was doing all this. It was like a compulsion. Some drive within her to bank good credit so that when the story came out, her family would be kinder to her. Or maybe it was an effort to scrub the guilt from her own mind. To wash away the sickening shame with unwanted acts of service. To cancel out her personal debt to the empty universe.

Or just to make herself feel better.

Mam came back from the surgery at three and didn't say anything about the party, so Sarah made dinner as well. She did the dishes and made everyone a cup of tea. She didn't complain when Elliot begged to play a board game.

She caught Moth and Mam looking at each other a couple

of times, but neither of them said anything until they got up to get ready for bed.

'Everything OK, kid?' Mam said mildly.

'Sure,' said Sarah. 'Everything's fine.'

She went to bed feeling completely hollowed out.

It wasn't until Monday evening that anyone mentioned the party to Sarah again. She didn't know if it had taken them that long to hear about it, or if they'd just decided not to mention it immediately. In the intervening time, Sarah had preserved six jars of nectarines and four of plums. She'd darned everything that had been sitting in the to-be-mended pile for the last six months, and she'd baked a loaf of bread.

It was almost starting to help. The rhythm of making things, of fixing things, was beginning to soothe her somehow. She felt lighter, calmer.

After dinner, Moth sent Elliot away with one of the books on his summer reading list. She'd given all the kids in school a reading list for the summer; she was insisting that they'd return to classes in the autumn as usual. Sarah wasn't sure if that was because she wanted to distract herself or the children.

After Elliot had left the room, Moth turned to Sarah and said, 'Is there anything you want to talk to us about, love?'

Sarah bit her lip but didn't reply immediately.

After a moment, Mam said, 'We heard—'

'Yeah, I know what you heard,' said Sarah.

'Hon,' said Moth, 'I know you're trying. But you have to figure out how to be kinder to people. To yourself. There's no good or right way to react to something like this. But you have to remember that everyone else is trying to deal with it too. This isn't something that's only happening to you.'

'Everyone else seems to be dealing with it just fine.'

'I promise you they're not,' said Mam. 'Why do you think I've been working so much? It's not like there's a flu going around.'

Sarah was silent.

'Everyone has their own way of getting through each day,' Mam continued. 'But that's what we're all doing. Just trying to get through each day. And it's easier when we help each other to do that.'

'We're so lucky, really,' Moth said. 'We're all here, our whole family. Our whole community. We're all still here, and we all still have each other.'

'It's like you've just forgotten about all your friends from before,' said Sarah.

Moth sighed. 'Of course I haven't. But I need to get out of bed every day too, and it's helpful to remember that I still have you. We still have our lives here. We can keep going.'

Moth's words fell into the empty pit in Sarah's stomach and sat there.

'But what's the point,' she said, 'if this is all there is now? If there's nothing left out there.'

Moth and Mam looked at each other. They didn't say anything as Sarah stood and left the room. She knew there was nothing they could say.

The Ferryman

It had been nearing dusk when someone noticed the ferry. That late dusk of the early summer, with the sun taking hours to gently lower itself through the sky.

There was an air of unreality in the village. Hushed disbelief had settled over the streets, occasionally spilling out into panicked speculation. Some had tried to call friends and family on the mainland, but the phone lines seemed to be out as well as the radio, and the line just rang endlessly. Some people couldn't bear to hang up, instead leaving the phone off the hook, with the faint sound of ringing still emanating from it.

There was a collection of people in the village centre, talking to no purpose. Wondering what they should do, when they could expect to hear news, how they could learn more. But some had chosen to shut their doors to the unknown, to stay inside, away from everyone, refusing to engage in the conversation, nurturing their fear in private.

No one really noticed the time passing. No one noticed the light beginning to fade from the sky, the long day of dead radios and falling planes coming to a close. But it was beginning to get dark when someone pointed at the water and said, 'Is that Arthur?'

It was the wrong day for the ferry. The wrong time for it. It arrived every Tuesday and Friday at 11am and departed for the mainland at 2pm. The ferry coming at the wrong time, on the wrong day, was the least of the strange things that had happened that day, but it was the one that galvanised the most people.

Word spread quickly and a crowd was soon gathered on the jetty, watching the slow progress of the boat through the water. There was a new energy – not hope, exactly, but a crackling, restless anticipation. Someone was coming, someone who'd been there, someone who would be able to tell them what had happened, if they were safe, if there was anything they needed to be doing in response to the events of the day.

For a while, that anticipation hummed through the crowd. All eyes were trained on the slow progress of the ferry. But as it drew gradually closer, it became clear that something wasn't right.

'It's listing!' someone yelled – and it was. It leaned gently to the right as it carved its way through the choppy water.

The crackle of impatience shifted into an intense debate. Was the ferry sinking further as it moved? Would it make it to the island at all? Did Arthur and whoever else was on board with him need help?

It was Thomas who broke off the argument, grabbing one of the other young men, Charlie, and striding towards the rowing boats that lined the cove. Gasps rang through the assembled crowd as the two men dragged a boat out onto the water before leaping into it and rowing towards the ferry.

By the time they began to close in on it, it was clear that the ferry was sinking fast. One of the boys – Marcus, it was – dashed off up the main street, and returned a few minutes later with a pair of binoculars.

'They've reached the ferry,' he said. 'Thomas is climbing aboard. Jeez, it's taking on loads of water.'

'Who's on it?' someone yelled.

'I can't see anyone,' said Marcus. 'I can't even see Thomas any— wait, there he is! He's with Arthur. He's bringing Arthur to the rowing boat.'

'They don't have much time,' someone else said. 'If the boat doesn't get away from the ferry soon, it could be sucked down with it.'

The crowd watched breathlessly, straining to make out the distant figures. For a few moments, fear for Arthur crowded out the larger, stranger fear of what had happened on the mainland, until Marcus finally announced that he and Thomas had made it to the rowing boat, which was now moving back towards the shore.

As it happened, the ferry didn't sink until Charlie, Thomas and Arthur were almost back to the jetty. Thomas and Arthur were both soaking wet, having had to jump into the sea in order to get to the rowing boat.

The moment they walked ashore, the villagers crowded around Arthur, flinging question after question at him.

'Leave him!' Thomas shouted, an arm around Arthur's shoulder as he tried to get him through the crowd. 'Look at him; he's all in pieces. Give the man a chance to recover.'

A hush fell over everyone. The minute they looked properly at Arthur, it was obvious that Thomas was right. The ferryman was pale and gaunt-looking, leaning heavily on Thomas. His eyes were wide and staring; it wasn't clear if he was even taking in the people around him.

It was a stark contrast to the gentle, cheerful man they knew.

Arthur had never been particularly garrulous, but he always had a smile for everyone. He was a comfortable person to be around, the kind of man whose company felt restful. Calming. Now there was a tense, nervous energy pouring forth from him. He was grasping Thomas's shoulder but he gave no sign of recognising him, or anyone around him.

'Who has a bed for him?' Thomas demanded. 'And where's the goddamn doctor when she's needed?'

He didn't leave Arthur's side until he was safely installed in Malcolm's spare bed, with Billie leaning over him, checking his vitals. For the next few hours, a handful of people circled around, looking after him. Malcolm, Thomas, Billie and Beth came and went, talking to each other in hushed tones, worried frowns creasing their foreheads.

The rest of the village buzzed with desperate speculation. This was their first chance to find out what had happened on the other side. Finally, they would know how catastrophic a situation they were in. They would know if there were other survivors; they would know how long they'd have to wait before they could go back to the mainland, or before other people came here.

But it soon became clear that their questions wouldn't be answered that night. Or, as it turned out, the next day. Arthur didn't reappear. As the days passed, the tension among the villagers didn't ease. The collective attention was focused on the small room above the pub, everyone was on edge, wondering how long they would have to wait before they got answers.

The team around Arthur acted as a protective wall. He wasn't well enough to see anyone, they said; he needed rest and quiet. They didn't know when he'd be up to seeing anyone other than themselves.

But they couldn't stop people speculating, and as the days passed, rumours spread swiftly around the island. Finally, Billie called a village meeting to address them.

'In normal times,' she said, once everyone had assembled, 'I wouldn't acknowledge speculation about one of my patients at all. A person's health is no one's concern but their own. But, well, these times are not normal, and I'm concerned about the effect of this on everyone else's health also. It's not good to be this anxious and keyed up for this long.' She looked around the room and sighed. 'The truth is it will be some time before Arthur can give us any idea of what he saw on the mainland. In fact, he may never be able to tell us anything at all. He is currently unable to speak.'

A ripple of shock blazed through the crowd.

Billie continued speaking. 'I don't want to contribute to further speculation – speculation that will, no doubt, only increase the anxiety we are all currently living with. But you all have a right to the truth about our situation. What little truth we have.

'It's clear that Arthur has been deeply traumatised. He has been physically weakened by his exertions, but he is recovering well from that. His psychological health is another matter entirely, and I cannot say with any certainty whether he will ever be able to tell us what happened to him.'

A stunned silence settled over the room.

Billie passed a hand over her face before she went on. 'I know you all know that Arthur has a family. A wife, children, grandchildren. He is obviously unable to tell us what has happened to them. We asked if they needed help, if we could try and get to them, but . . .' Billie's voice cracked briefly, and she seemed to struggle for words. After a moment she took a breath and straightened her back. 'Based on how he reacted to that question, we believe there is nothing to be done for them.'

Someone somewhere in the room was crying.

'I know that you were all – that *we* were all hoping to be able to learn something from Arthur. I'm sorry to have to tell you that that's likely not going to happen.

'The only thing left to say is to ask that you all keep him in your thoughts and that, when he is able to leave his room and join in a bit more with the rest of us, you treat him with kindness and patience. We have already put a lot of hard questions to him, questions that caused him a great amount of distress. Please consider your own questions already asked. Don't press him for more.

'He cannot help us.'

Chapter Eight

There was something about the fact that it had happened at the beginning of summer that had made it all feel temporary. Summer was always a step removed from routine, a small suspension of normal life. The children were on holiday, the crops were sown and growing, even those whose jobs didn't change from season to season found it easy to clock off early and enjoy the weather.

So it had been easy to believe that in the autumn, normal life, normal routines would return. No one necessarily put it into words, the assumption that there would be a resolution as the weather cooled. No one had a specific picture – just a vague idea, a dream of some international search-and-rescue team combing the country to find survivors finally reaching Black Crag on the first of September, just as the school children were sharpening their pencils.

But as summer drew nearer to its close, the radios stayed silent and the skies stayed empty.

Graeme saw the first leaves begin to turn and grew worried. He'd known this was coming; he should have started preparing sooner. But somehow, he'd still had hope. He still couldn't quite shake the feeling that any day now, the static on his radio would shift into speech. There would be news of the event, of rescue missions, of searches for survivors. A boat would appear on the horizon.

They would find out they weren't all alone after all.

Well, the feeling wouldn't leave him, but it started to feel less like hope and more like desperation. Impotent railing against the cold certainty that no one was coming to save them.

He knew he needed to ignore that hope. He knew he would have to be practical. If no one was coming now, then he would have to start acting on the assumption that no one was coming at all. It was the only way to survive.

He would have to call a meeting. He knew it wouldn't be popular, but Black Crag had to face reality, and if no one else was willing to say that, then he would have to be.

He put the word out, asking people to meet early that evening, and then set out to survey his farm.

He'd always loved walking through his fields. He'd grown up on his farm, started working on it when he was just a kid, when his grandfather was still alive. There was something grounding about it, about looking out over a field of crops and knowing that, year after year, he'd tended that patch of earth. And before him, his grandfather.

Graeme's farm was varied. There were a few fields of wheat, and some of corn. He had tomato vines and cucumber patches, and several varieties of potato. In recent years, he'd even dedicated a small corner to chilies, although he hadn't had great return on that yet. This wasn't surprising to him; he'd known it would be difficult, given the climate. But he'd always liked a challenge.

It had always brought him peace, surveying his farm, but today there was a crease of worry on his well-lined forehead.

He brushed a hand over the heads of golden wheat and felt a throb of sadness well up within him. It was petty, he knew, but it was real.

Within all the great grief of the past weeks, there were small things to grieve as well.

At five thirty, there was a reasonable number of people assembled, so Graeme decided to get things started.

He stood at the front of the room, looking out on the faces that were turned to him, and wished at his core that he didn't have to do this. That he didn't have to be the one to do this.

Well. It had to be someone.

He cleared his throat and started talking.

'As I'm sure you all know,' he said, 'summer is nearly over. Ordinarily, at this time of year, we would have seasonal workers starting to arrive. Maybe as many as a hundred people would be due to come and help us with our harvests. But they're not coming.'

'So what?' a voice rang out from the back. 'What's the point of harvesting anyway? It's not like we can sell anything.'

Graeme sighed. 'The food we grow on this island is now the only food we have to survive on. Harvesting it is even more important this year than it has been before.

'Now, there are, of course, some crops that are functionally useless to us. We do not have the tools to mill the wheat, for example, so most of that will be wasted.'

He felt that throb of grief saying it aloud. It would be a bitter pill to see so much of his work rot in the fields. He took a deep breath and continued.

'But the rest of it – the vegetables, the fruit – will all have to be harvested and preserved. And . . .' Graeme hesitated for a moment. 'We're going to have to decide on a rationing system for the winter.'

Someone sat forward in the front row. Thomas. It had been a while since Graeme had talked to him properly, although there had been a time when they were almost friends. Thomas had moved to Black Crag five or six years earlier, bought a farm to the south of the village. He'd had some trouble with his crops for the first couple of years, and Graeme had tried to help him out. Eventually, Thomas had stopped coming to him for advice and Graeme had left him to it.

In recent weeks, he'd become one of the loudest voices claiming they should be trying to reach the mainland. Graeme was starting to worry about the tension growing within that debate, but he was trying not to get involved. The way he saw it, his role was to make sure the village was able to survive the immediate future.

'Why are you in charge of rationing our food?' Thomas was saying.

'I didn't say I would be in charge of it. Just that it's something we need to do. There'll be no shipments from the mainland, so all we'll have to eat is what we've been growing here. And we should start planning now, so that as we harvest, we can put aside what we'll need to save.'

'What, you don't trust us enough to let us keep making our own decisions? You think we'll just rip through the food without your oversight?'

'This isn't about trust,' Graeme said. 'This is about care. It's possible we can survive the winter without it. But I think most of us would rather be certain. We can't bring in food from the outside anymore. All we have is ourselves.'

Thomas stood up. 'We don't know that.'

'What?' said Graham.

'We don't know that we can't get to the mainland. We haven't even tried. Because some craven weakling stopped us.'

An uneasy stir passed around the room. What had happened to the boats was naturally of massive importance, but Graeme had put it to the back of his mind, choosing instead to focus on what needed to be done on the island.

'I think it is wise to assume that it's not safe to cross to the mainland, even if we did still have an easy means of getting there.'

'It's cowardly, that's what it is. We're all sitting here happily accepting a situation we have no actual knowledge of.' Thomas turned to face the crowd. 'It's crazy. We should be trying to get there. Trying to find out what the situation actually is. Figuring out where we can get the things we're going to need.'

A hush fell upon the crowd. It seemed like Thomas was determined to drag this debate out into the public. As if they didn't know what everyone thought by now, after weeks and weeks of arguments all over the village.

'But the arm,' someone said from the middle of the room, followed by 'Yeah, there could be a disease out there,' from someone else.

'Arthur doesn't have a disease,' another voice chimed in.

'Yeah, but he's not exactly a ball of health,' someone in the back said. 'He's right, we just don't know.'

'Inconvenient that he can't just tell us, really,' said a voice to the side.

Thomas turned sharply, scowling. 'Inconvenient?' he yelled. 'That man is traumatised by whatever happened over there, and you call it inconvenient? The fact that we can all see the state he's in and still no one seems to think we need to investigate the mainland is exactly the problem.'

Graeme could feel the panic and anger rising in the room.

'Look, everyone,' he said, but the arguments continued over him. 'People!' he yelled. Slowly the hubbub died down.

Graeme waited for a moment, looking over his neighbours, his friends, as they quietened down. 'Of course, it's true that we don't know what it's like over there. But we do know that we're safe here. And for now, that safety should be our priority.'

'You don't get to decide for all of us,' said Thomas.

'I don't,' said Graeme. 'But we have limited resources. The ferry went down. Most of the boats are gone.'

'Not all of them.'

'We have a couple of rowing boats. They're not safe on the open sea – and even if they were, you couldn't row all that distance.'

'We can try the road.'

'We can, but we'd need to survey it. No one's used it in decades; there's no telling if it's still passable.' Graeme held up a hand as Thomas opened his mouth to respond again. 'I'm not saying there's nothing for us to learn out there. I'm not saying that at some point we shouldn't try to reach the mainland. Just that we have other priorities. We need to make it through the winter.'

'So you expect us to wait six months before we try.'

'I think that's wise. We can use that time to plan. To think about the risks, figure out the safest course of action.'

Thomas scoffed. 'A waste of time,' he said.

Graeme was close to losing his temper. 'Are you actually proposing we row to the mainland?'

Someone yelled from the back, 'There's old Patrick's sailing boat. It wasn't on the dock; it didn't get burned up.'

Graeme sighed. Patrick had died six years earlier, a solid decade after arthritis had put an end to his sailing career. His boat had sat at the jetty for years, until someone had noticed that it was listing to the side, and pulled it out of the water. Ever since, it had been on struts outside the pub, gently rotting away.

Graeme hadn't looked at the boat up close, but the sail was all but gone, and he was sure there was extensive damage to the hull.

He restrained himself from dismissing the suggestion out of hand, however. There was no need to get into a fight over nothing. 'There *is* old Patrick's sailing boat,' he said. 'I'm no expert on boats, but I think some extensive repair work will need to be done to make sure it is seaworthy.'

He glanced over at Thomas, who was still looking mulish, but didn't say anything.

'If there are some among you who would like to volunteer to assess the boat and carry out repairs so that we have that option available to us, I'm sure that would be fine.'

'We don't need your permission,' Thomas muttered.

'Indeed you don't,' said Graeme mildly. 'Now, if we agree that the sailing boat will be assessed and repaired, so that those who wish to travel to the mainland have a means of doing so' – he glanced at Thomas, who glared at him, but sat back down – 'let's move on to how we can manage the harvest, and storing food for the winter.'

*　　*　　*

Graeme was exhausted by the time he got home. He'd lived alone since the death of his wife four years earlier. He still wasn't used to it. He and Meg had been married for more than thirty years. It wasn't the same world without her, although he couldn't help but feel that she had been lucky to be spared all this.

But part of him was desperate for her company. Desperate for someone with whom he could talk through his own worries and fears.

He felt himself to be one of the community's elders. He knew there were people who looked to him for guidance, and he took that responsibility very seriously. He felt compelled to provide a sense of stability within the village.

Even if that sense of stability was a lie.

Graeme sighed heavily as he sat down to his solitary meal. It may be a mystery, what had happened over on the mainland, but one thing was certain. The world was in chaos.

He did not think it was safe to try and reach the mainland. There was no telling what was over there, or what exposure to it might do to a person. But then it wasn't safe to stay here, either. There was no reason to be sure that whatever had happened was over. That it wouldn't continue, that it wouldn't eventually reach them here.

It had always been true, really, he knew. Life was a vulnerable thing. It always had been. We trick ourselves into believing it isn't, and then every so often something happens to remind us we are feeble, brittle creatures, and we have to learn to forget again.

Because who can make it through the day constantly aware of how easily they can be broken?

Graeme felt it fell to him to help his neighbours forget their fragility. He felt he could be a steadying influence. Someone people could look to who could make them feel like things would be OK. Like they were safe. A reason to stay calm enough to keep going.

That way, maybe some of them would survive.

But without Meg, there was no one to make him feel safe himself. No one to hear his fears and convince him they were unfounded, even if just for a little while.

Graeme finished his dinner and carried his plate to the sink. He washed up carefully, and wiped the dishes dry before putting them away. He wiped down the table, even though there was no sign of crumbs or spills.

He took out the ledger he'd made of the villagers who'd volunteered to help lead the harvest planning. They'd agreed on a time for a meeting, so all he had to do was write up an agenda and copy it out for each of them.

He decided he would also begin drawing up a list of each farm and its crops, noting expected yields. Then he organised them by what would have to be left in the ground, what could be harvested but not preserved, and what could be kept for the long, hard months of winter.

It was nice to have something to do.

The Boats

The village of Black Crag had been woken by a roar in the air. It wasn't close, but it was loud. The roar was accompanied by a smell – acrid and bitter. The villagers scrambled out of their beds, pulling jackets and shoes on over their pyjamas, running outside, their shouts waking those who were still asleep in a domino run of alarm.

Out in the street, people scrambled in and out of each other's way, spinning on their heels to see what was happening, eventually joining the stream of their neighbours who were already heading towards the roar. Towards the glow over the water.

It looked almost like the sun was rising – but the sun was already up. It was early summer; the days were long.

It wasn't until you were almost at the shore that you'd notice that the heat on your face wasn't from the sun either. The villagers were jostling around each other to get a glimpse of what was happening, and a hush fell over the crowd as more and more people saw.

Every single boat that was moored to the dock was on fire. A few people were already trying to fight the flames, but it was clearly too hot for them to get close enough to have any real impact. It seemed like the ocean would put out the fires before anyone else had a chance to, as each boat finally sank.

Eventually, someone found and connected a hose, and sent a stream of water towards one of the boats. The villagers stood for what felt like hours, watching the flames die down. More than one of the boats sank before the hose ever reached them. The ones that remained listed sadly, promising to sink alongside their fellows if left on the water.

For a while, there was a hum of energy and activity as the crowd of people pulled the remaining boats up on to the beach, but once they were all safely out of reach of the tides, the atmosphere shifted.

There were only five boats left, and they were all clearly far from seaworthy. They seemed to be completely beyond repair. A chill spread through the crowd, despite the summer heat.

Chapter Nine

'So,' Sarah heard a voice say behind her. 'I heard about the party.'

She turned. It was Nathaniel.

'Are you following me again?' she asked, crossing her arms. She'd been thinking of taking her sketchbook to the fens. It had been a while since she'd painted anything. But she'd been dawdling. Somehow, she didn't feel like she had the energy.

Nathaniel was looking at her, a quizzical expression on his face. 'I should probably apologise,' he said.

'For goading me into a tantrum? The moment's passed.'

'Oh, no, not for that,' he said. 'The opposite. I should have kept going.'

'You should have what?' Sarah said.

'I honestly thought I'd done enough. That I'd helped you clear your head a bit. But clearly I underestimated you.'

'What are you talking about?'

'If I'd done my job right, you wouldn't have lost your shit at the party your best friend spent a week planning for the benefit of our fraught and beleaguered friends and neighbours.'

'It wasn't your job,' Sarah said. *He's so annoying*, she was thinking. *I should be annoyed*. But she wasn't quite. She didn't understand him, and he was infuriating, but there was something about him she found . . . funny.

'OK, so it was volunteer work,' Nathaniel said. 'Pro bono.'

Sarah rolled her eyes. 'So what, you're following me to put in another shift?'

Nathaniel chuckled. 'No. If you're not sorted by now, you're a hopeless case.'

'Oh,' she said. She felt puzzled and a little disappointed.

'But I'll come for a walk with you, if you want some company.'

Sarah shrugged and turned to keep walking as he fell into step beside her.

'Why are you paying so much attention to me, anyway?' she asked.

'Don't know,' said Nathaniel. 'I guess I find you interesting.'

'What, do you have a crush on me or something?' She knew it was a juvenile question, but she blurted it out before she could stop herself without really knowing why. She wasn't sure she was even interested in the answer. She just wanted to shove the conversation into clearer territory.

'No,' he said quickly. 'People can be interested in other people without it being a crush.'

'It's weird, though.'

He laughed outright at that. 'Don't you find yourself interesting?'

'Not particularly.'

'That's awful,' he said. 'Why not?'

Sarah turned her head to stare at him as they made their way through the wheat fields. 'People don't generally find themselves interesting.'

'I don't know about that,' he said. 'I find myself fascinating.'

Sarah laughed and scoffed. 'Oh, you do?'

'Yes,' Nathaniel said genially. 'For instance, I recently started hating caramel. Always loved it before. What's that about? I don't know, but I'm compelled.'

'You don't like caramel. That's what you find so fascinating about yourself.'

'Well, one of the things. I'm sure you could find things too, if you tried.'

'If I tried to find you fascinating?'

'Well,' he said, 'I meant yourself, but you're free to find me fascinating too, if you want.'

'I find you confusing.'

Nathaniel looked over at her with a smug smile. 'Well then, we're halfway there.'

Sarah found herself laughing, but she wasn't sure why. She didn't know anyone who talked like this, and she knew everyone in the village.

She managed to get some ordinary conversation out of him as they walked to the fens and back, but she wouldn't take out her sketchbook in front of him. She couldn't trust him to keep himself to comments like 'That's beautiful,' and she wasn't sure she was ready to hear him wax strange about her art.

It took three weeks for Ana to forgive Sarah for her outburst at the party.

'I mean, what am I going to do?' Ana said, when they ran into each other in the shop one evening. 'Be best friends with Rebecca Thorpe instead? She never stops talking about her pet pig. I wish they'd butcher that thing and be done with it.'

'I'll tell her you said that,' said Sarah, laughing.

'Do,' said Ana. 'Then maybe she'd get so mad at me she'd stop talking to me at all.'

Sarah didn't want to admit how relieved she was that Ana was speaking to her again. She was trying to spend less time on her own, trying to do things with people, and it was a lot harder to do that when your best friend was angry with you and everyone in town knew about it.

They walked together to the jetty and sat with a drink, looking out over the water. The sun was setting behind them, casting a glow across the gentle waves. The days were getting shorter. Soon it would be too cold and dark to spend the evenings outside.

Sarah didn't want to think about the months ahead.

'It's kind of nice it all happened when it did,' she said. 'Not that it happened, obviously. But if it was going to . . .'

'What do you mean?' said Ana.

'Just, I don't know. Imagine if it had happened a couple of months from now instead. Just as the days are getting so short and cold. If we were all stuck inside as well as stuck on the island.'

'God,' said Ana. 'Yeah. I hadn't thought about that. It's depressing enough here in winter as it is.'

'Yeah. So I guess it was nice that we had the summer to get used to it.'

'Sure.'

They were silent for a while.

'I know I was a dick at the party,' Sarah said eventually. 'I know I was drunk and self-involved and I ruined everything. But . . .'

'You are not about to make excuses, right?' Ana said.

'No, I promise. I just . . . Don't you feel that way too? Just a little bit? You used to say you wanted to try living in the city one day. To have a little apartment in the centre of town, to throw parties with more people than space. To go out on the prowl through glamorous cocktail bars. Aren't you upset that you can't anymore? Don't you feel like an entire life was snatched away from you?'

Ana took a sip of her drink and looked out over the water. 'Not really,' she said. 'It's like, I don't know, I used to think I'd be a famous ballerina. And then, of course, I realised that it was too late to start ballet lessons. I'd never catch up with all the kids who'd been dancing since they were four, not if I was just getting started now.'

Sarah laughed. 'I think living in your own flat in the city is a little more realistic a goal than becoming a prima ballerina without ever taking a single lesson.'

'I know, of course, but they both just always felt somehow removed from my own life. Something that other people did. I'm not saying I wouldn't have ever moved to the city, but I probably would have come home after a couple of years. I would always have wanted to come back here to settle down.'

'Oh,' Sarah said. She'd always known Ana wasn't as desperate to leave Black Crag as she was, but she hadn't realised that she barely wanted to leave at all. "I thought . . ." she said, before trailing off.

'You assumed,' said Ana. 'And maybe I let you assume. You were so cool, you know, when you moved her. The girl from the city. Maybe I wanted you to think I was as cool as you.'

'I'm not cool,' said Sarah. She sighed. 'I just always pictured us there together.'

'I know. And we might have been. But you would have stayed and I would have come back.'

Sarah sat in silence for a moment, digesting this.

'I don't hate it here,' Ana said. 'Not like you do. I mean, I'm not saying it's brilliant all the time. I'm not saying I'd never like to try something different. But this is my home. I like it being my home.'

Sarah nodded silently.

'It's not yours,' Ana said. 'You just live here.'

Sarah felt tears spring into her eyes. 'I've never said that,' she said.

'But it's true.'

Sarah knew Ana was right, and she felt a swell of guilt over it. Her family was so happy here. Elliot didn't remember anything else, of course, but even Mam, who'd grown up in the middle of the city, seemed to fit here. It was unsettling to realise that she didn't fit in the same place her family did.

'Well,' she said, 'it doesn't matter anyway. I'm never leaving now.'

'We'll see,' said Ana. Sarah looked at her in surprise, and she laughed. 'Look, this all just happened. We're stuck here for now, but next year, who knows? God, Sarah, we've just seen how suddenly and drastically the whole world can change, and you're here acting like it's never going to change again.'

The orange stain on the ocean started to fade as the sun sank behind the hills to the west, and a chill came into the air.

Ana shivered. 'Pub?' she said, and she and Sarah stood up.

'What happened with Marcus?' Sarah asked, as they walked towards the pub. 'Did you get to explore his teeth, or whatever it was you wanted?'

'I did, actually – and thank you for that.'

'Why thank me?'

'Oh, I was all upset after your tirade at the party, and I turned to him for comfort.'

Sarah burst out laughing. 'Slick,' she said. 'Very slick. How was it?'

Ana shrugged. 'Not bad,' she said. 'Might try again, see if he can't improve with practice.'

'Wow,' said Sarah.

'What? There's nothing else to do around here. It's not like I have cocktail bars to trawl.'

Sarah let herself relax into the evening. A few of her other friends were at the pub, and for the first time it felt comforting, rather than infuriating, to spend a normal evening out.

This might be all we have, she thought to herself. *Maybe I should be trying to enjoy it.*

Sarah woke up the next day to the sound of rain pummelling her window and her brother screaming at her parents down the hall.

'It's not fair,' he was yelling. 'You said I could go!'

Sarah heard Moth's voice in response, but she couldn't make out what she was saying.

'So what?' Elliot shouted back. 'I don't mind a little rain.'

Sarah had got out of bed and crossed to the window. It was significantly more than a bit of rain. It was pelting down outside, with strong gusts of wind appearing to grab the water in mid-air and hurl it around willy-nilly.

She pulled on her dressing gown and walked out into the hall. Elliot brushed past her into his own room, slamming the door.

Somehow, it was refreshing to Sarah. He should have been

throwing more tantrums. Even without the disaster, Elliot should have been making more trouble for their parents. He was fourteen; that was when you were supposed to rail against rules imposed on you.

Sarah blushed at the realisation that all the tantrums in the house over the last few months had been hers. She was supposed to be basically an adult. Old enough to leave home and go to university far away. But Elliot, all hormones and angst, had been an angel. Patient, kind, even to her.

She walked down to the kitchen, where Moth and Mam were making coffee and toast.

Mam raised an eyebrow at Sarah as she came in. 'Elliot wake you up?' she asked.

Sarah nodded. 'Him and the storm,' she said. 'What's he upset about?'

'He wants to go camping,' Moth said.

Sarah stared. 'In this?' she said.

'Apparently,' said Mam.

Moth laughed. 'It's the last weekend of summer,' she said. 'I'm making him start school again on Monday; he wanted one last big adventure with his friends. Never mind that none of their parents will be letting them out in this weather anyway.'

Sarah frowned. 'You don't have to make him start school,' she said. It seemed like a waste of time. Sarah had always loved school, but Elliot was different. He was much more interested in fishing, or in helping out on the farms. Graeme had said once that he was more helpful than any seasonal labourer, because he was so fascinated by the work.

She didn't know why Moth would want to force Elliot to do something he hated when surely it didn't matter anymore if he got a decent education. It would be much more useful for him to learn everything he could about farming.

'I know,' said Moth. 'But I think it's wiser. The kids need a sense of stability. Suddenly abandoning school would only make them more anxious, I think.' She smiled wryly. 'I am willing to abandon the official curriculum, however. Focus on what they enjoy and what's useful here, rather than making anyone do maths they'll never use.'

'What about the kids who want to do maths?'

Moth laughed and then sighed dramatically. 'Then I guess I'll let them. Take one for the team.'

'Anyway,' said Mam, 'they'll have more days off this year. We'll need them to help with the harvest.'

'Oh yeah,' said Sarah. 'I hadn't thought about that.'

'Graeme held a meeting last week. To put together a team to figure out what can be preserved, how to manage the food over the winter.'

Sarah couldn't believe she hadn't thought of that. How would they manage without being able to bring anything over from the mainland?

'Will we have enough?' she asked.

'If we can get it all out of the ground,' said Mam, eyeing her carefully. 'We'll need everyone to help out, of course.' There was an unspoken warning in her words. The time for dealing with this alone was over. Sarah was expected to rally, and start contributing.

If she'd said it a week or two earlier, Sarah was sure she would have flown off the handle. Too much to bear, too much pressure to take. But of course she would help. Everyone would have to help. That was all there was to it: they would each need to do whatever they could to help each other through the winter.

Sarah ate her breakfast and then carried some food up to Elliot's room. She knocked on the door and opened it in response to his surly 'What?'

'Hey,' she said, holding out a plate of toast and a cup of tea. 'Want to play cards?'

Elliot shrugged but let her in. His eyes were red. He suddenly looked very young to Sarah.

They played cards for a couple of hours, and she tried gently to pull him out of his black mood. Slowly, he seemed to relax. Slowly, he grew more invested in the games, laughing at Sarah's stupid mistakes, crowing when he won, demanding rematches when he lost. It occurred to Sarah that she'd missed this.

They played all morning and she barely noticed the time pass, until she suddenly realised she was starving. They packed the cards away for lunch, but as Sarah went to leave the room, Elliot hesitated.

'Sarah,' he said, 'are you scared?'

She looked back at him from the doorway. He was still sitting cross-legged on the floor, holding the pack of cards in his hands.

'Yeah,' she said, 'I'm scared.'

He nodded and looked away. 'I've been trying to pretend everything's normal. But it isn't, is it?'

'No. Nothing's normal.' She smiled sadly. 'But we're still here. We're not going anywhere.'

He nodded. 'I'm sorry,' he said.

Sarah frowned. 'What about? Because you had a freak-out? We're all having freak-outs. I mean, yours was nothing compared to mine. Any of mine.'

'No,' he said. 'I mean, yes, but that's not what I meant. I'm sorry you don't get to go away.'

A wave of affection swelled up in Sarah's chest. 'Yeah,' she said. 'Me too. I'm sorry you don't get to be rid of me.'

Elliot grinned. 'I guess we're stuck with each other.'

'Could be worse,' Sarah said, with a laugh. 'Could be a lot worse.'

Autumn

So it had been like this.

A storm that lasted longer than any storm should.

A plane seen careening drunkenly through the sky.

A sky stained an unnatural hue.

Radios that fell silent. Phones that were dialled but never answered.

A ferry that no longer ran.

A village that used to be part of a country, part of a world, became a world unto itself. People waited for weeks for someone to come, and slowly grew used to the idea that perhaps no one would. They made it through the apocalypse because they were so far removed from the world, and now there was no world but them.

The summer had been hard, heartbreaking. But as autumn began, the certainty that the months to come would be harder, more heartbreaking, seeped through the villagers. They had lived well enough through the warmth. Soon, they would have to survive the cold.

A chill was already felt, brisk sea winds winding through the cobbled streets, finding gaps in windows, making people shiver in anticipation of worse weather to come. But the sun still rose hot and the days were still long.

There was work to be done before despair could be allowed to set in.

Chapter Ten

For some, the return of routine had beckoned like a promise. A way to structure life that made things feel normal. Familiar. Even safe.

Seonaid had been looking forward to being back in the classroom. She'd had plenty to do over the summer, of course; she always did. But no matter how busy she was with planning the term ahead or writing and rewriting syllabuses, no part of the job could keep her mind as full and busy as actually teaching.

She'd always looked forward to coming back to school, but this year it felt even more crucial to her. She'd watched her children struggle over the last couple of months and had felt so powerless. She knew there was no way to navigate this kind of situation, she knew all she could do was be there for them, but it was agony to watch them break like this and have no solution. And she knew that her students were suffering in the same way Sarah and Elliot were.

Starting the school year at the same time and in the same way as every school year before it had started seemed to her like the best way to help the students. The best thing she could do for her community. She could give a sense of stability; she could establish patterns of behaviour that resembled normality.

She felt sure the children would welcome it, and she was certain their parents would. There had been no way to alleviate the strangeness of the summer. The eerie sense of the island being a step out of place or time. People going about their daily lives because they didn't know what else to do, but with an air of bewilderment about them. As if they were a moment away from waking up from a dream.

It was all made harder by the fact that the summer was supposed to be a time of leisure. Relaxation.

There had been moments when Seonaid had considered starting school early, just to get some sense of structure back into the village, but she knew it wouldn't work. It would only contribute to the sense of something amiss. And besides, the schoolhouse didn't have air conditioning, and the summer had been particularly hot that year.

So she'd waited, with more impatience than even her wife knew.

She'd sent notes to all her students a week ahead of term starting, reminding them of the first day of term and giving them a list of what to bring. Granted, there had been no shipments of stationery to the village shop, so they'd all be working a little bit more ruggedly than usual, but she'd done her best to account for that.

She was optimistic when she woke up on the first morning of term. Her daughter had made the family breakfast, and Seonaid found herself asking her if she'd like to come to school as well.

Sarah had just laughed. It had been asking too much, perhaps, but Seonaid had been genuine. Sarah had taken the situation even harder than Elliot, despite her age, but now she seemed to be coming through the other side.

Don't press her, Seonaid thought to herself. *She's nineteen; she has to find her own way.*

She was touched to see Sarah had also made her and Elliot school lunches. Sandwiches, made with the bread she'd baked the day before, an apple each. She'd even found some chocolate.

Seonaid felt settled and optimistic as she and Elliot walked the twenty minutes to school. So it was extremely disappointing to find only three other students there, rattling around the classroom that was built for forty.

For a while, she wasn't sure how to proceed. She'd known some people wouldn't see the point of sending their children back to school, especially the older ones, but she'd been sure that, for the most part, people would be as eager for a return to some semblance of normality as she was.

She looked round her sparse classroom and took a breath. The children who were there were at their desks, dotted around the room.

'Well, class,' she said, 'since it's the first day back and since there are so few of us, why don't we just sit in a circle and have a chat. You can tell me how you're feeling about things, and we'll talk through what the school year is going to look like. Hopefully, we'll be able to find a way to make it fun and interesting for you.'

After the school day was over, Seonaid sat for a moment to think about the best way to proceed. She should have done this ahead of time, she realised. She should have seen this coming and been prepared for it. *Well,* she thought, *we'll just have to deal with it now.*

She thought through the students who had been missing.

Julia and Abbie were best friends; if one of them came, the other would too, so she only needed to get one set of parents on board. Julia's would be easier to persuade, but Abbie's would be offended if Seonaid went to Julia's but not them, so it would have to be Abbie's.

Isaac and Paul might be tricky. Paul was seventeen, so already close enough to finishing school that his parents might think there was no point, or want him to be helping out on the farm. And if Paul got to miss school, Isaac would want to as well.

Rosie's mother would be difficult to get onside, but if she did agree to send Rosie back to school, she'd immediately go round to a few other parents to justify her choice, which might sway another few into the bargain.

Robbie's dad, there'd be no getting to. He'd either send him or he wouldn't, and trying to talk him round would almost definitely backfire.

After twenty minutes or so, she had a list of parents and had decided on the best order in which to approach them. She would start with Rosie's parents. Their house was near Seonaid and Billie's so she'd be able to drop by and pick up her bike to make the rest of her calls.

'I just don't see what the point is,' said Greta, Rosie's mum, after asking Seonaid in for a cup of tea. 'It's not like they'll be sending examiners round to test them at the end of the year.'

'Well, no,' said Seonaid. 'They won't. But really, school is about so much more than just having examinations. It's good for the kids' minds to keep them engaged, learning new things just for the sake of it.'

'I don't know,' said Greta. 'They hate going so much, it seems like a shame to force them into it when there's no real need.'

'That's why I'm planning on making it more student-led this year,' said Seonaid. 'We don't have to stick to the official curriculum, which is often rather rote and dry. We can study whatever we want. So the kids can tell me what they're interested in, and we can build their year around that.'

'Ha,' said Greta. 'My Rosie's not interested in anything but clothes, these days. Hormones.'

'That's great,' said Seonaid. 'We can study a history of fashion, look back through the styles of the past. We can even study sewing and design, so she can start making her own clothes. Which would be such a useful skill to have.'

'But if she really wants to learn that stuff, she can do it at home anyway.'

Seonaid took a big, steadying breath. 'Of course she could,' she said, 'but it's so much more fun to learn with your friends. And she'll need guidance as she learns, someone to make sure she's on the right track, to keep it interesting and fun even when it gets difficult. You don't have time for that yourself, I'm sure.'

'Of course not!' Greta cried. 'I've the shop to take care of. Besides, I don't know anything about the history of fashion.'

'Well, exactly,' said Seonaid. 'You have much too much to worry about without taking all that on as well. That's why I'd love to have Rosie back in school. I can teach her all this.'

Greta looked like she was starting to soften.

'How was Rosie this summer, anyway?' Seonaid asked mildly.

'Ah, you know,' said Greta. 'She had her rough days at the start, but she's young, she soon got distracted. Spends all her time off with her friends on the beach. When it's sunny, that is.'

'And when it's raining?'

'Oh god.' Greta rolled her eyes. 'When it's raining, it's a completely different story. She's always underfoot, often with her friends in tow. They come into the shop and try to get sweets from me. I won't let them have any, not now we need things to last as long as possible. But then they just hang around, as if they live there.'

'That must be frustrating.'

'And it's not like I don't enjoy the girl's company – she's a treat, always has been.'

'I agree, she's always been a delight to teach.'

'It's just that she doesn't notice when I'm trying to work.'

Seonaid nodded, but held back from saying anything herself.

Greta thought for a moment, chewing the inside of her cheek. 'All in all, I think it's probably best if she does come to school,' she said eventually. 'But I don't see the point in forcing her to read Shakespeare or whatever. She's no head for it.'

'I certainly won't force it on her,' said Seonaid. 'And I agree, I think it's for the best that she comes to school. Will I see her in class tomorrow?'

She smiled smugly to herself as she left Greta. That would take care of at least three of the other families, by her estimation.

Next up: Abbie's parents.

Seonaid spent three hours cycling across the village and talking to parents about why they should want to send their children back to school. Some were reluctant, some only needed a little persuasion, and some seemed completely taken aback by the idea.

A handful flat-out refused. Seonaid didn't press matters with them, but hoped that the children, when they saw their friends return to school, would want to come back too. Or at least that the reverse wouldn't be true.

She had decided to make one last call before she went home – one that she expected would be easy. Malcolm's son, Neil, loved school. He read constantly, was obsessed with history, was always asking Seonaid for more work.

She'd been shocked when he hadn't arrived for class, especially because he was one of the few students not from a farming family. His father owned the pub; there was no need for Neil to help out the way there sometimes was for some of the others.

She was surprised to hear raised voices as she approached the front door.

'. . . foolhardy mission,' she heard Malcolm say.

'There's still a world out there,' someone was yelling. 'And we're expected to sit here twiddling our thumbs?'

'You do whatever you feel you need to, son,' Malcolm said. 'But don't blame anyone for not wanting to throw in their lot with you.'

The door burst open just as Seonaid was raising her hand to knock. Thomas stood there, his lip curled in fury. He barely glanced at her as he stormed past her.

Seonaid raised an eyebrow at Malcolm as he waved her into the house. 'That seemed intense,' she said.

'Ah, he's not from here,' said Malcolm. 'He has family back over on the mainland.'

'So does everyone else,' she said. 'Even those that have lived here for generations.'

Malcolm nodded, but changed the subject. 'You're here

because Neil wasn't at school? He's had a stomach flu. No big deal, but I thought it best to keep him home. He'll be fine in a couple of days.'

'Ah, that's good news. He wasn't the only one not to show up, so I wondered. There are a few people around who think school is a waste of time, given the circumstances.'

'Can't really blame them,' said Malcolm. 'School seems so full of arbitrary things now.'

Seonaid laughed. 'Yes, well, I'm taking the opportunity to excise the things I personally find arbitrary. Of course, we may disagree on what those are.'

'Neil might have something to say about cutting things,' said Malcolm.

'I'll be replacing them, naturally. Hopefully with things that are more interesting and relevant to . . . well, the current situation.' Seonaid paused for a moment, frowning. 'By the way, what was Thomas trying to recruit you for?'

Malcolm sighed deeply. 'Ah, that fool. He wants to take a group out to check what state the isthmus is in.'

'What?' said Seonaid. 'Now?'

'That's what I told him. Weather's going to be unpredictable, which would be fine if the road was in a decent condition. Which it won't be. It was at least a full day's drive along the isthmus even when it was well-maintained, and that's if the weather was good. No telling how long it could take to cross nowadays. Once they get out on to the isthmus, if the weather gets bad, it could be dangerous. And we need all hands on deck to help with the harvest.'

Seonaid frowned. 'Has anyone looked into how much petrol we have? Is there enough to spare for this expedition?'

'That's a very good point,' said Malcolm. 'But I doubt you'd get Thomas to listen to it.'

Seonaid left Malcolm to his evening, and headed back home. They had all taken the summer for granted, she was beginning to think, and there was a hard road ahead.

The Aftermath

The destruction of the boats, the one solid method for discovering what had happened on the mainland, sent a schism through the people of Black Crag. Like a nail driven into a crack in a plank of wood, it split the village in two.

No one would admit to being behind the arson, but there were plenty of people who openly celebrated it. Who claimed that the risks of journeying over the ocean were too great, and if some people didn't see that, then it was for the best that they'd had the option removed from them.

But the violence of the incident, the destruction of so much property left everyone in shock – not to mention the strain it put on their efforts to survive. The loss of the boats meant they would no longer be able to fish in the open sea. They were left with small rowing boats that would keep the fishermen close to shore.

But more than that, the fire signified the removal of the last connection to the world. While there was still disagreement among most of the villagers about when it would be wise or necessary to cross to the mainland, there were plenty of people who were certain that eventually, someone would need to make that journey – and return. To have the option completely removed was devastating.

To those who had advocated for crossing, any suggestion that someone was sympathetic to the arsonist was as good as an admission of guilt. Endorsing the act, to some, was as bad as committing it.

The tension of the debate erupted on a particularly hot afternoon into a brawl that left a cluster of people nursing bruises, three with broken noses, one with broken ribs, and five needing stitches. After cleaning up the various injured, Billie took the fighters and agitators to task, stressing how limited medical supplies were on the island.

'A crime's been committed,' Thomas said, in response to her exhortations. 'We're trying to get justice.'

Billie rolled her eyes. 'If you want justice, then investigate,' she said. 'Don't just start punching anyone who disagrees with you.'

Chapter Eleven

The house was empty, and Sarah was surprised by how uncomfortable that made her. Moth and Elliot were at school and Mam was at work. It was just her.

This was it, then: the first real moment of divergence. She wasn't supposed to be here anymore. She should have been gone. She breathed in the empty house and let it settle around her. For a moment, she was at a loss. There was a lot of work to be done in the coming weeks, and she was prepared to do it, but that didn't help her in this moment. She felt restless, but not in the dark, upsetting way she'd grown used to. It was more that she was desperate to be productive.

But there wasn't much to do around the house. She'd cleaned and weeded and mended the whole house to within an inch of its life after the party, when she was trying to assuage her guilt.

She left the house and started off on one of her old walks, more out of boredom than anything else, but as she walked, it began to feel right. She knew she had to let go of her life as it was supposed to be, of the future she'd lost, and she was ready to.

But she needed to do it properly. Take the time and space on her own to release it, to bid it farewell. Otherwise, it would haunt her for months.

The sun was warm overhead, but it was windy. She decided to take to the hills, to stand overlooking the village, letting the blustery winds carry her old dreams away from her.

She felt exhilarated as she climbed. It had been a few weeks since she'd walked like this, and suddenly she felt like her body had been crying out for the exercise. It took her almost three hours to reach the top, and the wind took her breath away. It whipped her hair around her head as she stood looking back down over the fields, towards the village. To the curve of the bay, with the jetty thrusting out into the sea.

She knew it was too far to actually make out, but in her mind she saw the mainland. The highway curving through the fields. The villages and towns dotted across the landscape. And the vastness of the city in the distance. She imagined it deserted and ashen. Or crowded with desperate people, hurt or sick. Or piled with bodies. She imagined it as a crater.

She took a deep breath and pictured it as it would have been. As it used to be, when it was her home. She imagined the buzz of traffic, the hum of conversation. She pictured the tiny dorm room that might have been hers. The coffee stands she would have gone to every day. The lecture halls and study rooms.

She pictured the orientation parties she would have gone to this week. The people she would have met. The life she would have had.

She thought about the conversation she'd had with Ana. *Imagine if had happened a couple of months from now instead.*

She would have been there. In the city. She would have been in the middle of things.

So you didn't get the life you wanted, she thought. *But you still get to have a life. Be grateful.*

She wasn't sure how long she stood like that before she realised she wasn't alone. A little way down the hill, looking up at her, was Nathaniel.

Sarah stared. Had he followed her again?

'I'm sorry,' he said. 'I didn't mean to disturb you. I didn't think you came up here anymore.'

'How long have you been here?' Sarah asked.

'A couple of hours,' he said. 'I've been coming here a lot. I was here when you came up. I waved, but you didn't see me, and I didn't want to interrupt.'

'Oh,' said Sarah. 'OK. Well, I'm going back now. Enjoy.'

She turned to leave, but he called after her.

'Wait,' he said. 'Can we talk?'

She turned back slowly. Nathaniel was holding out a Thermos. 'I've got hot chocolate,' he said.

Sarah nodded slowly and moved towards him. He'd brought a picnic blanket with him and spread it out, with rocks piled on the corners to hold it down in the wind.

'Did you start coming up here because I was?' she asked.

He blushed. 'Kind of,' he said.

'That's weird, you know.'

'I wasn't trying to find you or anything,' he said quickly. 'It just seemed like if it was helping you, taking all those big walks all the time, then maybe it would help me.'

'Why do you think it was helping me?'

'I don't know. You kept doing it?'

Sarah shrugged. 'I guess,' she said. She sipped the hot chocolate he'd handed her. 'This is terrible,' she said.

'I know,' Nathaniel said with a grimace. 'My dad never lets

me put more than one spoonful in. Says it's a waste. He doesn't drink it, so he doesn't know how bad it is.'

'Why don't you just drink something else? Coffee, or tea. Or water.'

'I don't know, I'm kind of used to it.'

'OK,' said Sarah, dumping the rest of her cup out on the ground. 'Did you want to talk to me about something other than bad hot chocolate? Because I need to go.'

Nathaniel looked at the ground and bit his lip. 'I just wanted to tell you that, like . . . I understand.'

'You understand what?'

'Why you're so angry. To be stuck here.'

'I don't think I *am* angry,' Sarah said. 'Not anymore, anyway.'

'Well, why you were, then. I get it. I . . .' He trailed off and ran a hand over his face. 'I was going to get out too,' he said eventually. 'I wanted to leave. I spent years convincing my dad that I wasn't going to take over his farm. He finally agreed, and then . . .' He waved a hand in the direction of the mainland.

'Oh,' said Sarah. 'OK.'

'I, um, haven't been being very nice to him,' said Nathaniel. 'If he'd let me go when I first wanted to . . .'

'You'd probably be dead,' said Sarah.

'Yeah, but I'd have at least had some time. Some time not here.'

Sarah nodded. 'Aren't you, like, twenty-two?' she asked. 'Why did you need his permission?'

Nathaniel blushed even deeper. 'I guess I didn't. But I didn't want to just abandon him, you know? I'm all he has.'

Sarah held out her cup for more hot chocolate.

'You threw your last one away!' Nathaniel said in protest.

'I'll drink this one,' said Sarah. 'I promise.'

Nathaniel laughed and poured her another drink.

'What would you have done?' she asked. 'If you'd moved away?'

'I don't know, exactly. Probably just worked in a bar or something. I just . . . I want to know what it's like. If I'd fit better. Does that make sense?'

'Yeah,' said Sarah.

'How did you stop being angry?' he asked, frowning slightly.

'Talking to people, I guess. Also just time. I think we need to grieve the . . . I don't know.' Sarah waved a hand around in the air as she searched for the right words. 'The lives we would have had, I guess,' she said.

Nathaniel's frown deepened, but he nodded. 'That's a nice way of putting it. What are you going to do now?'

'With my life?' Sarah asked, with a laugh.

'Well, with the next bit of it, at least.'

'Help with the harvest. Help my parents with my younger brother. Try to survive.'

'Survive for what?' Nathaniel asked. Sarah was surprised by the bitterness in his face, even though it was a mirror of what her own feelings had been. He had always seemed so amused by Sarah's angst, she'd assumed he didn't have any of his own.

'Who knows?' she said. 'There's only one way to find out.'

Nathaniel gave a low bark of laughter. 'God,' he said. 'What a depressing thought. The only way to find out if life's worth living is to live it.'

Sarah didn't know how to reply to that. 'It's what we have,' she said, after a while. 'We can only do what's in front of us to do.' She took a sip of her hot chocolate. 'Oh god,' she said. 'I can't do it. I'm sorry.'

Nathaniel nodded as she dumped out her second cup.

'Well, I can't blame you,' he said.

Sarah felt strangely lighter as she walked home. The walk, the space, even talking to Nathaniel – something had changed for her. Something had solidified.

She was ready.

Sarah stood in the middle of a field of wheat. It had occurred to her that it was strange to have lived ten years in this village and still have very little idea how farming worked. She'd never helped out on the farms before; she'd never wanted to.

When her parents had brought her to Black Crag, she'd been so furious at having to leave her friends, her school, that she'd decided everything about this place was beneath her notice. Over the years, she'd slowly started to appreciate the peace and quiet that came with living in the country, the views of the rolling fields. But she'd still never thought that much about what it was like to work the land.

It had just never felt relevant to her. She was going to get out as soon as she was old enough; that had always been her plan.

Standing here now, though, the idea of the work felt powerful. To contribute, with the labour of your hands, to the survival of your community.

She noticed someone waving at the edge of the field and began moving through the wheat towards them. It was Ana.

'What were you doing out there?' she asked, raising an eyebrow at Sarah. 'We're not harvesting the wheat.'

Sarah smiled. 'I know,' she said. 'I just like it out there. It's peaceful.'

'Well,' said Ana, 'that's the only peace you're going to get. This is going to be exhausting.'

She was right. By the end of the day, Sarah's muscles were aching, her head was pounding, and she was covered in dirt. She'd spent hours crouching in the soil, pulling up potatoes, and she could feel it in every inch of her body.

She woke up the next morning stiff all over, knowing she had to do it all over again.

After the first week, she was regretting having agreed to help at all. She couldn't remember ever being so exhausted.

But in the second week she began to adjust. She was often working alongside Ana, so they could spend the days talking and joking as they worked.

She could feel herself getting stronger – and she could feel herself getting happier. It was strange.

She'd thought this would make her feel worse. That experiencing just how much work it was going to take to get everyone through would be demoralising. Depressing.

But somehow, it was the opposite. It was a lot of work, but she felt, unexpectedly, that she could do it. That she could contribute to this. She'd spent the entire summer feeling so separate from everything, from everyone around her.

It was good to feel like she was a part of things. Like she was working for the good of her neighbours. She knew her family could tell things had changed. They had been being patient with her. Now they were relaxed. It was only in the change that she realised how much they'd adjusted their behaviour to fit around her moods.

She tried not to let this add to her guilt.

All there was to do was move forward.

After a couple of weeks, Sarah found herself enjoying the harvest, but frustrated with it as well. There was something satisfying about it, yes, something about coming home covered in dirt with aching muscles that made her feel solid. Connected to the community.

But it meant that she was never alone anymore.

She worked all day surrounded by her neighbours, then she went home to her family. She was too exhausted by the work to get far enough out of the village to be truly on her own, even if she had time to.

After a few days of constant company, she wanted to flee to the fens forever. Instead, she wandered out to the end of the jetty and sat down, leaning back on her hands and closing her eyes against the sun. She'd been staying away from this spot, but once, before the end, she'd loved it. She liked thinking about all the life under the surface of the ocean, underneath her feet.

But it had felt too much like a broken connection recently. The beginning of the way to the mainland, to the city, to the world. The only part of that journey that remained. It had felt like an insult to her bitterness. But now she felt that bitterness draining away. She had turned her face to her community, to immediate needs, and her lost future didn't hurt quite so much anymore.

She found it comforting now to sit out above the water, thinking about the vast array of creatures down there, unaware of the tragedies above them.

For now, it seemed like enough to get by. Work to be done on the land, rest to be had by the water.

A few weeks into the harvest, Sarah noticed Nathaniel had joined the group of people working the fields. She waved at him and he nodded back at her.

It wasn't until they broke for lunch that she had a chance to talk to him.

'I see you've followed me again,' she said, draining a cup of water.

He laughed. 'Nothing better to do,' he said. 'Although doing nothing wouldn't hurt so much.' He stretched out his shoulders and made a face.

But Sarah wasn't sure he was enjoying being out in the fields as much as she was. He didn't seem interested in joining in with conversation. He kept his head down while he worked and, when everyone sat around to eat, he listened but didn't take part.

Sarah began to wonder if she was the only person he ever talked to. She tried to bring him into the conversation – she even invited him to work over with her and Ana – but although he was always polite, and responded when directly addressed, he still never voluntarily contributed anything.

'What's up with that guy?' Ana said, as she and Sarah walked home at the end of a long day.

'What do you mean?' Sarah asked.

'He just never has anything to say for himself. I don't know why you keep trying so hard with him.'

To own the truth, Sarah didn't know either, but she felt bad hearing Ana complain about him.

'I think he's just not very happy,' said Sarah.

'Yeah, OK, good for you, bud, no one's happy. We're the only ones left alive for miles. Hundreds of miles, maybe.'

Sarah was quiet for a moment. 'We don't know that,' she said.

Ana rolled her eyes. 'Sure, fine, for all we know everything's fine and dandy somewhere out there, but for us, right now, to all intents and purposes, the world around us has ended.'

'I just feel bad for him, I guess,' Sarah said. 'I don't think he has any friends.'

'Yeah, well, maybe there's a reason for that.'

'Ana!'

'OK, that was mean, whatever. It's just exhausting being around someone so awkward.'

'He's not that awkward,' said Sarah. 'Just a bit quiet.'

'It makes me self-conscious. Like, if he's not saying anything, it's because he's listening too carefully. Judging us all.'

'He's not judging us.'

'That you know of,' Ana said. 'I'm just saying he makes everything feel awkward and uncomfortable.'

'OK,' said Sarah. 'You don't have to work with him if you don't want to.'

Ana turned to Sarah, her eyes wide. 'But what if you choose him over me?'

Sarah laughed. 'Oh, you wouldn't let me.'

But after that, she stopped trying so hard to include Nathaniel. He was an adult, she figured, and he'd had no trouble approaching her out of nowhere. He could take care of himself.

The Inquisition

Thomas's attempt to discover the arsonist initially had the general support of the village. After all, even those who were most fearful of what might be brought back from the mainland acknowledged that a crime had been committed. No one was happy about an unknown person taking the situation into their own hands so absolutely.

In the weeks after the incident, when the summer was still bright and hot, people cooperated as much as they could – but it quickly became clear that no one had much to contribute to the investigation. The fire had started in the early hours of the morning, and no one had been awake to see anything.

There was no physical evidence. It was obvious that gasoline had been used to start the fire, but that didn't narrow things down. All the farms had generators, and petrol on hand to feed them, and no one bothered to lock their stores up.

As the leaves began to turn and the first autumn breezes drifted over the island, the investigation became less important to the village as a whole. But Thomas refused to let it go. He questioned people over and over again, insisting that there was some kind of cover-up happening, claiming that the village was against him.

In the end, it was an accident that uncovered the truth.

A farmer, Isaac, found a singed cardigan shoved into the broken fridge that had sat useless in his barn for a few years, smelling of gasoline. He recognised it as belonging to his wife, Helen.

When he confronted her, she admitted it immediately. It was because of him, she said. His brother had been on the third boat, and he'd been talking about going after him to find out if he was OK. Helen was terrified of Isaac going and leaving her alone. Dying over there on the mainland with no way for her to bring his body home.

The revelation to the wider village left people perplexed. No one was sure what should happen next. There was no court to hold a trial. No obvious sentence to mete out.

Nothing to be done.

Chapter Twelve

Sarah spent two days going around the village collecting as many jars and bottles as she could. Graeme was insisting that petrol needed to be preserved, so she hitched a cart to the back of Moth's bike and cycled back and forth across the island, an array of glassware jangling behind her.

A huge amount of vegetables and fruit had been harvested, and most of it needed to be preserved as soon as possible. Sarah had always liked preserving. Moth had taught her how when she was a child, back when they lived in the city. It had seemed like a strange magic to her back then. Something none of their friends knew how to do.

Her friends hadn't been impressed; they just bought fruit in cans and considered it much the same thing. But the process of taking an ordinary peach, and encasing it in glass, to sit golden on the shelf until it was wanted, struck Sarah as delicious alchemy.

She and Ana had taken over the pub kitchen. There were piles of food on every surface waiting to be brined or syruped, depending on their purpose.

'I can't believe you roped me into this,' Ana said.

'I didn't rope you into it,' said Sarah. 'You volunteered.'

'Only because you didn't want to join the hunting party.'

A group of the harvesters had been pulled from the fields to go out hunting rabbits, geese and boar. The meat would be smoked and dried to be laid up with the preserves. At first, Ana had jumped at the chance to go hunting, but Sarah couldn't bear the idea of shooting something, and Ana had decided to keep working with her instead.

'You know,' Ana continued, 'you really shouldn't eat meat if you can't bring yourself to kill the animals.'

'You really shouldn't eat pickles if you can't bring yourself to brine the cucumbers,' Sarah shot back.

'Not the same. I pulled those cucumbers from the ground, that's what matters. Also, I clearly am willing to preserve all this stuff. I just think it would be more fun to be out hunting.'

'Not to me,' Sarah said. 'And you didn't have to stay here just because I did. Marcus went hunting – you could have gone with him.'

Ana made a face. 'No, thank you,' she said.

'Oh,' said Sarah. 'OK.'

She knew that Ana and Marcus had been hanging out a fair bit since the party, and she'd assumed it was going well. Ana had never told her otherwise, although she'd never really talked seriously about him at all. She made jokes about him, that was all.

Ana raised an eyebrow at Sarah. 'Did you have a question?'

'Not really,' said Sarah. 'I just thought you were having fun.'

Ana laughed. 'I was having comparative fun. It was more fun to occasionally get off with Marcus than to not. I was bored, you know? Summer was boring.' She grinned and shrugged. 'But now I'm busy.'

'Fair enough,' said Sarah. 'How does he feel about it?'

'Presumably fine,' said Ana. 'He never did any of the work, you know. I presented myself in front of him and he went along with it. I've stopped presenting myself, and he's going along with that too.'

Sarah frowned. 'Are you hoping he'll start doing some of the work? Come after you?'

'God, I hope not,' said Ana. 'Then I'd have to turn him down, and that would be awkward.'

Sarah shrugged and let it go. She'd never really understood Ana's feelings about flirting, but they seemed to suit her well enough.

It had been a long, hard week, and Sarah was feeling old frustrations push against her newfound peace. She couldn't really tell what the problem was. Small things threw her off – a broken jar, a lost tool. Everything felt like a disaster, weighted with undue meaning. Like the smallest mistake could be the difference between the village surviving the winter and . . . not. She knew it didn't make sense, but she couldn't stop the dread of it from rising up within her.

She found herself almost snapping at her family again, and she hated how much she was having to hold herself back. It was like she'd fooled them into thinking they could relax around her, and now she was ready to blow again.

She wanted to run, to get out for a few hours, and she resented that she couldn't. That she'd made a commitment. There were people who were relying on her; she was part of something she couldn't turn her back on.

Walking home from the preserving station, she took deep breaths, trying to dispel the cloud that had been sitting over her for days. She turned towards the shore, hoping that some time alone with the sea would help settle her mood.

But as she turned on to the jetty, she saw that someone was already out there, sitting in her spot. Arthur.

Sarah let out a long, slow breath. She needed that space; she was desperate for it. But she couldn't be angry at Arthur. Not at poor, broken Arthur, who still barely spoke to anyone except to say yes or no whenever anyone asked him a direct question.

It was a strange place he'd made for himself in the village, she realised. A reminder of everything that had happened, a collective responsibility. The only person who had any knowledge of what had happened. The only person who couldn't talk about it.

Sarah turned away from the jetty and walked slowly along the beach instead. It was too late to go far, but it was better than nothing.

It must be lonely, she thought, as she walked. He was someone everyone was fascinated by and frightened of in equal measure. He was a living spectre.

It must be so lonely.

The Bodies

Thomas had never told anyone what he had seen on the ferry when he'd gone out to help Arthur. He wasn't even sure what it was he'd seen, and he couldn't see the benefit in opening it up for discussion.

The ferry had been swamped with water, and he hadn't been able to see where the water was coming from. But there were bullet holes in a couple of the seats on the deck, so it was clear someone had either fired at the ferry, or some kind of fight had happened on board.

Thomas hadn't thought much about this at the time; he'd been focused on getting Arthur out alive. But as he helped him down to the rowing boat, he looked around to see if there was anyone else on the ferry.

The first person he saw was sitting at the rear of the boat, facing away from him. Thomas yelled out, but the person didn't move at all. Then he realised the figure was strangely slumped. The rocking of the boat was shifting the figure from side to side, and they appeared to be doing nothing to stop it.

Thomas took a step towards it, and noticed another figure face down on the floor under the seats, being washed one way then the other by the water that had already spilled over the sides. There was a bloodstained hole in the person's back.

Thomas turned and dove into the water, pulling himself up into the rowing boat with Arthur and Charlie. He stared at Arthur, who was slumped exhausted in the boat, and let Charlie row them back to shore.

He didn't try to ask Arthur about it, and he didn't talk about it with anyone else. He didn't know if Arthur was responsible for the bodies on the ferry, and he didn't think it would do any good for anyone else to speculate about it.

But one of them had clearly been shot, and he had no reason to believe the other had suffered a different fate. He didn't know what had sparked it, but whatever had happened over there seemed to him to have been an outbreak of violence. Something like that wouldn't be contagious. As long as they were prepared to fight, he didn't see any reason they shouldn't confront whoever had been left standing.

Chapter Thirteen

While the village hummed with activity, the debate about trying to get to the mainland seemed settled, at least for now. For the most part, people started getting on with what was in front of them, trying to ignore the occasional comments and dark looks from the small faction that still believed getting to the mainland should be the top priority.

And for now, that faction was content to be ignored. They had their own plans. They were trying to make their own plans. Although, truth be told, they were happy enough if no one came poking around to see what those plans were. And how far they were from being realised.

Thomas had spent weeks going over the rotting carcass of old Patrick's sailing boat before he admitted defeat. It would take forever to fix it, even if he could get hold of everything he needed, which was a big if.

It had seemed like the most likely out, but he couldn't accept an option that wouldn't find fruition for weeks, if not months. He couldn't be here when winter hit. Then he really would be trapped.

It would have to be the road. He knew it was supposed to be in bad condition, dangerous in bad weather, but he was sure that was overblown. People assumed it was bad because they never bothered to go and see it.

He spent some time trying to find people who'd back his plan. He knew that Graeme would try to stop him and he would have support. Graeme, who always found a way to shoot down any opposition. Who threw his weight around, who thought he was the only one who could get the community through this.

Well, he could have it, as far as Thomas was concerned. Graeme could have Black Crag. Thomas was going to make it to the mainland and find out what was going on. And he would find a way to live there that meant he never had to come back.

Thomas was surprised by how much resistance he got. He'd thought Malcolm would be with him, but he practically laughed in his face, and he wasn't the only one. Even Charlie said it sounded like a long shot.

A couple of the younger guys were on board, and that would have to do. The weather would only get worse; they would have to go now. There was no other option.

He didn't know who had told Graeme.

Thomas had spent an afternoon looking over his car, making sure that if the journey failed, it wouldn't be because of some stupid, preventable mechanical flaw he should have seen. He'd gone into the village to grab a couple of extra cans of petrol, when Graeme accosted him.

'Evening, Thomas,' he said, as though it was years ago and he was just someone trying to help, as though they were friends, as though they were planning on settling in for a couple of pints. 'I heard you were planning on trying to drive to the mainland, and I wondered if we could talk that through.'

I wondered if we could talk that through. As though he weren't trying to ruin everything.

'Don't see that it's any of your business, Graeme,' Thomas growled at him.

'Well, you see, I think it's everyone's business,' Graeme said.

Thomas rolled his eyes. 'Graeme, get off my back. I'm not asking anyone to come who doesn't want to. The rest of you can hole up here for as long as you want. Till you all die.'

'Thomas, we need the petrol. We have to make it through the harvest. We have to be able to power the generators if the electricity goes out. Which it very well might. And beyond that, we have to prioritise next spring. We'll need to plant again.'

Thomas felt his lip curling in anger. 'It's not for you to decide, Graeme. You're no better than me.'

Graeme smiled, his expression infuriatingly bland. 'No,' he said. 'It's not for me to decide. The petrol is a village resource; it belongs to us all. We will have to put it to a vote.'

Thomas seethed. If there hadn't been other people watching, he would have laughed in Graeme's face and just driven away. But Malcolm was there, looking warily at him. He'd really thought Malcolm would be on his side. Everyone was so goddamn loyal to Graeme, just because he was older, just because he'd grown up here. Just because he kept organising village meetings. What was it with this place and their village meetings?

At the meeting, he sat in silence as Graeme explained to the assembled crowd just why Thomas shouldn't be allowed to use any of the petrol, why finding out what was going on across the water wasn't a valid use of resources. He had to listen to what felt like an hour of prosy nonsense before Graeme finally let him state his case. By that time, Thomas was almost too angry to say anything at all.

'Look,' he said. 'We have to get to the mainland. We're screwed if we stay here alone. I'm going. I want to drive. But if you won't let me have petrol, I'll walk. Anyone who wants to come with me, I'm leaving at eight tomorrow morning.'

Then he walked out of the room.

Thomas was sure people thought he was crazy. It would take several days of trekking just to get to the isthmus, let alone across it. And once across, it would be miles to the next village. But they were giving him no choice.

He had to get to the mainland, and they were taking away his only other option. He spent the evening packing up supplies for the journey. Then he walked around the small house on his farm.

He'd never really bothered to look around it. It was small and worn. It was a place to sleep. A place to stew over his latest failed crop.

He would be well shot of it.

He didn't know why he'd thought it would be a good idea to move here. Maybe he hadn't, not really. It had been a reaction.

His life had fallen apart and he'd run away from it. It had felt like action, it had felt like intention, but it had been shame and fear.

He'd come to this tiny, windy village at the edge of the world with a pile of books and the determination to do something right. To make a place for himself where he'd have complete control over the space around him.

And it hadn't worked. His farm had failed, year after year. Tiny, pitiful crops that barely covered the costs of planting them. For a while, he'd turned to the other farmers – turned to Graeme – sure that with the right advice, things would turn around. But eventually it had started to feel like they were laughing at him. He had broken his back to try and make this work, and he'd failed, and now he was stuck here. Stuck with his failure, with a pile of Graemes looking down on him, judging him for thinking he could be one of them.

Well, he couldn't be one of them. He wouldn't. He would get out of this place, even if no one else was bold enough to try.

Revenge

Helen had a vineyard on the edge of her farm. It was a pet project that both baffled and confused the other farmers. The climate of Black Crag was not suited to grapes. It was too cold, too unpredictable. It was a foolish hobby in such a place, but Helen loved it.

She devoted hours every week to its upkeep, to research on how to cultivate it. She sprang out of bed at the merest hint of wind, to ensure the vines were protected. Isaac joked that they could never have a baby, because it would take too much time away from the vineyard.

The day after the village discovered Helen had been the one who destroyed the boats, her vineyard burned down. She sustained massive burns trying to save it. She never had full use of her left arm again.

Chapter Fourteen

When Sarah saw the crowd of people gathered in the middle of the village, her stomach dropped and her heart began to race. She must have missed something. Some new development.

She was surprised at how frightened it made her feel. What could possibly make things worse? But as she got closer, she began to calm down.

There was worry and concern, but also laughter. People seemed entertained, even. As she approached the group she heard someone talking about a 'pack of idiots'.

'They'll be back before the day's over, tails between their legs,' someone else was saying.

Sarah's confusion must have been visible, because someone noticed her and said, 'It's Thomas. He and a couple of others have run off.'

It was Jeremy. One of the people who'd been working with Sarah and Ana on the harvest. Sarah hadn't known him that well before, but she liked him. He'd only lived in Black Crag for a year or so before the incident. He'd come over as a seasonal worker and decided to stay for a while.

'Run off?' Sarah asked. 'Where?'

'They're trying to reach the mainland on foot.'

Sarah stared. Jeremy laughed at her expression and said,

'Yeah, that's the prevailing view. Apparently there was a big fight about it yesterday, and an emergency meeting. I don't know, I wasn't here for that; I was out in the fields. But Thomas decided to drive that tinpot car of his across the isthmus and explore. I don't know how far he wanted to go, if he was planning on trying to get to the city, but a few people objected, said it was a waste of petrol. We need to have some saved for generators, you know, in case the power goes out.'

'Oh god,' said Sarah.

There was still so much about this that she hadn't thought about. Black Crag drew power from offshore turbines, so as long as there were tides, as long as there was wind, they'd have electricity. Sarah didn't know how regularly those turbines needed maintenance. How vulnerable they were to damage. The power they generated had to flow along lines under the ocean, through converters and into people's homes. Any part of that system could be damaged – and there was no one left to fix it if something did go wrong.

'So they gathered as many people as they could find,' Jeremy was saying, 'and held a vote. Thomas must have known that it wasn't going to go his way because he left before they even took it, saying he'd leave this morning whatever they said, on foot if he had to.'

'How long would it even take on foot?'

Jeremy shook his head. 'Don't know,' he said. 'Days, I think. They'll have to camp out in the middle of the road for at least a couple of nights.'

'But doesn't it get completely covered in high tide?'

'Apparently it's worth it. Hope they've got waders.'

Sarah smiled weakly. 'Yeah,' she said. 'Maybe he's not on foot, though. Maybe he took the car even though everyone voted him down.'

'Nope,' said Jeremy. 'Someone went to check at his farm. The car's still there, along with the spare cans of petrol he was going to take.'

Sarah was quiet as she walked on to meet Ana. They were still on preserving duties – as fast as they could bottle produce, the harvesters were pulling more from the ground.

Part of her was impressed by Thomas. He'd made her summer of angst seem petty and ineffectual. She'd thought she was trapped, she'd thought she was railing against the fate that had stolen the world from her and now he was just going. On foot.

It had never even occurred to Sarah to look for ways to get out.

She tried to explain it to Ana as they worked.

'Don't get me wrong,' she said, 'I think it's a crazy thing to do. But I didn't try to do anything. Anything at all, except storm around having a tantrum.'

Ana didn't respond.

'Yeah, I get it,' said Sarah. 'I know I was a nightmare, you don't have to keep making a point of it. And I suppose I'm glad that I never tried to do anything this mad, but still. Makes me feel a bit pathetic.' There was silence. 'OK, yes, I *was* pathetic. I am pathetic. Fine.' She looked over at Ana and noticed for the first time that she wasn't really listening. 'Are you OK?' she asked.

Ana looked up at her and gave a wan smile. 'Yeah,' she said. 'Sorry. I just . . . Marcus went with him.'

Sarah stared. 'Oh god,' she said. 'Are you sure?'

'Pretty sure. When I heard what had happened I thought he

might have, so I went to his place to check. His mum said he left early this morning, but didn't say where he was going. No one's seen him.'

'That doesn't mean he went with Thomas.'

'He did, though. He likes Thomas, he thinks he's cool. I don't think he has any real reason to want to get to the mainland, but it's more exciting than pulling potato after potato out of the ground, so.' She shrugged.

'Maybe he's just gone hunting.'

'Maybe.'

'It's just as likely he's gone hunting; more so, probably. Because hunting is a normal thing to do instead of a deranged one.'

Ana laughed quietly but still looked worried.

'It'll be OK. He'll be back by nightfall.' She could tell Ana wasn't convinced. Sarah narrowed her eyes at her with a small smile. 'I guess you weren't as bored with him as you said,' she said.

Ana frowned. 'No, that's not it,' she said. 'I just ... It's nothing, don't worry. You're probably right – and if you're not, then whatever. It's his business.'

But she stayed quiet and distracted for the rest of the day.

Ana was late meeting Sarah the next morning, and when she arrived she looked exhausted.

'He didn't come home?' Sarah asked.

Ana shook her head mutely.

'Oh,' said Sarah. She didn't know how to respond. It was clear that the relationship had been less casual than Ana had suggested, but she didn't seem to want to talk about it now.

'I'm sure he'll be OK,' said Sarah. 'Really, they just need to keep an eye on the tides, know when it's safe to make camp for a few hours. The weather's been OK. It's not super windy out there, so there shouldn't be unexpected waves. And if it looks like it'll get too dangerous, they'll turn back. They may have turned back already. They could be home by tonight.'

She rattled on for a while as they worked, only half aware of what she was saying. Ana worked mostly in silence as Sarah talked, occasionally nodding.

After a couple of hours of work, Sarah thought she was looking calmer, but then a jar of pickled onions slipped through her hands and crashed to the floor, and Ana burst into tears.

'Oh my god,' said Sarah. 'Are you OK?'

Ana sat limply in a nearby chair and nodded, but she kept crying.

'It's fine,' said Sarah. 'Don't worry about it. I'll clean it up. Do you want a cup of tea or something? Stay in that chair, there's glass everywhere.'

Ana sat silently, tears rolling down her face, while Sarah cleared away the shards of broken glass and mopped up the briny pool on the floor.

'See?' said Sarah as she finished up. 'It's all fine, no harm done. We were bound to break at least a couple. I'm surprised it took us this long, honestly.' She looked over at Ana, smiling brightly.

Ana looked stricken. She looked up at Sarah, her eyes red. She gulped a couple of times, and then bit her lip. 'I'm pregnant,' she said.

*   *   *

Sarah gaped. She moved silently to the chair beside Ana's and sat down.

'Oh,' she said.

Ana gave a sniff from beside her.

'When did you find out?' Sarah asked.

'Last week,' said Ana. 'I stole a test from the shop because I didn't want anyone to know.'

'Does Marcus know?'

Ana shook her head. 'I hadn't worked out how to tell him yet. And then . . .'

Sarah nodded. 'Then he went with Thomas.'

'And what if he doesn't come back?'

'He's going to come back. He's not going to die out there. He's just going to get a little bit wet.'

Ana swallowed. 'But,' she said, 'what if they make it across? What if they keep going? They could be gone for weeks. Months, even. If they take too long exploring, they'll have to find somewhere to stay for the full winter.'

Sarah hadn't thought of that, and for a moment the thought left her breathless. 'No,' she said, giving her head a little shake. 'They'll know that they can't stay for long. They'll know coming back is only going to get more dangerous the longer they leave it.'

'Do you think?' said Ana.

'Yeah, of course. They'll have thought of all this. I bet they decided on a return date before they even left. They'll be back in a couple of weeks. A month, max – I'm sure of it.'

'But what if—'

'Ana.' Sarah took her hand and looked at her, trying to steady her. 'It will be OK. He'll be back. And I'm here. We're all here. We can help you.'

Ana took a couple of steadying breaths and nodded. 'OK,' she said.

'OK,' Sarah said. Ana gave her a watery smile and they slowly got back to work.

She waited a while to make sure Ana was feeling better before she asked her if she'd spoken to Billie.

'No,' Ana said. 'I know I have to, I just . . . I don't want her to judge me.'

'It's illegal for her to judge you,' Sarah said. 'And she wouldn't, anyway.'

'I know she wouldn't. In my head, I know she wouldn't. I just can't quite convince myself to believe it.'

'I can come with you, if you want?'

Ana looked at her, brightening. 'Would you? I know I should bring my mum, but I just don't want to until I'm sure. Like *sure*, sure. I don't want to get her all worried and then it's a false positive. That can happen, right? The tests, they're not a hundred per cent accurate?'

'I guess,' said Sarah. 'I'm not really sure, though. I've never had to, you know . . . That's why you should see my mam.'

'Yeah,' said Ana. She was looking a lot more cheerful. 'You're sure you can come with me?'

Sarah smiled. 'Of course I'll come with you,' she said. 'And it'll be fine.'

Recriminations

The destruction of Helen's vineyard brought an unexpected if begrudging appeasement to Black Crag. The extent of Helen's injuries, the risk the fire had carried of spreading to the other crops – crops they now relied on for survival – the obvious spite of the act – all this made it clear that things had to calm down. They could not be allowed to escalate.

There was a general agreement not to respond to the fire, although most people thought they knew who was responsible. But that is not to say there were no consequences.

There had been an evenness to the disagreements in Black Crag up to that point. There was no fringe viewpoint, just different but understandable views. Those who ranged themselves with Graeme, insisting that the most pressing need was surviving the winter ahead, more or less sympathised with their opponents, who rallied behind Thomas and his belief that they needed to explore further afield as soon as possible.

But Thomas found his camp of supporters decimated after the fire. He insisted he hadn't been responsible for it, that he didn't know who was behind it, but no one believed them. And no one had the appetite for more investigation.

There was harvesting to be done, winter to prepare for. Justice was a luxury and there was no time to spare for it.

And the one person who could have proved Thomas's claim chose not to. He stayed out of the way, tending to his wife's ruined hands, praying no one would ever discover the truth. He would regret his drunken act of revenge for the rest of his life.

As for Thomas, he was busy with other things now. He was getting out, one way or another.

Chapter Fifteen

Sarah had never actually been in her mam's surgery before. Whenever she was ill, Mam took a look at her at home, usually just to decide whether or not she needed a prescription.

Elliot had been in there to have his arm X-rayed and plastered when he broke it on a hike with his friends, but Sarah had never broken anything. It felt oddly formal to go in and sit waiting by the nurse's desk while Beth sat there, writing up patient charts.

Ana was fidgeting nervously in the chair next to her. Sarah tried to give her an encouraging smile, but somehow on her face it felt more like a rictus grin. Finally, Mam came out and beckoned them in.

She asked Ana a few questions, and Sarah tried not to feel awkward about hearing the answers. Ana didn't seem to be embarrassed talking about any of it in front of Sarah; the least she could do was match her.

Finally, Billie examined Ana and confirmed she was pregnant.

'At least six weeks,' she said. 'But it's not an exact science.' She sat down, facing Ana. 'I don't know if you've thought about what you want to do,' Billie said. 'But we can talk through your options properly, so you can make your decision with all the information.'

Ana nodded. She suddenly seemed very young to Sarah.

'I always wanted to be a mother,' she said. 'One day, you know. But not . . .'

'I understand,' said Billie.

'It's just, I thought I'd be older. I thought I'd be married. And that the world wouldn't have just ended.'

Billie gave a small, sad smile. 'Well, that's one of the things we should talk about,' she said. 'We are limited with what we can do here, of course. Normally, if you decided not to go forward with the pregnancy, I'd refer you to a doctor on the mainland. In our current situation, I'd perform the procedure myself.'

'Is that . . . I mean, would you . . .'

Billie sighed. 'Before you make this decision, it's important that you know that this isn't a procedure I've performed on my own before. I know how to do it; I learned how to do it in med school. But I never worked in sexual health, so I don't have any experience there.

'I also don't have any experienced support, and I don't have any specialist equipment to deal with complications.'

Sarah sat, trying not to make a sound. The conversation felt so adult. So much bigger than she was prepared for. She couldn't imagine how Ana was feeling.

'What does that all mean?' Ana was saying.

'It means there are risks,' said Billie. 'There are risks to any medical procedure, and all of those are made worse by the fact that I can't send you to a hospital.'

'But if I . . .'

'If you choose to carry the pregnancy to term, there are also risks. In many ways, the risks are higher. There's a greater variety of things that could potentially go wrong. If the baby is breech, if you need an emergency caesarean section . . . And again, I have delivered babies before, but I'm not a specialist. If there are complications, well. It will be worse for you than it would otherwise.'

'Wow,' said Ana. 'So either way, it's scary.'

Billie nodded, but reached out to take Ana's hand. 'Look, I don't want you to dwell too much on what could go wrong. These are not the ideal circumstances for anything, but both abortion and childbirth are extremely common. They've both been extremely common for thousands of years, long before hospitals ever existed. Modern medicine has helped us be better at dealing with complications. Being stuck out here, we've essentially gone back in time. I don't want you to panic about this – it is a normal, natural thing and it will almost definitely be fine, either way. It's just that this is a big decision, and you need to face it with your eyes open.'

Ana nodded. 'But I need to make it quickly, don't I?'

'Quicker is better, yes,' said Billie.

Ana bit her lip. 'I haven't told the father. He's, um . . .' She looked to Sarah, who tried to smile, tried to be encouraging. Ana turned back to Billie. 'He went with Thomas.'

'I see,' said Billie. 'Well, you have to do what is going to be best for you. But can I give you some advice? Give yourself a deadline. It's natural to want to talk it through with the father, but if he takes more than a week or two to come back, then I would want you to be prepared to make the call without him.'

Ana nodded, but looked miserable. Sarah tried to think of something to say to make her feel better, but there was nothing. This was harder than anything Sarah had ever faced.

'Look,' Billie said, 'I have been pregnant, and I have watched people I love be pregnant. It's a big thing to put your body through. And your mind. Even in normal circumstances, pregnancy and childbirth are a huge sacrifice. What the father wants – that's important. But you're the one who actually has to do this. It's your decision to make.'

After Ana had gone back home, Sarah wandered down to the shore. She hadn't wanted to let anyone see how scared she was for her friend.

She hadn't fully comprehended how vulnerable they could be out here, without access to proper medical help. She'd trusted her Mam to do everything that was needed, and hadn't thought about how limited she was. Perhaps she hadn't wanted to think about it.

Mam had said that the chances of something going wrong were low, but now they were all Sarah could think about. She remembered every story she'd ever heard about disastrous pregnancies and labours. She only vaguely remembered her mam being pregnant with Elliot, but that had all been fine, hadn't it? She didn't remember any stress or panic. Just a more tired Mam and then a baby brother.

She wondered what she would do if it were her. She was pretty sure she wouldn't be able to go through with a pregnancy. She couldn't endure the months of fear with nowhere to go if something went wrong.

When she reached the shore, she could see Arthur sitting out at the end of the jetty again. Sarah turned to walk away, but after a moment she turned back. Arthur wouldn't bother her. He never bothered anyone. He still didn't really speak to anyone. Just the occasional 'yes' or 'no' when someone asked him if he wanted a drink or a seat.

Sarah had never tried to talk to him. It seemed to her that the villagers were split into two camps regarding Arthur. There were those who tried constantly to bring him out of himself, aggressively chit-chatting whenever they saw him, asking him questions and staring at him as they waited for an answer he wouldn't give.

And there were those who seemed to regard him as a spook. Who blanched when they saw him, and turned away. Who took pains to avoid him, afraid of what he'd seen. Of what he knew. Sarah realised she didn't want to do either of those things.

So she walked down the jetty, gave Arthur a small nod, and sat down. She'd thought it would feel awkward to sit there in silence beside someone else, but somehow it wasn't. It even felt somehow comforting. Comfortable. She didn't feel pressured to make any kind of conversation, but she didn't feel alone. It was nice, somehow, to just be near someone else, peacefully.

As she sat there, the sun lowering in the sky, she found she was thinking less of what could go wrong for Ana and more about what could be wonderful. Ana would be a great mum, she was sure of it. It felt so adult to think about, like Ana had taken a giant step forward in life. There was a strangeness to it, but something about it fit as well. So much of life had ground to a halt. It was nice to see this way that it could continue.

Sarah sat out there for hours, and when she eventually made her way back home she felt more rested than she had in a long time.

Sarah and Ana didn't talk about the pregnancy for the next two weeks. Sarah asked how she was a couple of times, and Ana just laughed at her.

'I don't think you've ever asked me that before in your life,' she said. 'Obviously, I'm fine.'

And she did seem fine. There was a lot to distract her.

Graeme had decided to butcher a couple of his pigs, and Ana and Sarah had volunteered to help. He didn't have that many, and he wanted to keep a few for breeding, but it would be harder to fish as the weather got colder, so he'd decided to store up some pork for the winter.

Sarah was surprised by how enthusiastic Ana was about the whole process. Graeme had a smoking shed, and she and Ana spent an afternoon hanging up meat.

They learned to make sausages, which were messy to look at, but which Graeme assured them would still taste just as good.

'And you'll do even better next time,' he said. 'Give it a season or two, and you'll be expert butchers.'

Sarah was strangely proud.

'I never thought I'd do this kind of thing,' she said to Ana, as they walked back to the centre of the village. 'I always thought farms were gross, unless you were seeing them from a distance. The rolling fields are pretty; the dirt and animals and meat are disgusting. But there's something satisfying about it.'

'I don't know, I think it's still pretty gross,' said Ana. 'But butchering is more interesting than preserving, at least.'

They chatted idly as they walked, but after a while, Ana fell silent.

'Are you . . . OK?' said Sarah.

Ana laughed. 'Fifth time you've asked me that today,' she said.

'No,' said Sarah. 'It's not.'

'It is, I'm keeping a tally.' Ana took a deep breath. 'I think

I'm going to keep it,' she said quickly. 'The baby. I told my parents last night.'

'Oh my god,' said Sarah. 'That's amazing!' She stared at her friend in awe. 'I thought you were going to wait for Marcus to come back.'

'Yeah,' said Ana. 'I need to talk to him about it, of course, but even if he doesn't want to, I think I will. Who needs him? He's boring, anyway. And my mum will help – and you'll help, won't you?'

Sarah felt a lump rise in her throat. She stopped walking and pulled her friend in close, wrapping her arms around her. 'Of course I'll help. And Moth and Mam will too. Everyone will. This will be the proverbial village that raises a child.'

Ana laughed. 'Yeah,' she said. 'I like that.'

They kept walking in companionable silence. Ana seemed calmer now. Happier. Sarah felt a sense of awe at her friend's decision. She was facing a future suddenly so different from the one she'd imagined. The one they'd all imagined. It occurred to Sarah that the village had been approaching their situation as something temporary. They were all waiting out the disaster, hoping that eventually someone would find them. Some kind of normality would return. But what if it never did?

Sarah saw a vision of the future on this island. A future where no one ever came to find them. Where they were left alone forever. They were managing to survive on the dregs of their old lives for now, but that couldn't last forever. If no one came for them, things would have to change.

By the time Ana's child was walking, they would have had to find a different way to live. But somehow, Sarah wasn't afraid of what that would look like. She'd grown to trust the people around her. They were resilient, creative. Somehow, she knew they could make something good.

Then she turned to Ana and said, 'What are you going to use for nappies?'

Ana stared at her. 'Oh god,' she said.

Chapter Sixteen

She wasn't the only one to think about that problem.

When Sarah's parents heard about Ana's decision, they sent her round with a pile of old baby things. Within a few days, the pile had more than doubled in size, thanks to a couple of family friends. Ana confessed to Sarah that, while she was grateful for the donations, she was worried about how many people seemed to know she was pregnant.

'It's my mum,' she said. 'I know it's my mum. I keep telling her I don't want anyone else to know until Marcus does, but she can't help herself. She just says, "I'm not telling anyone. It's just Doreen from next door and she won't tell a soul," but souls are being told and it's not me doing it.'

Sarah reassured her that the village at large hadn't heard the news yet, but she couldn't deny the slow but steady trickle of childcare supplies – and advice – that was coming in through Ana's front door.

Sarah and Ana were sitting mystified in front of a pile of old cloth nappies when Beth dropped in with a stack of rubber bottle caps.

'Oh,' she said, when she saw what they were looking at. 'These are easy. Just make a triangle and wrap the butt like it's fish and chips.'

She laughed at the look on their faces. 'This is what I grew up with,' she said. 'My mum couldn't afford disposables, so she used these. And I have three younger siblings I had to help with, so I know what I'm doing.' Her face paled for a moment, and her lip trembled. She gave her head a small shake and cleared her throat before continuing. 'So I can teach you how to use those. You'll pick it up in no time. You'll have to do a lot of laundry, but you'll be fine. The only thing is, with the old cloth ones, you can get a lot of nappy rash. I'll make a note to check how much emollient cream we have and put all of it aside for you.'

'Thanks,' said Ana, looking a bit startled. 'There are just so many things.'

Beth smiled. 'There are,' she said. 'But it will be wonderful. And we're all here to help.'

She stayed for a while, demonstrating how to use cloth nappies on one of the teddy bears someone had dropped off, making both Ana and Sarah laugh.

She was still there an hour or so later, when Jeremy dropped in with an old wooden toy train.

'Who told you?' Ana demanded, her eyes narrowing. 'Beth I get, she's the nurse, but you?'

Jeremy looked embarrassed. 'Oh,' he said. 'Your mum did. But she made me promise not to tell anyone else. And I haven't.'

Ana rolled her eyes. 'Well, thank you for the train.'

'Now, I know most people bring stuffed animals for a baby,' Jeremy said, 'but my mum always told me this was the only thing I'd have in bed with me. So just in case your baby is like me, I thought you could use it.'

'OK,' said Ana blankly. 'Thanks.'

'His name', Jeremy said, in tones of great importance, 'is Sir Peanut.'

Beth cleared her throat. 'And is it necessary to him that Ana's baby call him by this name? Or if they choose a different name for him, will he be comfortable with that?'

'Well,' said Jeremy, 'I cannot speak for Sir Peanut, of course, but I myself have always found him a genial and accommodating engine. I'm Jeremy, by the way. I'm sure you know that, we've seen each other around, but I don't think we've every properly met.' Beth's eyes were dancing.

Sarah burst out laughing. She was about to offer Jeremy something to drink when there was a shout from outside.

All four of them turned to the window. Jeremy went to the door and pulled it open. He called, 'What's going on?' to someone Sarah couldn't see.

'They're back,' they said. 'Thomas – he's back.'

Sarah turned to Ana, whose eyes were wide.

'Don't tell him' she whispered.

News of the return raced through the village, and without anyone calling for it, soon everyone was assembled for an impromptu meeting. Sarah and Ana crowded in at the back, craning their necks to see.

Thomas was standing in the centre of the crowd, looking battered and exhausted. It took a moment for Sarah to pinpoint Marcus – he was sitting to the side, his head in his hands. There were questions pouring forth from all sides, but Thomas was ignoring all of them.

'Wasn't there a third guy with them?' Sarah asked Ana. 'It wasn't just the two of them, right?'

Someone overheard her and said, 'Yeah, Will Dougan was with them, but they brought him back in pretty bad shape. Someone took him up to see the doctor.'

Sarah and Ana glanced at each other, and back over to where Marcus was sitting.

Finally, Thomas put up his hand. 'Yeah, all right,' he said. 'Everyone calm down and back off. I'll tell you what we found, but for god's sake, give us some space.'

Slowly, the crowd quietened down.

'Look, the road is impassable,' he said. 'I know a bunch of you said it was, and you were right, so bully for you. There are chunks entirely fallen away, sometimes a couple of feet wide. So even if you'd let me take the car, we wouldn't have been able to make it across.'

He looked defiantly out at the assembled villagers, as if he was expecting a chorus of I told you so, but it didn't come. There was complete stillness.

Thomas looked at the floor, and back up again. 'I think it's possible to make it by foot. But it's much harder than we thought it would be. There's a long stretch of road that has sunk below the high-tide line. I don't know how long it takes to cross that bit of road. We were in the middle of it when we had to turn back.

'It's . . . The water is unpredictable. Even when it's not high tide, there are swells that wash over the land. They can knock you off your feet. I imagine that they could drag you out to sea, even.'

There was a hush. Then someone close to the centre asked, 'What happened to Will?'

Thomas's mouth twisted into a grimace. 'That's why we

turned back. There are bits of road that have obviously been underwater for long stretches of time. There's algae growing on them; they're slippery. Treacherous. Will fell. He hit his head, and a swell came at that moment. It took a couple of minutes before we could get him out of the water.

'I think he's OK; he wasn't unconscious for long, and we helped him as much as we could on the way back. But we'd been walking for five days when it happened. Coming back . . . Coming back took longer.'

'So that's it, then,' someone said. 'We really are trapped.'

Thomas's eyes snapped to the person who'd spoken. 'No,' he said. 'We have to keep trying. The road . . . The road might be too dangerous. But we can sail across to the mainland in a few hours. We just have to fix that boat.'

Someone somewhere scoffed. 'That's a lot of fixing.'

Thomas scowled. 'Yes, it is a lot of fixing. Do you think I can't do it?'

There was silence.

'I'm going to reach the mainland,' he said. 'Anyone is free to help me. I know Graeme might tell you it's a wasted effort. He might tell you we should all just live here happily on our own forever. But we have to find others. We have to find out if there is a world to re-join.

'That's my mission. You can join me if you want.' He scowled. 'Now leave me alone. I'm going to get some rest.'

There was stillness and then a rising hubbub after Thomas had left. Sarah saw Marcus's mother take his arm and lead him away. He looked too exhausted to know what was happening to him.

Sarah turned to Ana, who looked shellshocked.

'Oh my god,' she said, her eyes wide as she stared back at Sarah. 'He could have died. He really could have died.' Tears were gathering in her eyes. 'I should go. I should go after him.'

'Look,' said Sarah, pulling her aside, 'not now. You saw him, he's barely upright. His mother's looking after him. She'll feed him, and then I guess he'll sleep for a million years. Don't go after him now.'

'But what if . . .'

'He needs time, Ana. At least a night. And you need to recover from the shock before you talk to him. About anything significant. You know.'

'Yeah,' said Ana. 'You're right. But he might expect me to be there.'

'He won't be awake enough to expect anything. And it's not like you're his girlfriend, right?'

'No, I guess. And we've barely even seen each other at all for, like, three weeks.'

'Right. And he doesn't know about the baby. So he won't expect you. And he's not ready to hear about it.'

Ana looked dazed, but she was nodding. 'Maybe you're right,' she said.

'Definitely I'm right,' said Sarah. 'Go see him tomorrow.' She thought about it for a moment. 'Quite late tomorrow, I'd say.'

Chapter Seventeen

In the end, it was two days before Ana could talk to Marcus.

The evening Thomas came back, Billie spent a few hours looking after Will, and confirmed he had a concussion and mild dehydration.

Sarah asked her for more details when she got home, but all she'd say was not to worry. The next day, she went off to check on Thomas and Marcus. Sarah couldn't imagine that Thomas would give her the time of day, but Mam said he'd been perfectly civil.

He had a few cuts and bruises that she'd cleaned out of fear of infection and, like Will, he was dehydrated, but largely fine. But when she went to check on Marcus, his mother wouldn't let her in. She said she wasn't going to wake him up, and that Billie could come by later.

Ana turned up at Sarah's in the afternoon, saying Marcus's mum wouldn't let her in either. She was determined to let him rest and recover for a few days before she let anyone, as she put it, 'pester him half to death'.

'Does she know about the baby?' asked Sarah.

'If she's heard, she hasn't mentioned it to me.'

'So why does she think you'd pester him?' asked Sarah.

'I don't know,' said Ana. 'But it doesn't really matter, because the moment he's caught up on his sleep, he'll be out the door on a bender with his friends, regardless of what she says.'

That prospect seemed to make Ana even gloomier.

'Isn't that good?' said Sarah. 'If he gets out of the house himself, you can talk to him without her even knowing, if you want to.'

'I don't think interrupting a raucous night with the boys to give him a piece of life-changing news is the play, to be honest,' said Ana.

'Right. Fair enough.'

'And then he'll be wildly hungover so won't want to see anyone the day after. What a nightmare.' Ana was chewing on the inside of her lip in worry.

'Is it so important you tell him right now?' said Sarah. 'If you've already made your own decision anyway?'

'I'm just worried someone else will tell him.'

'Oh,' said Sarah. 'I thought I was the only person who knew who the father is.'

Ana rolled her eyes. 'You're the only person I've *told* who the father is. That doesn't mean you're the only person who *knows*. It's not like there are other possibilities. Besides, if he hears I'm pregnant at all, he'll know it's him – and everyone knows I'm pregnant.'

Sarah couldn't argue with that logic. 'What are you going to do?' she said.

'I don't know. Try to catch him in the two minutes between him fighting his way out of the house and being three pints deep?'

Sarah did her best to keep Ana distracted. She wrote a long list of absurd baby names for her entertainment, and came up with a complicated plan to train the baby as a spy. Ana played along with it all, but she was distracted and morose, and left after a little over an hour.

Sarah sighed as she closed the door after her. She didn't know how to be helpful – and she wanted so much to be helpful.

Sarah and Ana spent the next day in the fields, and brought back a load of fruit and veggies to the shop. Anything that couldn't be preserved was put out for people to help themselves to as they needed.

When they came back outside after dropping off the food, there was Marcus, walking down the road. Ana put out a hand and grabbed Sarah's arm.

'It's OK,' said Sarah. 'Go talk to him. I'm here.'

But they were too late. A yell of 'Ey! He's out!' came from the left, and a couple of Marcus's friends barrelled up to him, dragging him off in the direction of the pub.

'Oh god,' said Ana.

'Maybe no one will tell him,' said Sarah. 'Do you want to go to the pub too?'

But Ana elected to stay away. She seemed nervous and fidgety, so Sarah offered to keep her company. They walked slowly to Ana's house, and Ana started absently looking through some of the bags of baby clothes people had dropped off to her, while Sarah desperately tried to think of something to say to distract her.

They'd been there less than half an hour when Marcus started banging on Ana's front door.

'Goddammit,' said Ana.

'Hi,' she said, after she let him in. 'You're looking well.'

'I can't believe you'd do this to me,' Marcus said.

'Hey,' said Sarah, standing up, and coming to stand with Ana.

'I know we weren't an official couple or whatever,' he continued, 'but you said you weren't seeing anyone else.'

Sarah stared at him in confusion. Ana seemed just as confused as she was.

'What?' said Ana. 'What are you talking about?'

'Whose is it?' said Marcus.

Sarah stared. She'd never thought that much of Marcus, but she'd assumed he was smarter than this.

'Marcus, you're not—'

He cut Ana off before she could finish her sentence. 'I know you're pregnant,' he shouted. 'So whose is it?'

Ana suddenly burst out laughing. She looked at Sarah, who gave an awkward smile in return.

'Don't laugh at me,' said Marcus. 'Tell me who the father is.'

'Oh for god's sake, Marcus,' said Ana. 'It's you.'

Marcus stood there blinking for a moment. 'What?' he said. He'd gone from red in the face to pale in less than a second. Sarah wondered if finding out he was the father was worse for him than believing someone else was. He didn't seem the type to embrace parenthood.

'You're the father. It's your baby,' Ana was saying.

'Are you sure?'

She rolled her eyes. 'Of course I'm sure. Why would I not be sure?'

'Oh.' He swayed a bit. 'I . . . I don't . . .'

Ana gave a sigh of exasperation. 'You're drunk. Let's not talk about this now.'

'But I . . .'

'Seriously,' said Ana. She put her hands on his shoulders and forcibly turned him around. 'Go back to your friends. We can talk tomorrow.'

'Right,' said Marcus. 'OK.' He stumbled back down the path. Sarah could see a few other guys hovering around the gate, and when he reached them, a general cheer went up, and they bore him away.

Ana sighed as she closed the front door. 'I hope the baby is smarter than its dad,' she said. But she was grinning.

Sarah tried to smile in return, but she could feel it wasn't convincing. Maybe she was wrong, but somehow she couldn't picture this little family unit working for long.

Nathaniel called out to Sarah as she walked home from Ana's.

'How's your friend?' he asked.

'You know her name,' Sarah said raising an eyebrow at him. 'You've known her longer than I have, surely.'

'Only in that we've lived in the same tiny village since we were born,' he said.

'That's what I'm saying,' Sarah said. 'You went to a tiny school with her for twelve years.' She didn't understand how Nathaniel always made her feel like she was supposed to introduce him to people. Like he was new here. 'You've lived here your whole life and you never seem to talk to anyone,' she said.

'Sure I do,' said Nathaniel. 'I talk to my dad. I talk to my friends.'

'What friends? Every time I see you, you're alone.'

Nathaniel clasped his hands to his chest and widened his

eyes in mock dismay. 'Wow,' he said. 'I can't believe you think I have no friends.'

Sarah rolled her eyes. 'Yes, sorry. I'm sure you're the belle of every ball, never a dull evening.'

Nathaniel laughed a little ruefully. 'I keep myself happy,' he said.

Sarah felt bad for a moment. Maybe she was prodding him in a sore spot. Maybe it wasn't by choice that he was so often alone.

They walked in silence for a while. They'd spent a fair bit of time together working in the fields, but somehow Sarah still didn't feel like she knew him at all. Maybe he felt awkward about everything he'd told her about himself. Maybe he regretted it.

'Are *we* friends?' she asked suddenly.

Nathaniel stared at her. 'I thought so,' he said. 'I hope so. Why wouldn't we be?'

Sarah shook her head a bit as she walked. 'I don't understand you. I never know when you're serious. You tell me something personal about yourself, and then you get all flippant and weird and I don't know how to talk to you. I try to make you feel comfortable with my friends, and you're all cold and rude. I don't know what you want.'

Nathaniel was silent for a while. They were almost at Sarah's house before he answered.

'I have a thing,' he said. 'It's probably really selfish. Mean, you know. But I get frustrated at having the same conversations over again. Do you know? Like, over and over again. And it happens a lot in a place like this. I feel like I've had every possible conversation with every possible person on this island.'

Sarah swallowed and nodded. She knew what he was talking about. It was one of the reasons she'd been so looking forward to leaving. To have days that were different. Conversations that were different. To have things to tell people that they'd never heard before. But she knew that wasn't really being fair on people. There was always something to talk about with Ana, for example. Even if they spent all their time together, they found something to keep them going.

It was only with the people she wasn't particularly close to that she had the same conversations. And somehow, she suspected that if she really wanted to, she could find something new to talk to them about too.

'Except me?' she said. 'There are conversations you haven't had with me?'

'I guess.' Nathaniel was looking at the ground.

'That *is* really mean,' said Sarah. 'To everyone else.'

'Yeah,' he said. 'It's probably not fair of me. I should try harder.'

'Well, if it helps,' said Sarah, 'I cannot imagine you ever having any conversation that follows predictable patterns.'

Nathaniel let out a shout of laughter. 'It does,' he said. 'It does help.'

Sarah laughed with him. As they walked slowly through the village, she decided she was enjoying this strange new friendship. She'd known Ana so well for so long – she could almost always tell how she was feeling or what she was thinking. It was a comfortable, reliable friendship.

But there was something refreshing about talking to Nathaniel, about not understanding him. About knowing she had a lot to learn about him. There was something satisfying about slowly figuring him out.

*   *   *

Sarah didn't hear from Ana at all the next day. She knew she would be talking to Marcus, and Sarah was desperate to know how the conversation had gone, but she figured that Ana would come and talk to her if she wanted to. Ana and Marcus needed space to talk to each other without interference.

But it was hard to keep away.

Late on the second day, she gave up. She grabbed Moth's bike and rode over to Ana's house, hoping she'd be there alone and ready to talk. To her surprise, Marcus was there, looking over the pile of toys people had brought round.

'It's all so old,' he was saying.

'Well, yeah,' Ana said. 'Everyone gave us their own stuff. It's not like they can go and buy new things.'

'I know,' said Marcus. 'It's just a bummer. Well. I bet when we make it to the mainland, we'll find loads of shops full of stuff we can just take.'

Sarah stared at him, and then at Ana. Surely, after the disastrous trip to the isthmus, Marcus would give up on the idea of going to the mainland, especially after he'd found out about the baby.

'Wait,' she said. 'You're not still planning on going with Thomas?'

Marcus turned to look at her as she stood in the doorway. 'Yeah,' he said. 'Of course. It'll be much quicker by boat, though. Once we've fixed it. But we can do that easy.'

Sarah looked over at Ana, who wouldn't meet her eye. 'Don't you think you should let someone else go?' Sarah said. 'Someone who doesn't have a baby on the way?'

Marcus shrugged. 'Nah. It's not like there's much I can do

till it's born. Or even after that, really, right? Ana will take care of all the early stuff.'

'Wow,' said Sarah, with a disbelieving laugh. 'Congrats on the antiquated views.'

'What?'

Sarah raised an eyebrow and opened her mouth to elaborate, but Ana interrupted her.

'Marcus,' she said, 'didn't you say your mum wanted you to bring her something from the shop? Why don't you go do that? I'll see you tomorrow.'

Marcus grumbled a bit, but left. Sarah turned to Ana, outrage still splashed across her face.

'So I guess he's decided not to be involved then,' she said. She was ready to launch into a tirade against him, against men in general, but Ana was looking back at her a little defiantly.

'You're wrong,' said Ana. 'Actually, he's really excited. We're going to try and do it properly. Together.'

Sarah stared. 'As a couple?'

'Yeah,' said Ana. 'I mean, we're not getting married or anything. Not going to move in together just yet, although maybe we will before the baby arrives.'

Sarah was taken aback. She hadn't understood why Ana was so attracted to Marcus, but that hadn't seemed to matter when it was just a fling. But what if Ana let herself get in deeper, just because of the baby? She'd always wanted to have a family; she'd always talked about falling in love and getting married. Sarah started to worry that she might convince herself to be in love with Marcus and wind up getting her heart broken.

'Ana,' Sarah said, as she sat beside her friend. 'Are you sure? He doesn't seem to have any idea what this is going to be like.'

'OK, but neither do I,' said Ana. 'Neither do you.'

'We at least know that it's not going to be entirely up to you to take care of everything.'

'No, but I am going to have to do most of it, in the beginning,' Ana said. The defiance was gone; she was talking earnestly. It occurred to Sarah for the first time that, however much she'd been thinking about this baby, Ana had been thinking about it much, much more. 'I checked the baby formula in the shop. Most of it will be out of date by the time the baby arrives. And the only breast pump on the island is hand-operated, so I can't imagine I'll use it much. So he's not wrong. For the first few months, I'll have to be with the baby all the time.'

Sarah sighed and sat down. She tried to rein back her frustration with Marcus, but she still couldn't believe how ready he was to dismiss his role in all this.

'So you're OK with him popping off to the mainland to explore god knows what carnage in a leaky boat?' she said.

Ana sighed. 'Look, I said he could be as involved a father as he wanted. This is how involved he wants to be.'

'OK,' Sarah said, frowning. 'I'm just worried he thinks this is, I don't know, completely involved. When it's actually only a very little bit involved.'

'Sarah, give him a break,' said Ana, but she laughed a little. 'He's only just found out. The man's literally never thought about what a baby *is* before in his whole life.'

Sarah laughed as well. 'I'm sorry,' she said. She took a deep breath and closed her eyes. 'I promise I will give him a chance.'

Ana smiled and said thank you, and that was that.

But Sarah biked home with a frown on her face. She could only hope that by the time the boat was fixed, Marcus would realise he had to stay behind.

Chapter Eighteen

Nathaniel didn't really know why he started talking to Thomas. He found him leaning on a fence at the edge of the village looking out over the ocean, and somehow he looked less belligerent than usual. A bit dejected, even.

Nathaniel waved a small hello at him and started to walk on, before some instinct prompted him to turn back. He leaned on the fence beside him and, for a moment, he said nothing. Thomas glanced at him, but didn't move.

'It's nice to have a few warm days this close to winter,' Nathaniel said, after a while. 'Pretty soon being outside for long will be unbearable.'

Thomas gave a grunt in reply.

'I hate winter in this place,' Nathaniel went on. 'Stuck inside with nothing to do.'

Thomas grunted. 'It's the dark for me,' he said. 'Sun barely comes out and it goes down again. Makes you feel sort of dead.'

Nathaniel nodded. 'Yeah,' he said. 'I know what you mean.'

'Hemmed in. That's what it is. No way out.'

They stood there for a while longer. The light was already beginning to fade. Nathaniel wasn't sure why, but he wanted to keep Thomas talking. He assumed that Thomas had plenty going on, friends he could talk to, pastimes that meant something to him. But every time Nathaniel had seen him around the village, he just seemed to be furious. Hemmed in was right, Nathaniel thought. He did seem trapped.

'Was it easier over there?' Nathaniel nodded towards the mainland. 'Winter, I mean.'

Thomas gave a short, humourless laugh. 'I didn't think it was easy when I lived there,' he said. 'But compared to here?' He shook his head slightly. 'There was nothing to stop you leaving whenever you wanted. Jumping in the truck and heading into the distance for however long.'

Nathaniel hesitated for a moment. 'Is that why you want to get back over there?' he said.

Thomas's mouth twisted briefly. 'No,' he said. 'No, that's not why.' He sighed. 'I just think it's crazy how happy everyone is to live in ignorance. We should be trying to figure out what's going on. How can they all stand it, just living day after day without knowing?'

For some reason, Nathaniel thought Thomas was holding something back. Which was only fair, he supposed. They didn't really know each other very well. There was no reason for Thomas to be completely honest with him. But he couldn't help wondering what it was he wasn't saying.

'Maybe they're hoping Arthur will be able to tell us soon. He seems to be recovering OK.'

Thomas scowls. 'Anyone who puts that question to Arthur will have to answer to me. I was the one who got him off that boat. What he saw broke him and for all we know asking him to relive it will send him right back there.'

Nathaniel didn't reply.

'It's laziness,' Thomas said. 'People only want the answers

195

if they come easy. They're not willing to put themselves on the line to get them.'

'Maybe', said Nathaniel, 'people do want to know. I'm sure plenty of them are desperate to know. But it seems too risky to try yet. I guess they're willing to wait till spring. And I suppose . . .'

Thomas turned to look at him as he trailed off.

Nathaniel cleared his throat awkwardly. 'I don't know,' he said. 'I think as desperate as people are to know what happened over there, they're also scared to find out. Whatever it was, it's going to be a horrible reality to face.'

Thomas scoffed. 'It's not going to get any nicer if we wait,' he said.

'No,' said Nathaniel. 'No, it is not.'

After that, Nathaniel started nodding to Thomas whenever he saw him. Eventually, Thomas started nodding back. Every so often, they said a few words of greeting to each other, occasionally commented on things that were going on around the village. Innocuous things, nothing concerning the big questions.

They grabbed a drink together a couple of times. Somehow, they developed something of a friendship, despite their ten-year age gap. It became clear that Thomas didn't really have other friends. There were a few others on the island that had ranged themselves on his side regarding trying to get to the mainland. But all they ever seemed to talk about was which tactics to use, how to fix the boat, who in the village might stand in their way.

It didn't seem that any of them really knew Thomas all that well. Nathaniel knew he'd only been in Black Crag for a couple of years, but it seemed strange – and sad – that in that time, there was no one he'd got to know particularly well. No one who'd got to know him.

So perhaps it wasn't so surprising that one night, after a few drinks, Thomas told Nathaniel why he'd come to Black Crag in the first place.

He'd been a chemist, he told Nathaniel. A pharmacist in a town he'd thought was small. Until he came to Black Crag and realised what small really was.

He'd taken the job there because it was the first one he was offered, and it had taken a good year of searching to find it. But he resented it from the start. Always wanted to live somewhere bigger, somewhere brighter, somewhere better.

After a while, he met a nice woman and got engaged. And he loved her, but somehow she also made him feel trapped. She was a tether to a place he thought he was above. He couldn't cope with how much he hated his situation, and he couldn't stop hating it.

He knew his fiancée never wanted to leave. She loved her life in this little town where she'd grown up. Loved being near her family. Wanted to raise her children in the same way she was raised.

The frustration and bitterness had curdled until he'd started looking for ways to shield himself from it. Which was easy, given what he had access to at work.

He was fired on the same day his fiancée told him she was pregnant. He was high and he'd just been fired, and he looked at her and said, 'Well, I guess I'm never getting away from here now,' and she stared at him for a moment. When he woke up the next morning, she was gone.

Her family wouldn't talk to him. For a week or so, he'd

walked around in a daze, working through the stash he had left over from the pharmacy, waiting for her to come home. But she didn't. Eventually, one of her friends told him she'd moved to the city. Found a job in an office. An apartment downtown.

That was when Thomas got angry. He'd stayed there in that backwater town because of her, and now she'd moved on without him, gone to live the brighter life he'd wanted. He thought of going after her. He didn't know what he'd do if he found her – beg her to let him stay, or rail at her for leaving. He stewed all through the night, but when morning came, he knew he wouldn't follow her. The idea of crawling after her, whatever the reason, was repellent to him. He wanted to go as far in the other direction as he could.

It's likely that he would still not have left, that he would have stayed simmering in his rage. But his old boss came by asking questions, and he realised it was only a matter of time before it would become clear that he'd been stealing money as well.

The story trickled out of Thomas like rain through a leaky roof. He spoke slowly but incessantly, in a low monotone, his eyes on the drink in his hands. Nathaniel wondered if there was a relief in the telling. Like lancing a boil. It seemed to him that Thomas wasn't completely aware that he was talking.

But then he looked Nathaniel dead in the eye. 'I don't even know', he said, 'if she had the baby. I don't know if I had a kid out there, when . . .' He trailed off and looked back down at his drink. After a moment, he drained what was left of it and walked out.

For a while after that night, Nathaniel didn't see Thomas. He didn't know if he was avoiding him, embarrassed about everything he'd revealed. Nathaniel was ashamed to admit it to himself, but he was a little relieved not to have to make conversation after all that.

He didn't know what he would say. He suspected there wasn't anything. But it felt callous to go back to ordinary conversations as if nothing was different.

He found himself chafing against the village's attitude towards Thomas. It seemed suddenly strange that everyone had an opinion about him without really knowing him at all. They must know they'd only seen one side of him.

But then, he reasoned, if they knew what Nathaniel did, maybe they'd judge Thomas even more harshly. An addict, a thief. Someone who'd driven his lover away with his casual cruelty. But that all seemed like symptoms of something else to Nathaniel.

He didn't know what had really started making Thomas so unhappy, but he was willing to bet that it was more than just hating the town he'd lived in. Maybe Thomas didn't know himself. Maybe that's part of being human. You don't always know what makes you feel the way you feel. You don't always know how to deal with it.

And your ordinary human faults don't always disappear when you're living through disaster.

Injuries

One of the kids helping with the harvest sliced his hand open and, for a while, Billie thought she'd have to amputate it. An infection developed that didn't immediately respond to the limited treatment she could provide.

Her supply of antibiotics had been almost used up by Helen's burns, and there was nothing else Billie could do except keep the wound clean. As she monitored its progress, she considered her dwindling supplies. There were still plenty of bandages, but the medications she kept on hand were all running low.

What would happen when she ran out of Beth's dad's meds? Of her own son's asthma medication? What if there was another infected injury?

She and Beth carried the awareness of the situation between them without discussing it. Billie didn't bring her fears home. If they were careful, if there were no unexpected issues, she thought they could just about make it through the winter. She tried not to think too hard about what would happen beyond it.

She tried to simply do what was in front of her to do.

When the kid's infection began to clear, she tried to take it as a sign. She tried to let herself believe that they could make it.

Chapter Nineteen

After a night of hard frost, the village woke to find that one of the cows had escaped its enclosure and spent the night outside. The cow was OK, but a few of the farmers were concerned about the dangers of it happening again.

'We're lucky this happened this early,' Graeme had said. 'Any later in the year and the cow could have frozen to death. We can't afford to lose any livestock.'

He drew up a list of all the barns and enclosures on the island, and sent out pairs of workers to check they were all secure enough to hold through the winter.

'Any small repairs you feel you can handle yourselves, feel free to take care of them. But make a note of what you do. Anything you feel is beyond your capabilities, or that needs additional materials or tools, add it to the list and we'll return to it over the next few days.'

Sarah saw Ana pair up with Marcus, a hopeful smile on her face, and felt a swell of concern. She couldn't help wishing he and Thomas had made it across the isthmus and spend the next few weeks exploring the mainland. Or that he'd come back and decided he wanted nothing to do with Ana.

She didn't really understand why she felt so worried about him. She'd never paid much attention to him before now; she didn't know him as well as Ana did, so she should be happy to let Ana make her own decisions. And it was true that he was young, that this was the first time he was facing any real responsibility. It was only natural that it would take him a while to get used to the idea of being a father.

She would have to let this go.

She sighed and turned. She was a little surprised to find Nathaniel standing beside her, holding a toolbox. 'Well,' he said, with a smile, 'shall we?'

Sarah found herself relaxing in Nathaniel's company. It was nice to spend a whole day with someone without feeling like there were important things they should be discussing, or painful truths they needed to be distracted from.

He asked how Ana was doing again, and made a couple of snide comments about Marcus that Sarah laughed at. She didn't say anything about him herself – that felt disloyal – but she found it comforting to know that it wasn't just her who found him wanting.

The day passed quietly. They found a few things they could fix themselves, but there was plenty someone would have to come back for.

They walked slowly together over the fields. The day had been clear and bright, but cold. There was still frost on the ground, and their breath crystallised in the air in front of them.

'I've always wanted to ask you,' Nathaniel said, after a while. 'What was it like, living in the city?'

Sarah looked up at him, surprised. 'You've always wanted to ask me that?' she said.

He laughed. 'I remember when your family moved here,'

he said. 'I don't think there had ever been a new kid at school. Everyone else was born here.'

'But I'd been here a lot before we moved,' said Sarah.

'Yeah, but that's not the same.'

'Why not?'

He thought for a moment. 'I don't remember. Maybe I never actually saw you.'

Sarah laughed. She'd never really thought about how her arrival had been seen by the other villagers, by the kids at school. She'd been thinking about herself, about how much she missed her old friends, about how annoyed she was at her mums for making her move.

'But then you started coming to school, and you were different, you know,' Nathaniel said. 'You wore different clothes and your hair was cut differently. You talked differently to everyone else.'

'Oh,' said Sarah. 'I didn't realise I stood out so much.'

'You did to me,' said Nathaniel. 'You were from *the city*, you know? From this mythical place. I was desperate to talk to you about it, to find out what it was like.' There was a self-deprecating edge to his voice.

'Yeah,' said Sarah. 'You and every other kid. All asking me if it was true that cars kept driving even in the night-time. If I had to live in a house with other people. If anyone ever went to sleep at all.'

Nathaniel gave her a sceptical look. 'No one was asking you that,' he said.

Sarah laughed. 'Well, maybe only the very young kids.'

He nodded sombrely. 'Then you should have treated those questions with the gravitas they deserved.'

Sarah smiled. 'What would you have asked?' she said

'I would have asked how many different people you knew, and what they were like.'

'Oh,' said Sarah. She glanced up at him. No one had ever asked her anything like that. 'I don't know how to answer that.'

Nathaniel laughed. 'It just always seemed so wonderful to me, the idea of being surrounded by strangers. Everyone here, I've known forever. I love them, of course, but I know them. I know what our relationship is; I know how I feel about them now, how I'll probably feel about them in ten years. The idea of turning a corner and meeting someone new – that's what I wanted to ask about.'

'I've never really thought about it like that,' said Sarah. She tried to remember how it had felt to live so anonymously, but she couldn't. The people around her in her memories weren't really more than backdrop. She'd never expected to turn a corner and meet someone new. They'd always just be someone to brush past. 'There's something nice about knowing exactly who's around you and how you fit within them,' she said. 'Even if how you fit is badly. But I don't know, maybe there is something special about having that, I don't know, *possibility* all around you.' She laughed. 'I don't know, we moved here when I was nine. I wasn't really old enough to have a comprehensive take on country versus city.'

Nathaniel nodded, but he looked a little pensive. 'You moved back because of your mum, right?' he said.

'Yeah. Well, because of her parents. She grew up here. Always said she'd never move back, but things change, I guess. She doesn't seem to regret it.'

'Can I ask you something weird?' he said.

'Weirder than "What were the people you knew like?" Sure.'

'Why do you call her Moth?' he asked.

Sarah laughed. She'd been expecting something much less weird than that. 'I guess it's what Mam called her from the start,' said Sarah. 'It's short for mother, really. She didn't want to be called just mother, because she says it made her feel like her own grandma. And mum is too close to mam, and we already had one of them. Confusing to have two. So Mam – Billie – shortened it.'

'I like it,' said Nathaniel.

'Yeah,' said Sarah. 'Me too. I mean, I've never really thought about it that much, but I do.'

Nathaniel was quiet for a moment. 'Is that why she left? When she was younger?' he asked. He wasn't looking at Sarah anymore; his eyes were on his hands.

'What do you mean?'

He bit his lip and looked away. 'I mean . . . because she wanted to date, you know . . .'

'Oh!' said Sarah, as understanding dawned on her. 'I don't think so. But I've never actually asked. She's talked about a couple of girls she dated in high school, and she went to high school here, so . . .'

'Doesn't mean no one had a problem with it,' Nathaniel said quietly. He still wasn't looking at her.

'I guess,' said Sarah. 'But she's never told me if they did. I think she was just bored here. She wanted to be able to, I don't know, go and dance in a crowd of strangers at one in the morning. She wanted to see plays and concerts and things. She didn't like every day being the same as the one before.'

'Can't've hurt though,' said Nathaniel, 'that there'd be a bigger dating pool.'

'Sure,' Sarah said. 'But that's true for everyone.' She almost said, *Ana wouldn't need to resort to Marcus,* but managed to stop herself. She was supposed to be giving him a chance.

'No, it isn't,' Nathaniel said. 'Not to the same degree.'

Sarah glanced over at him. He was still looking down.

'I see,' she said slowly. 'You wanted the larger dating pool.'

He nodded silently. He stopped walking and rested his elbows on the fence they'd been strolling alongside. Sarah propped herself next to him.

'It just feels,' he said, after a while, 'that I don't get to figure out who I am anymore, you know? Like, it's easy to say I'm into both boys and girls, fine. But it feels . . . I don't know, academic. Just a theory.'

'And also like if you can't figure out a way to be attracted to one of the people you've known since you were born, then you'll never have anyone at all?' said Sarah.

Nathaniel laughed. 'Yeah, well, there is that,' he said. 'And well, even . . . Even trying to figure out how I really feel about, well, you, for example. I don't know what's real and what's just the best available option.'

Sarah stared at him. 'How you feel about me?' she said. 'So you were lying. You do have a crush.'

He blushed. 'I didn't say that.'

'You kind of did.'

'Well. Don't let it go to your head. There's a limited selection.'

Sarah settled her head in her hands, looking out over the rolling fields. The sun was lowering in the sky, giving the wheat an unearthly glow.

'Do you think this is what it was like in the past?' she asked. 'Like, before everyone had cars, before cities became the places where most people live? Everyone just in tiny villages, reaching adulthood and thinking, "Well, this person who is near me is the least loathsome, so I guess that's that."'

Nathaniel shrugged. 'They could at least visit a couple of neighbouring villages,' he said.

'Sure, but I've been to enough of them to know that that doesn't really improve the odds of finding romance.'

Nathaniel gave a bark of laughter. 'That's not fair,' he said. 'Some of them are even smaller than Black Crag.'

'Because it's easier for people to get further away from them,' Sarah said.

'OK,' said Nathaniel, sitting up a bit straighter, his voice a bit brighter. 'If it falls upon us, upon the village of Black Crag, to continue the human race, who is your least loathsome option?'

'You want me to fuck, marry, kill every male on this island between the ages of, what, seventeen and twenty-nine?'

Nathaniel took a moment to think, before nodding firmly. 'Yes,' he said, 'yes I do. Although I suppose expecting marriage is a bit much; we could all just band together to make as many pregnancies as possible and raise the resulting babies altogether.'

Sarah laughed, shaking her head a bit. 'We can't,' she said. 'There aren't enough of us.'

'There are more than three hundred people in this metropolis. I think we could manage to raise a couple of dozen children.'

'Not enough to continue humanity,' said Sarah. 'It's a genetic bottleneck. We need at least a couple of thousand to really make it work long term.'

'Huh,' said Nathaniel. The mood had shifted slightly. 'So that's just it, then. If we're the only ones left, then humanity is actually over.'

Sarah suddenly regretted her comment. It had felt, at the time, like another joke, another quip from the gallows, but now it was just depressing.

'We're not the only ones left,' she said, her voice low and unsteady. 'We can't be.'

'You can't know that,' said Nathaniel.

'No,' she said. She gave her shoulders a shake and looked up at him. 'But statistically, it's true.'

Nathaniel just looked at her.

'It is!' she cried. And as she talked, she didn't know if she believed what she was saying, or if she was just trying to convince herself it was true. 'There's nothing special about Black Crag. We only feel like it's different here because we compare ourselves to the mainland. But there are loads of places like this. So why shouldn't other places have survived? And if it comes to that, it's a pretty big assumption that whatever happened over there happened everywhere. It could just be here. We could be just on the outside of a circle that's actually only a few hundred kilometres wide. It's knocked out our radio and our phones, but that could just be damage to local infrastructure.'

Nathaniel was looking at her with concern in his eyes. Did she really seem that crazy?

'But someone would have come,' he said gently.

'Maybe they have,' said Sarah. 'Maybe right now, there are rescue and clean-up crews over there, and they just have so much to do that they haven't found us yet. Really, when you think about it, it's far more likely that this is a localised disaster.'

Nathaniel looked at her, frowning. 'Is that really what you believe?'

Sarah sighed. How was anyone supposed to know what to believe? What to have faith in, what to doubt? 'I don't believe anything. I don't know anything. None of us knows anything. I'm just saying the actual apocalypse is—'

'Statistically unlikely?'

'Yeah.'

'So we just all have to sit here and wait for the rescue crews to find us?' Nathaniel said.

'Maybe,' said Sarah. 'Or . . .'

'Or Thomas has to succeed in his attempt to find them.'

Sarah laughed ruefully. 'It could happen,' she said.

'Yeah,' said Nathaniel, his brow furrowed. 'It could. It could happen.'

Winter

So it had been like this.

A storm that lasted longer than any storm should.

A plane seen careening drunkenly through the sky.

A sky stained an unnatural hue.

Radios that fell silent. Phones that were dialled but never answered.

A ferry that no longer ran.

A summer spent hoping in vain that it would all be temporary. That someone would come and bring the world back to Black Crag. An autumn spent in acceptance, and work to shore up supplies for a long winter.

And now the days were growing short. The mornings were full of mist and frost. The wind had a bite to it. People were frantically darning gloves and socks with whatever scraps of wool they could find.

The green in the sky had started to slowly recede, but no one had noticed that yet. They wouldn't for a few more weeks, partly because of the weather, partly because how often do you really look at the sky?

The harvest was in, and once again the activity of the village shrank. But this time, it was not with a spirit of transience and relaxation. Now it was time for endurance. And it felt like it would last forever.

Chapter Twenty

The first snowstorm of the year lasted three days and buried the village up to its knees.

It came out of nowhere. Sarah hadn't realised how much they'd all relied on weather reports before then.

She and her family huddled around the oil heater while the snow pelted down, with no way of knowing how everyone else was faring. Finally, on the fourth day, they woke to blue skies and the sound of someone running a snow plough up the street outside.

Billie left the house immediately to call in on a few patients with chronic conditions, and make sure everyone had come through the storm OK. Sarah and Elliot went into the front garden to make a snowman.

Sarah had always liked the winters in Black Crag. There was something so comforting about how total they were. When they'd lived in the city, life had been expected to go on as normal. The streets were salted and ploughed, and everyone went out every day, battling the cold, trudging through slush thrown up by car tyres, just because they didn't have a good enough reason to refuse.

But in Black Crag, everyone hunkered down. If you went out in the snow, it was because you wanted to, because it was worth it. Nothing was expected.

School stayed open, of course, but on the understanding that if it was too hard to get there, you didn't have to go. Waking up and seeing the world covered in snow was like being given permission to ignore your obligations. Keep yourself warm: it's your only job.

At first, she felt the same now. They'd all been working so hard all autumn to make sure that there were enough supplies to make it through the winter, but now winter was here, that job was done.

By the end of the day, though, she was terrified.

Graeme called a village meeting that afternoon. There was no heating on in the hall, so everyone huddled in their coats and gloves, each releasing a cloud of vapour with each breath.

Graeme stood at the front of the room. 'Let's try and keep this brief,' he said. 'It takes an age to heat up this room, so it just seemed better to get things over with as soon as we can, instead of waiting for it to get comfortable.'

He looked around the room. 'First, I want to thank all of you for your hard work during the harvest. We managed to set in store a decent amount of food. But unfortunately, we did not get all of it.

'None of us expected this kind of snow this early, and it has left us a little shy of the point we wanted to get to.'

A murmur of worry swept over the room.

'Now, I think we still have enough to get through,' said Graeme, 'if we are careful. Very careful.'

The atmosphere in the room was getting tense. Sarah felt her stomach sinking. They'd worked so hard. It had seemed like there was plenty of food. How much more had he expected them to put by?

'What we have to remember,' said Graeme, 'is that we have no way of knowing how severe the winter in general will be, or how long it will last. This early snow could mean we're in for a hard few months, so we should plan for a late thaw. Much better to have extra come spring than run out with weeks of winter left to go.'

A restlessness was developing in the room. People were muttering to each other, looking around to see how everyone else was taking the news.

'With that in mind,' Graeme went on, 'I've drawn up a rationing system for the coming months. Now, it may seem at first glance like a difficult system to keep to. But I think it is necessary to get all of us through. And if you find yourself truly struggling to manage, then you can come and talk to me, and we'll see if there's wiggle room.'

'Who put you in charge of rationing our food?' said a voice from the back corner.

Sarah looked behind her to see where it was coming from. It was Thomas.

She turned back to Graeme, who sighed. 'Well, Thomas, no one put me in charge of it. But since I was the one overseeing the harvest, I'm the one who knows how much food we have to share between us all. You are welcome to look at the plan and check my maths, of course.'

Billie leaned forward beside Sarah. 'Thank you for all the work you've done, Graeme,' she said. 'I just wanted to check if you've planned for people who are ill, and might need a bit more nutritional care. For example, expectant mothers.' The evenness of her tone seemed forced to Sarah, and it did little to dampen the crackle of tension.

'Yes,' said Graeme, 'A good question. I have accounted for people where their conditions are known to me. But if you are able to make sure everyone's needs are being catered to, that would be appreciated. And perhaps you could keep watch for any signs of people not getting what they need.'

'This is outrageous,' said Thomas. He'd stood up and was staring around the room. 'He's going to starve us all winter, and for what?'

Graeme took a breath. 'As I've said, I've worked things out so we have enough to survive on day by day, and enough to get through the winter, even if it ends up being a longer one than usual.'

'You can't tell us what to eat, Graeme.'

'If you have an alternative suggestion, I'm sure we'd all love to hear it,' Graeme said. He spoke quickly, and Sarah was surprised by the bite in his voice. She'd never seen him lose his patience like that, he always seemed so good at holding back his own frustrations.

'We need to eat what we need to eat,' said Thomas. 'If we run out, we can always butcher another couple of pigs or cows. And we don't need to last the whole winter. Just long enough until we make it to the mainland.'

There was a ripple of surprise across the room. A few people laughed. But Sarah saw a couple of people muttering and shooting dark glances at Graeme.

'I don't think it would be wise to attempt to reach the mainland again before spring,' Graeme said.

'I'm not asking you to do it,' Thomas retorted.

'How are you going to get there?' someone yelled.

Thomas didn't reply immediately. 'We have to sail there. We have to fix up the boat.'

'Boat's under a couple of feet of snow, pal,' came a voice from the back. A few people tittered in response. However they felt about the food being rationed, it seemed like most people were not going to back Thomas in his attempt to reach the mainland. But there was a handful of people, of young men, looking at Thomas intently. Looking at him like they wanted to believe in him.

'It doesn't matter,' Thomas yelled. 'It's the best option we have, so it's what we'll do. I'll dig it out and fix it, and make it to the mainland.'

'OK,' said Graeme, his eyes flicking briefly to the ceiling. 'But as we can't know how long that will take you, or whether you will manage to find anything to help us when you get there, I think it's still best that we plan for a long winter with only the food we have now to sustain us.'

'You don't get to decide what we eat,' said Thomas. 'You don't get to turn this into your own petty dictatorship.'

Graeme sighed, but then said briskly, 'Well, then, we can put it to the vote.'

'Yeah, and we all know how that's going to go.'

'Thomas, if you don't expect the vote to go your way, then I'm baffled as to why you think this is a dictatorship.' A few people laughed at that.

Sarah felt Moth stirring beside her. She turned to see her standing up.

'All right,' Moth said. 'It's freezing in here. I think we've debated this enough. Graeme, I assume you have your rationing plan written down for everyone to look over. Why don't we plan another meeting to vote on it when everyone's had a chance to read it.'

There was a murmur of assent, and some people began to get up and move towards the door.

'Don't bother,' said Thomas. 'Starve yourselves if you want, I don't care. Anyone who wants to do something actually useful, you know where to find me.'

Thomas was as good as his word. Sarah walked past the boat the next day on her way to visit Ana, and he was there, with a group of others, digging away at the snow that covered it.

She spent the day at Ana's and didn't ask her if Marcus was still going along with Thomas. She hadn't seen him with the group at the boat, but that didn't mean he'd given up on the plan. Ana didn't talk about Marcus at all.

When Sarah walked back home Thomas was still digging. As she passed by, a few flakes of snow fell on her face. She glanced at Thomas, who swore and threw his shovel to the ground.

By the time Sarah got home, the snow was falling thick and fast, with no sign of stopping.

Chapter Twenty-one

It soon became clear that Thomas was not going to stop. Every morning, he would check if the sky was clear or not and, if it was, he'd wrangle as many supporters as he could to keep digging out the boat. There were a few false starts, and each time fewer people came to help him.

But after a week or so of on-and-off snow, there finally came a day that broke blue-skied and still. Four or five people rallied alongside Thomas to dig out the boat, and Sarah made several thin excuses to walk past and check their progress. By midday, it looked like they might make it.

Sarah was idly leaning against a wall, trying not to look like she was watching them, when Nathaniel came up and joined her.

'Wow,' he said. 'I'm actually impressed.'

'Me too, honestly,' said Sarah. 'I don't know what he's planning to do when they do get it out, though. They'll just have to do it all over again the next time it snows.'

'He has a barn ready for it,' said Nathaniel. 'He's been emptying it out all week. That's why he's brought his car in, so he can tow it back to his farm.'

Sarah stared at him. 'How do you know that?' she asked.

'He told me.'

'Oh.' She didn't know how to process this information. She didn't know Nathaniel and Thomas knew each other.

'It's actually interesting, what they're planning,' Nathaniel was saying. 'Thomas lived in one of the towns on the other side, so he knows the area. Knows where there are shops that should be well-stocked, knows some of the farms on that side.'

He was talking in a mild tone, as if all this was normal, unsurprising, but Sarah was still staring at him, shocked and confused.

'And Charlie's been over there a lot, too, so he has a lot of ideas,' Nathaniel went on. 'I think the main goal is to eventually explore far enough to find out a bit about what happened, but I don't think that'll be part of the first trip. That's going to be more focused on finding resources.'

He fell silent, and for a moment, Sarah scrambled to find something to say.

'I didn't realise you were so interested in all this,' she said, eventually.

'Well, yeah, aren't you?' said Nathaniel. 'I know there are other priorities, and it's a big thing to try and do. And dangerous, of course. But I think it's important to be talking about it. Even if it's a few months before anyone can actually go. And now the harvest is over, it's not like there's anything else to do.'

'Right,' said Sarah. She gave a weak half-smile.

She didn't want to tell Nathaniel how surprised she was. She thought Thomas was being crazy; she'd assumed everyone thought he was being crazy. Everyone she knew well, at least. His insistence on trying to go as soon as possible instead of waiting till spring seemed incredibly stupid; she couldn't imagine why anyone would buy in to it. The way Nathaniel was talking about it, as if it was so rational, was off-putting. She'd thought she was starting to understand him, but now she wasn't so sure.

It was one of those strange moments that seemed to create a slightly new reality. After that conversation, Sarah started to see Nathaniel everywhere, talking to Will, talking to Marcus; she even saw him having a drink with Thomas.

She wondered how long he'd been friends with them. She must have seen him with them before, maybe repeatedly, and just not noticed. It was as if her ideas about who Nathaniel was were so incompatible with her feelings about Thomas and Marcus and their cronies that her mind had refused to unite them.

It threw off her understanding of the situation so drastically that she started to question whether she was right about Thomas at all.

'Thomas *is* crazy, right?' she asked Moth, one day. 'What he's doing is crazy?'

Moth shrugged. 'It definitely seems like a bad idea to be pushing it so hard in the middle of winter. And I'm not sure he's an expert at fixing boats. Or that the boat in question is fixable.'

'Right,' said Sarah. 'It's a terrible idea.'

'I do think eventually we have to try and see what the world is like beyond our shores,' said Moth. 'But right now, the priority has to be making it through the winter.'

Sarah frowned. 'But if he genuinely thinks the best way to survive is to get over there as soon as possible, then what he's doing does make sense.'

'Sure. But he's putting the long term before the short term.

Which, in this situation, is a bit too risky for me.' She glanced over at Sarah. 'Why are you thinking about this now?'

Sarah sighed. 'I don't know,' she said, 'I just . . . I thought I knew what I thought about it all. Then I wondered if maybe I was wrong. Short-sighted or something.'

Moth gave a small, quiet laugh. 'Well, it's good you're questioning your own assumptions. Even if you end up in the same place you started.' She turned to look at Sarah properly. 'The problem is, none of us know what the best thing to do is,' she said. 'We're all flying blind. Maybe we are making things harder for ourselves by locking down like this. Rationing food, rationing petrol. For all any of us know, there could be help for us on the other side of the water. Maybe everything's not as bad over there as it seems.

'But I think if we were going to try to get over there, we should have done it at the beginning. The point where it would have been the best choice has past. Now we need to wait for it to come around again.'

Sarah was silent for a while. 'Moth?'

'Yeah, love?'

'What do you think happened?'

Moth sat back in her chair, and stared out the window. She sighed and shook her head slightly. They'd never talked about this before, but Sarah could tell Moth had been thinking about it a lot. 'I don't know,' she said eventually. 'The arm, the storm . . . seems like it must have been something chemical. I have no idea what kind of chemical reaction could knock out the phone lines and the radio, though.' She shrugged. 'But what do I know?' she said. 'Why are you asking?'

Sarah took a moment to reply, trying to find the right words.

'It's like . . . I've got so used to it that I forget sometimes that it happened,' she said. 'The whole of reality shifted, and now I can't make sense of how the world used to be. It feels like we're just alone. Like we've always been alone. Sometimes.'

Moth smiled sadly at her. 'I think that's just how people work. We adapt quickly; it's how we survive. But we haven't always been alone. And there will come a time when we won't be alone again.'

'How do you know?'

Moth waved a hand in the air vaguely. 'Statistics,' she said. 'Wildly unlikely that the whole world is dead except for us.'

Sarah gave a shout of laughter. 'That's what I said!' she said.

Moth laughed. 'Well, you're your mother's daughter,' she said. 'And your mother is very smart.'

While the island was being pelted by snow, Sarah realised she missed sitting on the jetty with Arthur. She had got used to sitting out there with him. She'd found she liked the feeling of silent company, and she'd developed a habit of looking for him there a couple of times a week.

Sometimes she brought him a drink or something to eat. Once, he'd pointed out an albatross cutting a dramatic path across the sky. They sat in a companionable silence for hours. Sarah wasn't sure he even knew her name. She found herself feeling sad on the days she ended up sitting out there alone.

After the snow had stopped falling, on a sunny but windy day, she made her way down to the jetty hoping to find him there, and surprised herself at how relieved she felt when she saw him. She'd brought out a Thermos of tea, and they sat drinking it for a while. Ten minutes at least passed in silence, as usual. And then, 'There was a dolphin,' Arthur said.

'What?' said Sarah. It was the first time he'd ever said any-thing to her, other than 'yes', 'no' or 'thank you'.

'A few minutes before you got here. Came up right near here.'

'Huh. They don't normally come in this close, do they?' Sarah asked.

'Used to,' said Arthur. 'When I was a boy. Not so much recently.'

Sarah looked out into the water for a while, hoping the animal would return. 'My parents took me out to swim with them once' she said. 'They borrowed someone's boat. We had to sail for ages, and when we found some, the water was too cold to stay in. I moaned the whole time.'

Arthur was looking down at his hands, but he seemed to be listening.

'I was mad at them for moving us here,' Sarah continued. 'They were trying to show me that there were things here to like. Things that would make up for losing my friends, my school, trips to the cinema.' She laughed a little. 'I wouldn't have liked anything they showed me at that point, but getting freezing and wet just for a dolphin that wouldn't come near me didn't help.'

Arthur didn't say anything but he gave a small grunt that might have been a laugh.

Sarah wondered if she could get him to talk a little more. She didn't want to push him, but it felt like there was a wall coming down. Surely, it would help him to be able to talk about things.

'So you grew up here?' she asked.

Arthur nodded. 'Lived here till I was sixteen, then moved over the way.' He nodded across the water. 'Always meant to go further, but . . . Well.'

'What happened?' Sarah asked. For a moment, she thought

she was discovering a kindred, someone who'd become trapped in this tiny corner of the world while longing to be somewhere bigger. Somewhere further, brighter, better. But Arthur's eyes suddenly glinted, and he gave a sheepish half-smile.

'Met my wife,' he said simply.

Sarah stared at him. 'You met your wife when you were sixteen?'

'Ah no, it was a couple of years later.'

'How did you meet?'

He was looking down at the movement of the water, but that small smile was still playing across his face.

'She took my ferry. It was only a few weeks after I started working on it. I didn't pilot it then; I was there to help load and unload things, you know. And she comes on with nothing, which is unusual, you see. People usually have something with them, that's why they're coming: to bring things here. Or if they're from here, they're going over to the mainland for a week and they have luggage.'

Sarah nodded. Black Crag wasn't the kind of place people came on a day trip.

'So she gets on the ferry with nothing but herself, sits right at the front the whole way over. Then when we get here, she walks up and down the beach for a while, then gets straight back on the ferry for the trip back.

'I asked her what was going on, and she said she'd never been on a boat before. Wanted to see what it was like.'

'Never?'

'She'd just moved out here. Grew up in the city. Said she'd always wanted to live by the sea. Got me thinking that maybe she was right. Maybe waking up in the morning without the sound of the waves would feel stale. Dead.'

Sarah was silent as they sat looking out over the sea. The constant noise of it had kept her awake when she'd first moved to Black Crag, but now she wondered if Arthur was right. She couldn't imagine moving through the day without the crashing of the waves. The calling of the gulls.

Maybe it would feel stale to be without it.

'What was her name?' she asked.

Arthur sat for a moment without answering. The smile had faded from his face, and he swallowed hard before saying simply, 'May. Her name was May.'

Chapter Twenty-two

The next day when Sarah walked through town, the boat was gone. All that was left were the tracks taking it away, and the piles of snow around the hole where it had been.

With the boat went the small, ragtag group of young men Thomas had gathered around himself. Even when the snow had been falling, Sarah had seen them around, talking together in the pub, or sitting out on the jetty, like they'd claimed it. But once the boat was gone, they were too. She supposed they must have moved to Thomas's barn.

She found herself walking through the village a lot, on the pretext of checking up on Ana, or running an errand for her parents, and as she walked, she looked around at who else was out.

It was interesting, she thought, that she didn't see Nathaniel. But then he was probably just staying home. She would have thought he might have come out to see people, to spend an evening drinking mulled wine at the pub. She would have thought he might have come out to see her.

But maybe they hadn't become as close as she'd thought. Maybe they'd just worked alongside each other for a few months and now it was over.

It was strange that he wasn't around, but that didn't mean

he was with Thomas, she found herself thinking. There was no reason to think he wanted to join the expedition just because he found the idea interesting.

Sarah couldn't stop worry from mounting in her chest. She found it annoying. What business was it of hers what Nathaniel did or didn't do?

But still, a couple of times a day, she found an excuse to leave the warmth of her house and trudge through the cold to the other side of the village.

A week went by with no sign of Nathaniel. With no sign of Marcus or Will or anyone of a handful of others who would normally be lurking on the jetty or outside the pub.

Black Crag felt peaceful. Quiet, in its blanket of snow.

Sarah wondered if anyone else was feeling as tense as she was. She wondered if anyone else was fighting to quell the feeling that the peace and quiet was a lie.

'This is the worst time of year to be pregnant,' Ana moaned. 'I love mulled wine.'

Sarah grimaced at her in sympathy. They were sitting in a cosy corner of the pub, watching Malcolm and Arthur play chess at the bar.

'Malcolm,' Ana called over to him. 'How much wine do you have left?'

Malcolm glanced up. 'Enough for the time being,' he said.

'Enough for the next year?' Ana asked.

He just shrugged in reply.

Ana turned back to Sarah. 'I swear to god, if this is the last winter we can have mulled wine and I don't get to drink any because I'm bloody pregnant, I will be furious.'

'You'll hold it over that kid's head for the rest of its life,' said Sarah, laughing at her.

'I absolutely will. That and the fact that it's forced me to keep having to see its father.'

Sarah looked at her. 'Is that not going well?' she asked. They hadn't talked about Marcus in weeks. Sarah hadn't brought him up, knowing she couldn't trust herself not to say something harsh about him. And Ana hadn't mentioned him – maybe because she couldn't trust what Sarah would say either.

Ana let out a low bark of laughter. 'No,' she said, 'and apparently now I don't get to just be done with him.'

Sarah's eyes widened. 'What happened?' she said.

'I mean, it's not working.' Ana shrugged. 'We don't like each other. But he won't let me break up with him.'

'I didn't think that was an option' said Sarah.

'That's what I said! I told him it wasn't working and it was over and all of that, and he just said, "Well, you can't do that because of the baby." And I said that it was nothing to do with the baby, and I wasn't about to stay with a guy who's such a big pain in the ass when I could just be a single mother instead. And he said, "I'm still the father," and I said that I'd never said he wasn't.'

'What did he say to that?'

'Nothing. But he keeps coming round, and I don't know if he thinks we're still together or if he just thinks he gets to do that because he's the father of my baby. There may not be that much distinction between the two states of being.'

Sarah laughed. She felt strangely giddy. It was relief, she decided. Not that Ana was trying to break up with Marcus necessarily, but that she didn't have to guard her tongue anymore.

She could say whatever she felt about him, without worrying Ana would be upset. 'Is he still helping out with Thomas's boat?' she asked.

Ana rolled her eyes and snorted. 'It's all he ever talks about. Which parts of the hull are rusted through, what's wrong with the rudder. And he's always so excited when he's telling me, like he thinks this will prove they know what they're doing. Everything he says makes it sound like even more of a terrible idea.'

'Wow,' said Sarah. 'What are you going to do when they're ready to sail?'

Ana laughed. 'Honestly, I don't think they ever will be. They'll have to realise eventually that the boat's past saving.'

Sarah hesitated. Maybe Ana was right, maybe there really was nothing to worry about. But she couldn't dismiss the creeping dread in her gut. She tried to keep her voice light as she said, 'But if they do sail?'

Ana was quiet for a moment, then she shrugged. 'I'll tell him he can't go. That he can help fix the boat up as much as he wants, that he can help plan and whatever, but that he's going to be a dad and he needs to stay here for the baby.'

'Will he agree to that?' Sarah asked. She didn't have a lot of faith in Marcus's ability to compromise.

'He doesn't have to agree. He just has to do it.' She laughed again. 'Look, it's not going to come to that.'

Sarah bit her lip and looked at the table. 'But if it does,' she said, 'you can't really forbid him, not if you're broken up.'

Ana grimaced. 'Well, he doesn't seem to have agreed to the break-up, so as far as he's concerned, I can.'

At that, Sarah laughed too.

'He can't have it both ways,' said Ana breezily. She spoke as if she was laying out unassailable logic. 'He's either involved or he's not. And if he's involved at all, the baby has to be a priority. He can't go off on a death boat after the faint possibility of help from outside.'

'Well,' said Sarah. She didn't know that Marcus would follow the logic, but maybe it wouldn't come to that anyway. 'You're probably right. The boat may never be able to sail, anyway.'

For some reason, the thought of that was comforting. But there was still something like dread gnawing at her stomach.

Sarah was walking on the beach a little way out of the village when she finally ran into Nathaniel again. She'd wanted to stretch her legs, to get some space, but walking too far in the snow was difficult, and she knew it could be dangerous.

There wasn't any snow left on the beach. It had been swept away by the tides, leaving no trace.

She'd thought she was alone, until she heard Nathaniel call out to her.

'Hi,' he said. 'I haven't seen you recently.'

Sarah frowned. 'I've been around,' she said. 'You haven't been.'

Nathaniel smiled and winked at her. 'Maybe we've just been around at different times.'

Sarah paused for a moment before replying. 'Maybe you've been around somewhere else.'

He laughed at that. 'Where else would I be?' he asked.

'I don't know,' Sarah said. 'Maybe in Thomas's barn. Working on his boat.'

Nathaniel looked confused. 'I've been there once or twice,'

he said with a shrug. 'I went to have a look at things. I don't know if that qualifies as *being around* there.'

Sarah felt a twinge of annoyance. She wasn't sure where it was coming from. Nathaniel couldn't know that she'd been so worried about the boat, about his friendship with Thomas. And, when it came to that, why was she? They were friends, yes, but he didn't owe her anything. She tried to shake off her irritation.

'How's it all going over there?' she asked.

Nathaniel cocked an eyebrow at her. She had the feeling he knew she was annoyed and found it funny. 'There's a lot of work to do,' he said. 'That boat must have been sitting there rotting for twenty years.'

'Do you think they'll be able to fix it?'

'No idea,' he said, casually. 'I don't know enough about boats.'

Sarah turned to walk back to the village, and Nathaniel fell into step beside her. They walked in silence for a while. Sarah steeled herself to ask the one question that had been rocketing around her brain. But she tried to sound indifferent. She tried not to let it show how stupid an idea she thought it was.

'Are you going to go with them?' she asked. 'When Thomas and his gang set sail, are you going to go too?'

Nathaniel looked down at her, his brow crinkling, his mouth twisting into a half-smile. 'No one's setting sail any time soon,' he said. 'There's no point in thinking about who's going and who's not.'

Sarah didn't think that was a particularly good answer, but she didn't feel she could press him. She was surprised and annoyed that he hadn't just said a firm no. Did he really think it was a good idea?

Was he really so ready to leave them all behind?

Chapter Twenty-three

There was tension rippling over the village. It had been there for weeks and Graeme was exhausted. He was exhausted and he wondered if he'd been exhausting everyone else. It was draining, he realised, worrying so much about how to survive. Questioning every decision in case it would hurt you in the long run. Wondering how long you could make it before everything fell apart.

He tried to give the village a sense of stability. Everything he'd done had been to make sure they were all OK. He didn't think he'd been wrong; he just thought everyone needed a rest.

A rest from worry, a rest from rationing. A rest from thinking. He remembered that some of the young folk had thrown a bonfire on the beach in the summer. At the time, he'd dismissed it as teenage selfishness. Ignoring the reality of the world so you could have fun. But now he wondered if he'd been wrong. If there was some greater benefit in pretending, if just for a few hours, that everything was OK.

He took a walk into the village and went to see Malcolm.

Malcolm sat him at the bar with a pint and they chatted for a while before Graeme came to the point.

'I think we need to have a party,' he said.

Malcolm stared at him, a confused smile on his face. 'A party?'

'A Christmas party,' said Graeme.

'Ah,' said Malcolm. 'You want to have it here?'

'I was thinking it would be the best place.'

Malcolm nodded slowly.

'Do you have a plan for food?'

Graeme sighed. 'We can't have a great feast, of course. But we can go a bit over the daily allocation.'

Malcolm thought for a moment. 'I've got a couple of cases of champagne out the back. Been saving them for a special occasion.'

'Well then,' said Graeme. 'That should be fine.'

He went to see Greta in the shop to see if there were any cards or decorations leftover from the previous year, and she managed to find some old fairy lights, and a box of three hundred and fifty cards – just about enough for everyone.

He spent the afternoon carefully writing out the cards, wishing everyone a Merry Christmas and inviting them to gather in the pub for a celebration on the twenty-fifth of December.

Graeme was surprised by how many people volunteered to help with preparations for the party. The anticipation of it spread through the village, and the mood shifted palpably. Sarah Harrison offered to bake some cakes for it, and Beth offered to decorate. She said her friend Jeremy would help.

Graeme smiled a little at Beth's claim on Jeremy. It had been Graeme's farm Jeremy had worked on when he first came to Black Crag as a seasonal worker. Graeme had been surprised when he'd decided to stick around after the previous year's harvest, but now he seemed to have settled into life here well. And clearly he'd become significant to Beth. There was something nice, he thought, about romance blooming in the midst of everything.

Life goes on.

Ana and her mother offered to help out in the kitchen, and Ana said she'd make Marcus pitch in for the clean-up.

There was a genuine sense of excitement in the air; people seemed lighter, and determined to make sure the party happened and went well.

The weather was bad in the lead-up to the day, but Beth and Jeremy still managed to trek out to the hills to cut down a pine tree. They dragged it back on a sled, along with piles of extra foliage to festoon the pub. They'd even managed to find some holly.

Graeme dropped in on Christmas Eve to check everything was ready, and felt himself becoming overwhelmed by the transformation. There was greenery everywhere, strung up along the tops of the windows, looped around poles. Every table was adorned with bunches of holly. Malcolm had swept the chimneys and laid firewood out in the big fireplaces that sat on either side of the pub. He normally just used electricity, but he said the fires would be cheerier.

He found Sarah in the kitchen, putting the finishing touches on her cakes – he knew she'd been working with severely limited ingredients but they looked amazing. It looked like she'd painted them with food dye, creating a fairy tale forest with the whorls and crests with the icing.

Malcolm came up beside him as he looked around the room.

'I think it's looking OK,' he said. 'Might be a decent party.'

Graeme nodded, tears welling in his eyes. 'I think so too,' he said. 'I think we've done all right.'

People started trickling in to the pub at around midday. There were gasps at the decorations, and cries of delight at the hams Graeme had dressed and displayed ahead of the meal.

Malcolm was circulating with champagne, and a few people had raided their own drinks cabinets to contribute. There were bottles of brandy and whisky people had been saving for special occasions being shared around with a generous hand.

Greta had taken over the piano in the corner and was playing Christmas carols that a few other villagers were warbling along to. Graeme found himself smiling, his eyes misting as he looked out on it all.

After a couple of hours, the gathering settled into a mellow, comfortable vibe, and he invited Malcolm to carve the ham and serve it out to everyone. He knew it couldn't match the Christmas feasts of previous years, and he knew it couldn't fix the fear and struggle of the past months. But seeing everyone happy and safe for a few hours had a certain magic to it.

As the darkness pulled in outside, Graeme stood and cleared his throat.

'I won't interrupt you all for long,' he said, 'but I wanted to make a small toast.' He looked around at the assembled villagers. 'You have all shown yourselves to be extraordinary people over the course of the last six months,' he said. 'I never could have imagined the resilience and compassion I've seen from each of you. It gives me great hope for the future.

'I know the thought of the future is daunting. There is a great unknown hanging over all of us. But you have all proved yourselves equal to whatever might come. And I am humbled by that.

'Thank you all for coming today. It is, I believe, vital that as we discover our capacity for survival, we do not lose our capacity for joy. There is always something to cherish. Always something to celebrate. I hope we never stop looking for those things.

'I want to toast to all your hard work. To your strength and patience. And I want to toast to our hope for the future. Our hope that, one day soon, we will find we have not been left entirely alone. Our hope that there is nothing lost that cannot be rebuilt.'

He raised his glass and said, 'God bless you all.'

There was a chorus of *Cheers* around the room, and glasses clinked against each other. Greta returned to the piano, this time to play something a little more upbeat. Graeme saw Jeremy pull Beth on to the dance floor, followed by Seonaid and Billie.

A group of younger kids were playing some kind of elaborate game under the tables, and Arthur had pulled out a deck of cards and was dealing out a game of poker in the corner.

Suddenly, Graeme was aware of a tussle behind him, voices in a low argument.

'I don't care,' someone said. 'I'm going to tell him.'

He turned to see Thomas bearing down on him.

'You've got a nerve,' Thomas said. 'Talking about hope for the future. What future are you hoping for other than to keep everyone stuck here under your thumb forever?'

'Thomas,' said Graeme, evenly. 'I'm glad you could make it. Merry Christmas.' He tried not to let his irritation show. If he was honest with himself, he'd been hoping Thomas wouldn't come. He had as much right as anyone to be there, of course, but Graeme had suspected that if he came, it wouldn't be to have a good time.

'Acting like finding we're not alone is something that's just going to happen.' Thomas's voice was thick and slurred, and he was swaying a little on his feet. 'Not something we have to do for ourselves.'

One of the younger men at his side looked worried. 'Come on, man,' he said. 'You're drunk. Don't ruin the party.'

But he was the only one. The other two with Thomas were also looking at Graeme with mutinous gazes.

'You should watch your step, Graeme,' Thomas spat. 'People won't put up with you for much longer.'

'Thomas, I really think this energy would be better spent fixing that boat of yours than railing against me.'

Thomas sneered and then, before Graeme realised what was happening, he'd pulled back a fist and punched him in the face. Graeme fell to the ground as chaos erupted around him, and then died down into a crackling tension. He took a moment to find his bearings, and then sat up.

He could see Thomas – also on the ground, holding a hand to his cheek. Beth was kneeling beside Graeme, trying to check he was OK.

Thomas was looking up at someone balefully. Graeme followed his gaze and saw Jeremy standing over him.

'Stop whining,' Jeremy was saying. 'I barely hit you. Go home and sleep it off.'

Thomas struggled to his feet and took a couple of steps towards Jeremy, but this time his friends held him back.

'Come on,' said one of them. Nathaniel, Graeme believed. 'You need to get out of here.'

For a moment, it looked like Thomas was about to hit him as well, but finally he relented. He spat at Graeme's feet, and then stormed out of the pub.

Nathaniel looked to one of the others. 'We'd better go after him,' he said. 'Make sure he gets home OK.' They headed out of the door after him.

Graeme noticed a hush had fallen over the pub. He brushed himself off and gave a little laugh.

'Nothing to worry about,' he said. 'Just a few too many.'

Jeremy nodded at him and shook out his hand. 'I shouldn't have hit him,' he said, with a smile. 'It bloody hurt.'

There was a ripple of nervous laughter.

Graeme gave Greta a look, and she shrugged and started playing again.

'I'm fine,' he assured Beth, who was still fussing over him. 'He didn't hit me that hard, just threw me off balance.'

'He's a menace,' she said. 'He would have kept at you if Jeremy hadn't stepped in.' She looked up at Jeremy with a smile. 'You were very brave, hon,' she said.

'Oh, does that impress you?' Jeremy said, with a laugh. 'Unbridled male aggression?'

She winked at him. 'Just this once.'

Graeme settled into a chair and tried to look like he was still having a nice time, but he couldn't help worrying. He didn't know what to do about Thomas. It had seemed wisest to leave him to his own devices, let his ire burn itself out on his fruitless project. But that didn't seem to be working. And some of the cronies he'd gathered around him were very young. Graeme wondered if he was putting them in danger by not stepping in.

But then trying to confront the situation might just make it worse. He sighed. There were no right answers. And there was nothing he could do at all tonight.

Slowly, the party got going again around them, but it was muted. There was a buzz of conversation under the music, worried glances. He saw Ana having a whispered argument with Marcus.

Graeme forced his face into a wide smile and strode up to one of his neighbours, clapping a hand on his shoulder and wishing him a Merry Christmas. He spent the rest of the evening doing his best to be genial and energetic. He knew he was pushing it too hard, he knew he was overcompensating, but he was damned if he was going to let Thomas ruin the celebration everyone had so desperately needed.

Chapter Twenty-four

Sarah had enjoyed the Christmas party. She and Ana had danced together, with Ana resolutely ignoring Marcus for most of the evening. And she was extremely proud of her cakes, although she'd had to make some odd ingredient substitutions. They didn't quite taste as they should, but she'd made sure they looked amazing.

Nathaniel sat and chatted to her and Ana for a while, and the three of them had fun together, joking and gossiping, speculating about what was going on between Beth and Jeremy.

'They're definitely together,' Ana said. 'Look at the way they're dancing.'

'But wouldn't we know?' said Sarah. 'Mam would know, and she would have told me, if they were.'

'Maybe they've always been together,' said Nathaniel. 'Maybe they came to Black Crag separately as a cover.'

Sarah laughed. 'A cover for what?'

'They're spies,' he said. 'They were sent here to gather intel on small independent farmers and take it back to foreign governments.'

'Come on,' said Ana, 'be serious. When do you think they hooked up?'

The three of them darted back and forth, Nathaniel bringing

THE HORSES

up more and more absurd possibilities while Ana tried to bring things back to real life. Sarah laughed at both of them, letting their speculation run wild, but really she felt warmed by the possibility of Beth and Jeremy getting together. It felt like such a normal thing to happen, and nothing had been normal recently.

When Thomas came in, obviously drunk, Nathaniel stood up, a look of concern on his face. As he walked away from the table, Ana shook her head.

'He's a weird guy,' she said.

Sarah laughed and nodded. 'Good weird,' she said.

Ana peered at her through narrowed eyes. 'What's going on there?' she asked.

Sarah glanced at her in surprise. 'What?' she said. 'Nothing.'

Ana looked sceptical.

'Honestly,' said Sarah. 'We're just friends.'

'You're not into him at all?'

Sarah laughed. 'No,' she said. 'Definitely not.' She thought for a moment, her brow furrowed. 'I feel weirdly responsible for him, though,' she said. 'I don't really know why.'

'But not attracted to him,' said Ana.

Sarah laughed again and shook her head.

'Hmm,' said Ana. 'I wonder.'

Sarah didn't reply. She knew if she kept denying it, Ana would just take it as proof she was lying. Part of her was annoyed that she couldn't just be friends with Nathaniel without people speculating there was more going on. But there was something different about him. Something unusual. It wasn't romantic; it was more that she felt like they were from the same place somehow. Like everyone around her lived in one world, and she and he lived in another, one that was slightly different.

She watched as Nathaniel followed Thomas out of the pub. She hoped he wasn't getting too drawn into his plan. But she didn't think he'd take it well if she voiced her concerns.

Despite the fracas, the good mood of the party held in the following days. Boxing Day dawned bright and clear, and the good weather stayed for the next couple of weeks.

The days were starting to get longer again, and though it was still very cold, there was a cleanness and brightness to the cold that was invigorating. It was easy to believe that this year would see a turn. That things would start to feel less dire.

Sarah found herself looking forward to the coming year. She hadn't been prepared for that, and she didn't have any explanation for it.

It felt like they'd got through the worst of it. There were still two months of winter left, but the darkest days were behind them. They could make it through, and when spring came, they'd all be able to plan that much better for the next winter.

They could do this. They could learn to live alone.

Slowly, Arthur had begun to let stories about his life, about his family, filter into his conversations with Sarah.

He told her about the little cottage on the mainland he and his wife had lived in when they were first married. On the outskirts of the village, practically right on the beach. With a cramped, smoky kitchen and a tiny loft bedroom, but with one great window that felt almost as if it was letting the ocean right into the house.

He told her about the three perfect years they'd spent living there, how much time they'd had to spend fixing the plumbing and the electricity. How sad they'd been to leave it.

'But there was no room for a baby,' he said. And then he laughed as he told her it had been condemned as soon as they'd moved out.

He talked about the sensible three-bedroom house they'd bought in the village proper, the room they'd done up as a nursery, May standing on ladders painting it sage green when she was eight months pregnant.

'Would never take it easy,' he said. 'Would just stare at me if I told her to give it a rest, to let me do it all.'

He talked about how, even though they'd been happy in that house, they'd spent thirty-five years trying and failing to make it feel as magical as the tiny cottage on the shore.

They'd been married for four years when their first son was born. Fergus. It had been an easy pregnancy, an easy labour, and May had been very flippant and smug about it, Arthur told Sarah. '"Don't know what everyone makes such a fuss about," she'd say. "There's nothing to it."'

But the ease of the pregnancy had set them up with false expectations for parenthood. Fergus had been difficult from the start, contrarian and fractious. Rejecting all his toys, grabbing for hot pans and sharp knives.

'It was like he was always trying to test the world,' Arthur said. 'He wouldn't take our word for it that something would hurt him; he had to make sure for himself.'

But he'd been a generous and thoughtful child as well, always quick to take care of someone if they were sick or hurt, eager to share what he liked about the world with anyone he met.

Arthur and May's second son had been the complete opposite. It was a difficult pregnancy; May had had intense morning sickness for months, and started spotting late in her second trimester. She'd spent the final weeks of her pregnancy on bedrest, and had an excruciating labour that lasted almost thirty hours.

'And then little Bertie was the sweetest child you could imagine,' Arthur said. 'Never had to tell him anything twice. Often didn't have to tell him once. Five years younger than his brother, he was, but they were the best of friends.'

There were stories of sailing trips and holidays. Of blackouts that led to the whole family huddled in the living room, telling ghost stories. There were broken legs and fevers and failed exams. There were Christmases and birthdays and first dates and broken hearts.

Eventually, Fergus had moved away to go to university, and he'd never moved home again. He'd become a psychologist, fallen in love with a chef called James, and they'd got married and settled down in the city with two dogs and a cat.

'We were so excited when they got married,' Arthur told Sarah. 'Thinking we'd have grandchildren soon, you know. But it was always something they were planning for the next year, and then the next. That's the problem when you have to plan so much for a child – it's always easy to delay. Now, Bertie and Kate, their first was a complete accident. They weren't even married yet.'

He smiled warmly as he talked, describing the crowded waiting room. Fergus and James had come out for the birth and insisted on waiting with Arthur and May and Kate's family. He laughed about how unprepared he felt when he held his grandchild for the first time.

'You're supposed to feel unprepared when your own first child is born,' he said. 'Everyone expects it. Everyone knows it's impossible to be ready. But a granddad is supposed to have wisdom. The peace of experience. Instead, I felt terrified that I'd lived my whole life without ever learning anything that would be useful for my grandchildren.'

Sarah didn't ask how long ago Arthur's first grandchild had been born. She didn't ask how many others had followed. If Fergus and James had ever got around to setting a date on their own plan for children.

She'd noticed that Arthur had never ventured an opinion on Thomas's fervent determination to reach the mainland. He never argued against it, but he showed no sign of wanting to go with Thomas. He never suggested that Thomas had a point.

It seemed to Sarah that, with everything he'd had over there – a wife he adored, children, grandchildren – he must have a pretty good reason for not wanting to go back. And she did not want to know what that reason was.

The Sky, Again

No one talked about the green in the sky for a long time. Perhaps some people didn't want to jinx it. Others weren't sure they could trust what they were seeing. After all, from one day to the next, there was no difference to see at all, and who can remember what the sky looked like a week ago?

Arthur, sitting on the jetty for the first time after several days of snow, wondered to himself if the green wasn't a little bit further away than it had been before the storm. But he couldn't swear to it, and didn't tell anyone.

Sarah, while painting a few weeks after New Year, noticed that the sky had a little more blue in it than it did in a similar painting she'd done before Christmas. She couldn't be sure, though, if she'd painted the sky accurately.

It was like this all over the village. People wondering if it was changing, and dismissing it as an illusion. Looking back again and again, unsure of what they were seeing. Eventually, someone would mention it to a friend, 'Don't you think it's different?', ready to dismiss it all if they were challenged.

There weren't many long conversations about it. It was a light game of speculation, and no one was ready to take it any deeper.

No one was ready to ask the question that simmered under it all. If the strange tint in the sky really was receding, what was changing on the mainland?

Chapter Twenty-five

Sarah didn't notice the power had gone out at first. It was the middle of the day, and the sun was bright outside. There was no sudden darkness to signal the change, just the slowly growing awareness that something had changed. Sarah stood in the middle of the hallway for a moment, trying to work out what felt different.

Eventually she realised – it was the silence. The low static of the radio that was always on in the kitchen had disappeared.

She walked through to the kitchen, and it was sitting on the countertop, dead. At first she thought the radio itself was broken, but then it occurred to her to try the light. She flicked the switch back and forth a few times.

'Shit,' she said.

The oil column heater in the living room was still giving off waves of heat, but the light on the end of it was off. Sarah knew it was only a matter of time until it went cold. The house had a couple of fireplaces, but they'd been boarded up for years, and Sarah had no idea how to reopen them. And even if they managed to do it, they'd still have to go out and get firewood.

She stood there for a moment, unsure what to do. She was home alone – Mam was at her surgery, and Moth and Elliot were at school. Finally, she decided to go and see what other people were doing. Someone must have made a plan for this. She knew the farms had generators; there had to be some system for sharing power from those.

She threw on her coat and went outside, to see people emerging from their front doors all along the street.

They started moving towards the centre of the village together, picking up more people as they went. Sarah saw Mam standing outside the door of her surgery and waved to her.

'Is it out at the house too?' Mam called to her, and Sarah nodded.

The crowd was growing larger with every passing moment, and Sarah heard a familiar voice in the hubbub behind her.

'And where is Lord Graeme when something goes wrong?' Thomas was saying. 'Nowhere to be found.'

'I'm sure he's on his way,' someone said in reply. 'His farm's a wee way out.'

'This is exactly why he shouldn't be keeping us trapped here . . .' Thomas went on.

Someone near Sarah muttered, 'For the love of god,' under their breath, but Thomas was too far away to hear.

'We're all vulnerable here. What are we supposed to do? We can't fix the power grid. We can't even find out what's gone wrong with it. So now we're stuck with no heat in the middle of winter.'

He walked past Sarah, continuing his tirade but moving far enough away that she could tune him out. But there were murmurs in the crowd around her.

'Do you think Graeme does have a solution?' someone said.

'God knows,' someone else replied. 'I don't really see what solution is possible. Not immediately, anyway.'

'There are generators, right?'

'Sure, but if they have to power the whole village, we'll be out of petrol within a couple of days. And then what?'

'Graeme will know what to do,' someone else said, but there was uncertainty in their voice. 'He has to.'

Up ahead, Sarah saw Thomas pulling himself up on to a low fence. He looked like he was about to address the crowd, when someone yelled out, 'There he is!'

Graeme was hurrying up the street towards them all, but before he could do or say anything, a wave of panicked questions and complaints poured forth. Sarah couldn't make out any of the individual words; they merged together into a wave of noise.

She could see Graeme at the front of the crowd, his hands up in front of him, trying to calm people down so he could respond, but no one would stop talking. The more people talked around her, the more they panicked, the more Sarah could feel fear curling in her own stomach. There were still weeks of winter left; how were they supposed to survive without electricity?

Suddenly a shrill whistle cut through the crowd. Sarah couldn't see who was responsible for it, but the noise quietened down. There was a moment of silence, and then Graeme cleared his throat.

'OK,' he said, 'I know you're all worried, but it's going to be alright.'

But he looked as scared as anyone else.

'How is it going to be alright?' someone yelled, while someone else said, 'What are we supposed to do?'

For a moment, it looked like the crowd was going to devolve into shouting again, but Graeme put up his hands and the noise died down once more.

'Look, I don't have any firm answers yet, but Walter is looking into the situation, and I'm sure he'll have some information for us soon.'

There were a few sidelong glances and a couple of people scoffed, although Sarah saw others nodding, looking reassured. Walter was around twenty-four – only a couple of years older than Nathaniel – and he still lived on his parents' farm, helping them out. He'd never done any proper training, but he collected old appliances and tried to get them working again in his spare time. He had enough working knowledge of electronics to help people out with some basic repairs that couldn't wait for an electrician from the mainland, but he was not an expert. Going from being able to rewire a lamp to fixing a village-wide power cut seemed like a pretty big step up.

Graeme noticed the scepticism in the air and sighed. 'I know it's a lot to ask of him,' he said. 'And I know that if he can't deal with this, then we have a real problem on our hands. But let's not borrow trouble. It'll probably take him a couple of hours to find the problem, so while he does that, we can come up with some back-up plans.'

'Back-up plans like freezing to death?' Sarah recognised Thomas's voice.

Graeme ignored him. He looked towards Malcolm, saying, 'Do you have firewood laid by for the pub?' he asked.

Malcolm nodded. 'Enough for a couple of days, I'd say. But usually we'd have the fires going with some electric heating on as well. They don't really fill the room, you see.'

Graeme nodded. 'We'll be working with what we have,' he said, and turned to the crowd. 'Can I get a show of hands: who has working fireplaces – I mean, recently maintained fireplaces – and enough wood to light them? And who has generators with full tanks of petrol?' A few people put up their hands, including Graeme and Thomas.

'OK, so for now, I think everyone who can should wait it out in the pub. We need to conserve petrol, so let's stick to places with firewood for the afternoon, and we'll reassess the situation once Walter has had a chance to properly look into things.'

No one seemed very happy about this, but it didn't seem like anyone had anything else to suggest, so slowly the crowd moved into the pub. Initially, it wasn't too uncomfortable, but after an hour or so, it became clear that Malcolm had been right – the fires didn't really reach the whole room. People huddled at tables, shoulders hunched in their coats, scarfs pulled over their noses. The atmosphere was tense, and as dusk began to fall, people started looking nervously towards the door. Malcolm had put out candles, but the darkness around the pub was absolute. The prospect of making it home only to huddle under blankets in a freezing house was terrible, but surely everyone couldn't sleep in the pub?

Sarah could feel panic creeping up her spine. She looked over at her parents to see if they were scared as well, but they were busy chatting to their friends and didn't seem to have noticed that night had fallen outside.

Sarah was just about to go over to them to ask them what they were planning to do when deafening music blared out from the sound system, and lights flickered on around the room. A few people screamed, and then nervous, relieved laughter broke out.

'Sorry,' yelled Malcolm, as he turned the music down. 'Sorry. I'd turned it up earlier so it would be clear when the power came back, but I forgot.'

There was more laughter, but it had an edge to it. The day had been hard, and there were still nerves in the air. Most people stayed in the pub, hoping they'd be able to learn more before the night was over.

It was another hour or so before Walter returned. He talked about damage to the substation, using a string of words Sarah didn't understand, and said there was more repair work needed. He'd have to cut the power for a few hours every day until it was all done, but he'd done enough to prevent the network from being overloaded for now.

'Pfft,' someone said. 'And you think you're the man for the job?'

Sarah couldn't see who it was, but she assumed it was one of Thomas's cronies. She couldn't imagine anyone else being so dismissive of what Walter had just managed to do.

Walter, who looked exhausted, rolled his eyes. 'Well, no. So if you want to go out there tomorrow and risk electrocuting yourself instead of me, be my guest.'

The was no response. The mood in the room had shifted. Sarah could see relief on people's faces, but there was also uncertainty. Clearly, Walter had managed, but was he really going to be able to fix things properly? Enough that they didn't have to worry about it going out again?

'What if it doesn't work?' someone asked. 'What if he can't fix it all?'

In unison, the crowd turned to look towards Graeme.

'Are we meant to spend the rest of the winter ready to go sleep in the pub?' someone yelled.

'Of course not,' said Graeme. 'I apologise, we should have had a plan in place for this sooner. Tomorrow, we'll get started putting better systems in place in case the power goes out again.'

The crowd quietened a little, but people still looked uneasy.

'Please bear with me,' said Graeme. 'I promise there is nothing to fear.'

Everyone was nervous that night and the next morning, but the power didn't go out again. Walter seemed to have done his job well. At around midday. Jeremy showed up at Sarah's house, a clipboard in his hand.

'So,' he said, after she'd invited him in, 'Graeme asked me to do a wee survey of the village to check on what everyone needs in order to stay warm and safe if the power goes out.'

'Oh,' said Sarah. 'Sure. Well we have fireplaces, but they're boarded up. We've never used them.'

'Yeah, that's the case for most people, I think. But it's good, really. All we have to do is open them up again, make sure the chimneys are clear. And a bunch of us will go out and chop down some trees, get firewood for everyone.'

'There's loads of driftwood, too,' said Sarah. 'Just a little way out of town. A lot washes up.'

'Good point, yes. Do you have a store of candles or anything?'

'I don't think so,' said Sarah. 'Does anyone?'

'A couple of people, but most only have one or two. We might have to find a different solution for light.'

Sarah nodded, but after Jeremy left, she felt suddenly overwhelmed.

All these things they relied on could fail. And it felt not just probable, but imminent. And terrifying.

*　　*　　*

Sarah clung on to a desperate blind faith in Graeme – that he would have a better solution than just fireplaces and darkness and hoping Walter's self-taught electrical skills were up to the job. Something dramatic, creative. Something that would mean they didn't have to worry about power at all.

Of course, he didn't.

There was a meeting to talk about the situation, and Sarah could tell immediately that people were losing faith in him. They'd all looked to him to keep them together, and so far, it had worked. He'd got the harvest in, he was keeping them fed. He seemed so sure of everything, so unshakeable. Everyone had fallen into the trap of thinking Graeme could solve every problem.

Everyone except Thomas.

The atmosphere in the room was tense. People were not as openly frightened as they had been the day before, but they were worried. Graeme stood at the front and thanked everyone for letting him know whether they had fireplaces.

'If you haven't spoken to anyone about this, please come and see me at any time,' he said. 'Over the next week or so, I'm arranging work crews to sweep all the chimneys and make any necessary repairs. We'll do this in spots, so there's at least one house in each street with working fireplaces as soon as possible. We have a small amount of firewood already, but we're arranging for another work crew to gather more. If you're able to help with this, please also let me know.'

'Is that all you've got?' Thomas called out, and a murmur of agreement passed around the room.

'Warmth is the most pressing need,' said Graeme. 'Once

we've assured that no one is going to freeze, we will of course have other issues to address.'

'The reality is, you don't have a solution,' said Thomas. 'We're completely dependent on a power network we have next to no knowledge about. Just some kid who likes tinkering in the backyard and is flying blind. And what if something goes wrong further out than the substation? There could be a serious problem with the turbines; we wouldn't know how to find out, let alone fix it.'

There was a restless energy to the crowd as they listened to Thomas. Sarah could see a lot of people nodding along to what he was saying, mixed in amongst those who were still looking at Graeme with fear and hope on their faces.

Thomas continued. 'This is what I've been saying from the start. We can't afford to be complacent. To just sit here and assume we'll be OK. Any number of things could go wrong here and we have no support. We need to be looking out there for help, not assuming we can make it on our own.'

'Oh please,' someone said from the middle of the room. 'Whatever Graeme does is the wrong thing for you. But you have no solution, either. Just a ridiculous plan to explore the mainland for help that probably isn't there. Everyone on the mainland is dead. You just can't accept that we're all you have now.'

Sarah sighed and put her head in her hands. The arguing was grating on her brain, making her itchy and frustrated.

'We don't know anything about what's going on over there,' said Thomas. 'We only know what's happening here. And what's happening is that we could freeze or starve to death because we were too scared to look out there.'

'For all we know, you did this on purpose,' someone else said.
A crackle passed over the room.

'What?' said Thomas.

'You've been trying to destabilise us for months. For all we
know, you sabotaged the power supply so we'd panic and turn
on Graeme. Support your mad quest for glory.'

'That's ridiculous.' Thomas looked around defiantly.

Sarah couldn't see who was speaking, who was accusing
Thomas of all this, but she wished they would stop. They'd
only make him angrier. None of this was going to help anyone.

'Is it?' the voice said. 'Seems like it would be a good plan
for you. You've turned half the room against Graeme, when
the truth is the power was fixed within a day and it's been fine
since.'

'OK,' said Graeme loudly, holding up a hand to try and quell
the voices. 'Thomas didn't sabotage the power. Apart from that,
everyone is right here. The power may be fine for months. It
may be fine for years. Walter may be able to keep it maintained
perfectly well. But he may not. It may go out again tomorrow.
And we don't know if we'd be able to fix it. There may be help
for us on the mainland. And there may be nothing at all.'

There was a hush. This wasn't the comfort and security
people had been hoping for.

'We have limited options, and that is scary,' said Graeme.
'But we do have *some* options. For now, for the time being, we
need to make sure that, if there is another problem, a more
permanent problem than we had yesterday, we will survive it.
That is my only goal right now.

'But in the longer term, we will have to do more. We are not
experts here, but we're not entirely lacking technical knowledge.

We can examine the electrical system. We have a few people who are experienced divers, who have been diving in these waters before. We can send them to check on the turbines.'

Sarah wanted to believe that he was right, that between them all, they could solve this problem, any problem. But it seemed so unlikely.

'But we can't do that now,' Graeme continued. 'It's too cold, the weather is too unpredictable. When it's warmer, in the spring, we will look for permanent solutions. Right now, we just need to worry about getting through the winter.'

Graeme looked at Thomas for a response, but Thomas said nothing. Sarah suspected it was more because he couldn't think of an immediate reply than because he agreed. There was an uneasy silence in the room.

'OK,' said Graeme. 'That's all for now. Stay safe, stay warm. We can get through this. We can get through it together.'

Chapter Twenty-six

The strain of the long, cold winter was taking its toll on people. Couples were snapping at each other, parents were short of patience with their children, firm friendships seemed suddenly brittle. The fear of another power cut led to sleepless nights; the prospect of more winters ahead like this one led to a sense of doom that pervaded the island.

Nathaniel saw Marcus and Ana fighting outside Ana's house as he walked into the village. He'd never been able to figure out why they were together, although he wasn't sure if they even were anymore.

Ana was always talking. She was the sort of person you thought at first was flighty, just because she talked so much, but that was only because you kind of assumed that anyone who talked that much must be talking nonsense. The kind of person that, when you listened to them for more than five minutes, you realised they were actually really sharp.

Marcus barely talked at all – and when he did, what he said was baffling. When Nathaniel had asked him why he'd wanted to help Thomas with his boat, why he'd gone with him across the isthmus, he'd just said it seemed rad. That he thought they might see some fucked up shit.

He was sure Marcus had more going on. That there was

another side to him that he showed to the people he was closest to. Like Ana, presumably. But Nathaniel couldn't imagine it.

He tried to pretend he couldn't see the argument as he walked by it, but Marcus saw him and called out a greeting.

'Marcus,' Nathaniel heard Ana say, with a dangerous note in her voice.

'I have to go,' Marcus shot back. 'I don't have to do what you say.'

He jogged away from her to catch up with Nathaniel.

'You going to Thomas's?' he said.

'Yeah, maybe,' said Nathaniel. 'Thought I'd check how things are going.'

Marcus nodded and the two walked in silence for a few minutes.

'That woman is crazy,' Marcus said, after a while.

'Ana?' said Nathaniel. 'She's always seemed pretty sound to me.'

'Yeah. She's pretty,' said Marcus. 'But it's not worth it.'

Nathaniel didn't correct him.

Marcus spat on the side of the road as they walked. 'She thinks she gets to tell me what to do about everything,' he said. 'I think I'm going to have to break up with her.'

'Hmm,' said Nathaniel.

'She's always mad at me because she doesn't like Thomas. She thinks he's stupid, that all his ideas are dumb.'

'Right.'

'Like this morning, I came by just to see how she was doing, with the baby and everything, and then she got all mad at me because I mentioned the boat.'

'What did you say about it?'

'Oh, you know, just that it might be ready to sail soon, and how cool it would be to get to take it out on the water.'

'Ah,' said Nathaniel. 'Do you think it will be ready soon?'

'Oh yeah,' said Marcus. 'There's hardly anything that needs doing to it now.'

Nathaniel wasn't so sure of that. The holes in the hull had all been patched up, but Thomas hadn't tested them yet, and it seemed more than a little likely that at least one or two might not be entirely watertight.

'So she's mad because it's nearly ready?'

'Yeah. Because she's so clingy. She's all paranoid about me going away for a couple of days. Like I don't do enough for her already. Like she can't get along without me.'

'Yeah,' said Nathaniel. 'I guess she's worried it won't be safe. That something will happen to you.'

'Yeah,' said Marcus. 'Like I said, she's clingy.'

'Hmm.' He let Marcus rattle on as they kept walking. He didn't know if it was true that the boat was nearly ready, but he was sure he didn't want to be stuck on it with this guy.

When they got to Thomas's, it was clear that he agreed with Marcus. He was buffing the hull furiously, running his hands over the patches that covered what had been pretty serious holes. There was a handmade sail piled on top of the boat, with a coil of rope beside it, and Thomas instructed Marcus to start rigging it to the mast.

'Wow,' said Nathaniel, looking over it all. 'I didn't realise how far you'd got.'

'Yeah, no thanks to you,' said Thomas. 'I thought you were going to help us out. You've barely been here recently.'

'Yeah, sorry about that. I've had some things to take care of at home.'

This wasn't entirely true. He'd been staying out of the cold and having an intense Monopoly tournament with his dad, more than anything else. One of the things he liked about living in a place like Black Crag was the imperative to hunker inside in the winter. No one expected anything of you; no one was surprised if they didn't see you for a few days.

Besides, he'd never promised to help with the boat. He had some sympathy towards Thomas, and he was worried about the expedition. He suspected he was the only one near the project who wasn't sure the boat was going to work. It seemed sensible for there to be at least some scepticism in the room. Not that anyone listened to him.

'Well, you have a decision to make, kid,' said Thomas. 'You coming or staying?'

'What, now?'

'Next couple of days.'

'Oh,' said Nathaniel. 'OK. I thought . . . Are you sure you don't want to wait till spring? It'd only be a few more weeks.'

Thomas gave him a hard look. 'Are you sure you want to bring that attitude to me and not Graeme?'

'It's just . . . I didn't realise you were so close,' Nathaniel said. He knew Thomas was determined, but he'd thought he'd want to make sure it was safe first. He'd *hoped* he'd want to make sure it was safe.

'Yeah, well, I am,' said Thomas. He was still looking at Nathaniel. 'I thought you understood why we're doing this. I thought you agreed.'

'Yeah,' said Nathaniel slowly. 'Sure.' He walked round the

boat. 'I wonder if it wouldn't be a good idea to set the boat in the bay for a day or two before we go,' he said. 'To check for leaks.'

'And let someone light it on fire? Waste all our work? No, thank you. Besides, I've checked for leaks.'

'In the barn?'

'Yep.'

'Are you sure that's a good enough test? Wouldn't it be worth a little delay to be sure?'

'Look,' said Thomas, 'I blasted my high-pressure hose on every inch of this boat. Nothing got through. It's sound. We're going.'

Nathaniel bit his lip. He didn't want to set Thomas off, but it seemed obvious to him that this was reckless in the extreme. 'OK, well, if you're sure,' he said.

'I *am* sure,' said Thomas. 'So you can be sure.'

Nathaniel walked slowly as he made his way back through the village, his eyes on the ground. He heard someone calling his name, and saw Sarah walking towards him.

He sighed. A few months ago, he'd thought she was the only person who felt the same way he did. Like there had been a future for her away from Black Crag, and it had been taken from her. The way his future had been taken from him.

Not just his future. His future self.

But it didn't feel like that anymore. She'd found a rhythm here. A way to not feel so trapped. And he'd tried to as well, he'd really tried. He'd helped out wherever he could. He'd spent hours trying to talk himself past it, willing himself to get over it.

But he just couldn't do it. He couldn't commit to this the way Sarah had.

'Hi,' he said, as she walked up to him.

'Hi. You seem troubled.'

'Oh, I'm OK.'

'Are you sure?' She seemed sceptical.

'Just a lot to think about,' he said.

Sarah turned and fell into step beside him. 'I hardly see you anymore,' she said. 'It's actually making me look forward to spring, when there'll be all that work to do. Sowing new crops and whatever it is you have to do on a farm in the spring. Because you'll be around again. Helping out.'

'Yeah,' said Nathaniel.

Sarah turned to look up at him.

'Are you sure you're OK?' she asked.

He gave her what he hoped looked like a genuine smile. 'I'm fine, I promise. Just a bit tired. Having one of those days.'

They walked in silence for a while.

'Were you at Thomas's?' Sarah asked.

He nodded.

Sarah stopped walking. 'You shouldn't go there,' she said. 'He's dangerous.'

'He's not dangerous. He's just a bit intense.'

'He almost turned the whole village against Graeme.'

'He just disagrees with him. That shouldn't be a bad thing.'

'It's a bad thing when he stirs people up for nothing.'

Nathaniel didn't reply. He understood why she was worried. Thomas sometimes appeared a bit unhinged. But she'd obviously forgotten how desperate she'd once been to leave. How desperate he still was.

'I just think he's going to get someone hurt,' said Sarah.

Nathaniel gave her a smile. 'I promise that if things get too weird, I won't go there anymore.'

She stared at him for a moment, and then shook her head as if she was trying to clear water out of her ears. 'Do whatever you need to,' she said. 'This is just advice, you know. Just my opinion.'

'I know,' said Nathaniel. 'And I'll be careful. I promise.'

She nodded, and they kept on walking.

Chapter Twenty-seven

There was a brick of dread in Sarah's stomach, and she didn't know why. She wasn't even sure when it had appeared there, but now it was all she could think about.

She told herself she was being irrational, that she was just hungry or tired and would feel better in the morning. But when she woke up, it was still there.

It was bigger.

'Is everything OK?' Moth asked, as Sarah picked at her breakfast. 'You look pale.'

'I don't know,' said Sarah. 'I feel . . . I don't know. It's probably nothing. I'm just worried.'

'What about?' said Mam.

'I don't know. I'm just . . . really worried. I'm sure it's just lack of sleep or something.'

Her mam moved over to her and put a hand on her forehead. 'I'm not sick, Mam,' said Sarah. 'I'm just worried.'

'For no reason that you're aware of.'

'Yeah,' said Sarah. 'I think I just need some air.'

But the feeling didn't leave her as she walked through the village. She went to see Ana, who also felt her forehead.

'Jeez, Ana,' said Sarah. 'Can you wait to mother me until you actually *are* a mother?'

'I practically am,' said Ana, running a hand over her stomach.

'I think you'll take that back once the baby's here,' said Sarah. She paced around the room. 'Can we go for a walk, or something? I'm all on edge, I feel itchy. Can't sit still.'

They walked back and forth up the village streets for a while, but the feeling still stayed.

'OK, we've walked around enough. I need to sit down somewhere,' said Ana. 'I'm walking for two, remember?'

'Yeah,' said Sarah, 'all right.' But as they turned to head back, they heard a commotion coming from down the street.

Thomas was striding along, ringing a big bell.

'Where on earth did he get that?' said Ana.

He was yelling as he rang it. 'Meeting,' he shouted. 'Village meeting. For anyone who gives a shit.'

Sarah and Ana looked at each other and shrugged. They followed Thomas into the hall, along with a few other people. Thomas waited for a while, until there were around forty people in there. He looked over the group and sneered.

'Not quite the same turnout Graeme gets, is it?' he said. 'Well, it doesn't matter. You can pass the word on. If it pleases you.

'Anyway. I've said all along we need to get to the mainland, and that I'd be the one to do it. And I will. I've fixed up my boat. Old Patrick's boat. And we're leaving tomorrow. Me and anyone who wants to come.'

Sarah and Ana gaped at each other.

Ana was suddenly pale. 'He can't be serious,' she whispered to Sarah.

'Don't suppose many of you will be brave enough,' said Thomas. 'But if you are, we're setting off from the jetty at eight. So that's it.'

He strode out of the room with the same fury he'd summoned the meeting.

Ana swallowed hard, her eyes wide and panicked. 'Is he here?' she said, craning her neck to look around the room. 'Is Marcus here?'

Sarah couldn't see him. 'It's OK,' she said. 'It'll be OK. We just need to go and find him.'

They left the building and set off in a hurry towards Marcus's house. He wasn't there, so Ana told his mother why they were looking for him. 'If he comes home, tell him don't do it. Tell him not to go.'

His mother nodded, and they took off again. As they drew close to the centre of the village, they saw Marcus coming out of the pub with Will and a few of Thomas's other cronies. Including Nathaniel.

Sarah felt a strange coldness wash over her. She realised that she was disappointed in him. He'd been so insistent on the two of them becoming friends, and then he'd come over all cold. Like he didn't want to talk to her at all. She hadn't understood. Now it seemed like he'd simply wanted to spend his time with Thomas and his crew of acolytes instead.

'Marcus,' Ana called, hurrying up to him.

He turned to watch her approach him. His expression was stony. 'What?' he said.

'You'd better not be going,' she said. 'You'd better not get on that boat.'

'Why do you think you can tell me what to do?' he said.

'You said you wanted to be this baby's father. You said you'd be around.'

'Yeah, and I will be.' He rolled his eyes. 'It's just one boat trip.'

'One boat trip to god knows what,' said Ana, her voice rising. 'We don't know what's over there; it's not safe. You are risking your life.'

'Don't be so dramatic,' he said. 'We're just going for a couple of days. You're not even close to having the baby yet. You don't need me.'

Ana stood up a little straighter. Her eyes narrowed. 'Marcus, I told you.' Her voice was low and hard. 'You are either here completely, or you're not involved at all.'

'What does that even mean?'

'It means,' Ana said, glaring at him, 'that if you get on that boat, then you are not this baby's father. If you go on this trip, you will have nothing to do with me or this child. Assuming you make it back at all.'

Marcus rolled his eyes again, but he looked a little shaken. 'God,' he said, 'fine. Whatever. I don't get why you need everything to go your way all the time.'

Sarah was looking at Nathaniel, who wouldn't meet her eye. She didn't have a right to ask him to stay. They were just friends. Recently, they were barely even that. And she knew how much he hated being stuck here.

So she said nothing. She followed Ana as she stormed away, and spent her afternoon telling her that of course Marcus wouldn't go, of course he'd put the baby first.

And then she went home and went to bed, and didn't sleep at all.

At seven the next morning, Sarah got up from the bed she hadn't slept in and went downstairs. As she was making herself some coffee, there was a quiet knock on the door.

It was Ana.

'He's going,' she said. 'I was just at his house. His mother said he'd left for the boat already.'

'Oh my god,' said Sarah. 'Do you want to go down there? Try and stop him?'

Ana shook her head. 'I don't think it would work. He's made his decision.'

Sarah nodded and poured her a cup of coffee. 'I know you're not supposed to. But I think one is OK.'

Ana pressed her hands around the mug, and sat staring down at it. 'I don't even want him,' she said. 'I don't like him. And he'd be a terrible father. I just . . . I didn't want to be having a baby with someone who didn't want it.'

They sat together, watching the clock on the walk tick closer to eight.

'Do you want to watch it leave?' said Sarah, as the clock reached seven-forty.

'No,' said Ana, shaking her head. 'No, I don't.' She drank a bit more of her coffee. The minutes ticked by.

'Yes,' she said, at five to eight. 'Yes, I want to watch.'

Sarah grabbed her coat and they walked through the village. There were a few other people around, also heading towards the jetty. More joined them as they walked. The further they got, the faster Ana walked. As they drew close to the jetty, she broke into a run, but she was too late. The boat was already pulling away.

There was a crowd of people behind them as Ana and Sarah walked out onto the jetty, watching the boat glide across the water. Ana let out a sigh and sat down on the ground.

Sarah was looking back at the crowd around them, scanning the faces. 'He's not here,' she said. 'Nathaniel's not here.'

Ana looked up at her from her seat on the ground. 'Maybe he's on the boat too,' she said. 'He was with them all yesterday.'

Sarah suddenly felt heavy and tired. She dropped to sit beside Ana. 'Yeah,' she said. 'Yeah, he was.'

Ana looked at her sharply. 'Are you—'

'No,' Sarah said. 'No, we're just friends, I told you. I just didn't think he'd go.'

The Ferryman, Again

By midwinter, Arthur had become as much a fixture in Black Crag as anyone else. It had taken a while. He'd been a symbol of everything they didn't know, everything they were afraid of for so long.

For the first few months, he'd kept largely out of sight, staying in his room at Malcolm's, seeing only the doctor and the handful of others who'd appointed themselves his caregivers. Eventually, when he'd recovered enough to spend some time outside, people had stayed away from him and he'd stayed away from them.

No one wanted to ask him to relive whatever it was that had left him so traumatised, and plenty of people were glad to have the excuse not to delve into the reality on the mainland. Once he had begun talking at all, he'd told Malcolm and Billie that he didn't think anyone was still alive in the village where he'd lived, and they'd shared that information.

So, for a while, he was left to himself.

People saw him sitting out alone on the jetty and left him there. Sometimes if they walked past him in the street, they nodded hello, but no one stopped to chat.

But slowly, bit by bit, the rhythms of daily life overtook the fear that Arthur had symbolised to so many people. He was a fixture at the pub, always ready for a game of cards. He still didn't speak much, but he seemed to enjoy hearing about other people's lives.

People finally felt at home with him, and he seemed to feel at home in Black Crag.

Chapter Twenty-eight

Nathaniel didn't know why he hadn't said aloud to anyone that he wasn't planning on getting on Thomas's boat. He hadn't said anything to make people believe he *was* going to get on the boat either, but he suspected that just having spent time with Thomas was enough to suggest he was.

He could tell his dad was worried he was going. He'd been looking at him like there was something he wanted to say, but couldn't. Nathaniel could imagine the thoughts going through his head: *He's an adult, let him make his own choices.*

A couple of times, he almost broke and told him. *It's OK, Dad. I'm not going. The boat doesn't seem safe to me, and I'm pretty sure it's not going to make it across. I've told them all I don't think they boat is safe, but they think I'm being a coward – by the way, how culpable do you think I'll be for their deaths if it does go down? Shouldn't I have done more to stop them than just tell them I think it's a bad idea?*

Somehow, he couldn't quite say the words aloud. He was still baffled by the conversations he'd had with Thomas, with the crew of young men he'd gathered around him. They rolled their eyes at his concerns, told him he'd been mollycoddled, said he'd feel stupid when they were all standing on the dock on the other side.

None of them seemed to think his concerns might stop him coming with them. They were all so sure they were right, all so determined to get there, to be the only people in the village who were actually going to figure out what was going on. They didn't take Nathaniel's fears seriously, so they assumed he wasn't really serious either.

He wasn't sure why he hadn't told them. He suspected they wouldn't believe him.

He hadn't told Sarah, either. She hadn't asked. He knew she didn't understand why he'd been spending time with Thomas, helping him with the boat. She didn't want to understand. And he didn't want to explain it. He didn't think he could, without revealing more about Thomas than felt right. He didn't know how to express the obligation he felt to at least try and make the boat a little more seaworthy.

He and Sarah had become such good friends over the past few months. She was probably the closest friend he had right now. Maybe that was why he didn't bring it up. She should be able to trust he wouldn't do anything as reckless as getting on that boat. He felt justified in assuming that she knew he wasn't going – and if she wanted to ask him, she could. But he wasn't going to bring it up.

If he was honest with himself, he knew he'd been avoiding her. He didn't want the topic to come up. Didn't want her asking questions he'd refuse to answer. It was easier to keep his distance until . . .

But the *until* was also something he was avoiding. Did he think things could just go back to normal after the boat had left? If it went down, like he was sure it would, did he think their friendship would just pick up where it had left off?

When Thomas called his meeting and announced the departure, Nathaniel couldn't meet Sarah's eyes. He knew he was a
coward. He was hoping no one else had realised that.

It was five in the morning when Nathaniel left the house the
next day. His dad was still asleep. He tiptoed through the house,
pulling on his hiking boots and collecting his supplies. He was
not looking forward to the walk.

The worst of the winter had passed, but there was still snow
on the ground, and he didn't know how deep it would be on the
hills. But he didn't feel like he had a choice. He hadn't been able
to convince Thomas and the others that the boat was unsafe.
The least he could do was try to make sure someone knew what
happened to it.

He trudged away from the village, dread curling around his
stomach. He headed towards a ridge, hoping the snow wouldn't
be so deep there, and picked his way carefully uphill. It felt
like he was moving through tar. His mind went over the same
possibilities, the same fears, over and over.

Finally, he was at the top. He pulled out his telescope and
steeled himself to look. There was a crowd assembled around
the jetty, watching the boat as it left the harbour. It looked like it
had only just cast off. Nathaniel wondered if they were surprised
at him for not being there. What they were saying about him.
If they'd waited for a while, in case he turned up.

The cold sank into him as he watched. He realised he should
have built a fire, but it was too late now. He couldn't look away.
He stamped his feet to get his blood moving, and flexed the
fingers of each hand in turn.

As the hours passed, his mind grew quieter. He felt suspended in time. When the boat finally went down, it took a moment for him to realise he could leave.

He packed up his things and headed back down the hill, his heart like lead in his chest.

Chapter Twenty-nine

It had been a while since Sarah had sat out on the jetty with Ana. Over the last few months, it had become her place with Arthur, but a year or two earlier, it had been hers and Ana's.

The two of them had spent a lot of time over the years sitting out there, away from their parents. In the summer with ice cream, in the winter with hot chocolate. It was always the best place to talk if you didn't want to be overheard.

They didn't talk as they sat there now. They gripped each other's hands as they watched the boat get further away. The crowd behind them grew a bit, but then shrank again. They'd been watching for an hour when they saw the first sign of trouble.

'It's wobbling a lot,' someone in the crowd said. 'Maybe it's windier out there than it is here.'

Sarah stood and put a hand over her eyes, squinting against the sun to see more clearly. The boat did look like it was struggling. Ana grasped her arm.

The boat kept wobbling as it grew smaller and smaller.

And then it was gone.

A hush spread over the crowd.

'Did it go down?' someone asked.

'Nah,' said someone else. 'It's just gone over the horizon.'

'I think it went down,' came another voice.

'It was just being buffeted a bit, by the wind. They must be nearly halfway now. If they made it that far, they can make it all the way.'

Ana looked at Sarah, her eyes wild. 'What did you see?' she said. 'Do you think it went down?'

Sarah shook her head mutely. 'I don't know,' she said. 'It was too far away to tell.' She felt suddenly cold and still and somehow as if the world was moving around her without her being part of it.

'I have to get away from all these people,' said Ana, and her voice sounded as if it was coming from far away. 'I have to walk.'

Sarah nodded and the two of them wove through the crowd of villagers lining the jetty and heading up the beach.

'It could be fine,' Ana was saying. 'It didn't show any signs of leaks or anything when it was close. If it was OK for long enough for them to load it up and take off, then it's probably OK for the whole trip.'

Sarah nodded beside her, but didn't say anything as Ana kept talking. Her mind felt strangely blank. She couldn't let herself wonder about Nathaniel. They walked up and down for a while, until eventually Ana said she needed to sit and suggested getting a drink.

They walked back into the village and went into the pub, sitting in a table tucked into the corner, away from everyone else.

'I can't believe I told him I wouldn't let him be involved anymore,' Ana said. 'That was so mean. I'm so mean. Of course he'll be involved; he'll always be involved.'

They sat drinking their hot chocolates while Ana kept up a constant stream of chatter.

'I wonder if we should have another look,' she said, after a while. 'Maybe our eyes were just tired from staring for so long. It was so bright outside. Maybe now we've rested our eyes inside, we'll be able to see better.'

They got up and walked back down the jetty, peering out over the sea, but there was nothing there.

'That was stupid,' said Ana. 'Of course we can't see anything. Tired eyes – I don't know what I was thinking. Do you think Graeme needs any help with anything today?'

Graeme didn't need any help, but he brought Sarah and Ana inside and gave them lunch. He didn't comment as Ana explained what had happened and speculated over whether something had gone wrong. He didn't comment as Sarah sat there in silence.

He didn't comment when Ana stood up suddenly and said, 'Well, thank you very much, but we have to go now. We have to see if Sarah's mums need anything.' She turned to leave.

'We can't go to my house,' Sarah said, as they walked away from Graeme's farm. 'I don't want to go to my house.'

'Oh,' said Ana. 'OK. Where do you want to go?'

But Sarah didn't reply. She was staring down the road ahead of them, her eyes wide. Walking across the fields was Nathaniel.

'Oh,' he said, as he approached. 'Hi. I came to see Graeme.'

'You didn't go,' said Sarah. She felt strange, like she wasn't getting enough oxygen. There was a lump in her throat. 'You weren't on the boat.'

He frowned. 'No,' he said. 'I, ah . . . I need to talk to Graeme.'

'Where were you?' said Sarah. 'I looked for you . . . you weren't there.'

Nathaniel looked down at the ground. 'No. I went for a walk.'

'Oh.' She stared at him, confused. 'What aren't you telling me?'

'Look, I need to talk to Graeme,' he said. 'I might see you later.' And he turned up the path to the house.

'That was weird,' said Ana, as Sarah stared after Nathaniel. 'I wonder what he needs to talk to Graeme about. I wonder where he was. I've always thought he was a bit weird. Haven't you always thought he was a bit weird?' She was still talking in a fast, agitated tone.

'I don't know,' said Sarah. 'He's interesting.'

Sarah and Ana walked slowly back to the village centre and took a seat in the pub. It was busier now, full of people speculating over the fate of Thomas and his crew. Sarah thought Ana would want to leave again, but before she could bring it up, Graeme walked in.

Malcolm turned down the music so Graeme could address the crowd.

'I'm sorry to interrupt,' he said. 'We need to have a village meeting. Immediately. But I suppose since so many of you are here and it's warmer here than it is in the hall, we may as well just talk here.'

He waited a few minutes for those who hadn't already been in the pub to file in.

'As I'm sure most of you know,' he said, 'Thomas set sail this morning with a crew of four or five others. I'm not sure how many exactly he took with him. Nathaniel came to see me a few minutes ago with some news of that journey. I've asked him to tell all of you what he told me.'

There was a deathly stillness in the room as Nathaniel stepped forward. He looked pale, and his eyes were on the floor.

'Hi,' he said, a little awkwardly. 'I've been keeping up with Thomas's work on the boat over the last few weeks. I was considering going with him when he left. I ultimately decided not to join him, because I was uneasy about the amount of testing he'd done on his repairs.'

He hesitated for a moment and cleared his throat.

'This morning, before the boat was due to leave, I hiked to the top of the hill to the north of the village,' he continued. 'I knew we would only be able to see the boat from down here for so long. I took a telescope with me so I could watch its journey and make sure it arrived safely.'

It felt like everyone in the room was holding their breath. Ana was gripping Sarah's hand

'For the first hour or so,' Nathaniel went on, 'the journey was uneventful. They had a good steady wind, and were making decent enough progress.

'But then they lost a bit of control. Part of the sail detached from the rigging. And they started to take on water. They managed to keep going for another twenty minutes or so, but then . . .' – he wiped a hand across his eyes – 'then the boat did go down.'

Sarah felt the air go out of the room around her. She felt like her arms and legs were somehow disconnected from her body, like she'd become nothing more than a heart pounding in a chest. Nathaniel's words echoed around the inside of her head.

'I'm so sorry,' he was saying. 'I'm so sorry to have to tell you all this.'

There was absolute silence. For a moment or two, the room felt crystallised, immovable. And then a thin, quiet wail started up somewhere on the other side of the pub. Marcus's mother.

Sarah could see Will's parents standing in the middle of the room, as if turned to stone.

Slowly, life began to return to the room. Muffled, broken life. People staring at each other in shock. Sobs. Murmurs of grief and attempts at consolation. Mere moments ago, the place had been alive with debate over whether the boat had made it or not, but now there was just confusion and pain.

Stricken, Sarah turned to look at Ana, whose eyes were wild. She put a hand over her mouth.

'What do I do?' she whispered. 'What do I do now?'

Spring

So it had been like this.

A storm that lasted longer than any storm should.

A plane seen careening drunkenly through the sky.

A sky stained an unnatural hue.

Radios that fell silent. Phones that were dialled but never answered.

A ferry that no longer ran.

A hard winter that strained nerves that were near breaking point to begin with. Division, doubt, fear. A tragedy born of desperation and fury.

But all things are temporary. Life's periods of trial, as well as its times of wonder, all come to an end eventually. The bite slowly faded from the wind that swept over Black Crag. The snow retreated to the hills and pale, scrubby grass began to show through.

Now, there are daffodil shoots poking through the soil; there are buds showing on the cherry tree someone planted years ago despite the inhospitable climate. It never bears fruit, but always flowers in spectacular fashion.

Now, the green across the sky is halfway back to the horizon. The long winter is over. The heather on the hills is beginning to show purple again. The leaves are sprouting on the trees.

There are lambs near to being born and there are new seeds to be planted.

The world is still turning.

Chapter Thirty

The first flowers of spring were starting to show, and nobody wanted them.

There was a pall hanging over the island that felt irrevocable. How had they let themselves pretend that this couldn't touch them, Sarah wondered. That whatever had happened to take them out of the world wouldn't also take something from them?

The day after the boat had gone down, the skies had opened. It had rained solidly for three days, the first real rain of the year. It poured down, turning what remained of the snow to slush. There was something fitting about this, but it also felt strange. It kept everyone indoors, in their own homes, when Sarah felt like they should all be together, grasping each other's hands.

Malcolm had sent round a note of a funeral to be held on the beach.

Sarah wondered why it had come from him and not from Graeme. Perhaps Graeme was reluctant to be involved because of the enmity between him and Thomas. Perhaps he felt guilty. Perhaps he was angry.

After all, Thomas had taken four others along with him, three of whom had been young. Just twenty years old. She'd been at school with them.

She didn't know how to process the loss. Part of her felt

completely torn apart. She'd never known someone her own age to die. She'd lost her grandparents, and that had been hard, but it had also felt natural. They were old and they'd been so sick. There had been time to prepare.

But this felt wrong. She'd known the boat was dangerous; she'd thought it was a stupid, reckless plan. But knowing it had failed, knowing that everyone on board had drowned, took her breath away and left her battered and confused.

And then she felt guilty for claiming so much grief for herself. She hadn't known any of them that well. Even the three she'd been at school with were hardly her friends. She'd barely seen them over the last couple of years – even Marcus. Somehow, feeling any grief at all felt like an insult to everyone who'd really known them. Who'd loved them. Who'd relied on them.

Sarah walked through the rain every day to see Ana. They sat together and talked about nothing, and every so often Ana would start to panic and Sarah would hold on to her until she calmed down.

After Ana had decided to continue with her pregnancy, she'd been ready to dismiss any fears about the risks. Billie had said complications were unlikely, and Ana was ready to believe her. She'd let herself fall into planning. Putting together a nursery with whatever was available, listing possible baby names, happily speculating about whether she was having a boy or a girl.

But after the boat was lost, all the possible nightmares became real to her again. She would suddenly become sure that the baby would be breech, that the umbilical cord would be around its neck, that she'd go into early labour and it wouldn't be able to survive without an incubator.

Sarah would sit with her and let her talk through all her fears, and when she ran out of steam, would say simply, 'But probably not,' and Ana would look at her, wild-eyed, and nod.

'Right,' she would say. 'Probably not.' But when she'd managed to calm her fears about the birth, she was flooded with guilt about Marcus.

'Do you think if I hadn't kept telling him he couldn't go, then he would have stayed?' she asked, after one of these panics. 'Do you think I drove him away?'

'No,' said Sarah. 'That's ridiculous.'

'He was just so annoyed at me for telling him what to do.'

'I think he always would have gone. I think if you hadn't told him not to, it would never have occurred to him that there was another option.'

'Maybe,' said Ana. 'I don't miss him, you know? I'm not going to miss him. I feel so guilty about that.'

'Yeah, well, he was a pain in your ass.'

'But he was still a person. He deserves to be missed.'

Sarah leaned forward. 'Hey,' she said. 'He is missed. He will be missed. You feel the way you feel, and there's nothing wrong with that. You don't owe him anything.'

'Don't I? I'm carrying his baby.'

'You weren't married to him. You weren't even dating him really, not for long. You just had what you had and you got pregnant. That doesn't mean you're supposed to suddenly be in love with the guy.'

'Yeah,' said Ana. 'I suppose.'

'You can tell your kid that their dad was brave. That he tried to help us at the end of the world.'

Ana snorted. 'Their dad was an idiot,' she said.

'Yeah, well. They don't need to know that.'

The day of the funeral had dawned bright and clear. The sun was warm as it glinted on the last remnants of snow. People gathered on the beach, where someone had built up five stacks of driftwood, with evergreen leaves woven through them.

As people arrived, some of them walked up and added mementos to the stacks. Photos, books, even a couple of battered old toys. Ana went up to Marcus's stack, and placed down a folded scarf.

'It's the only thing I have of his,' she said to Sarah in an undertone. 'And it's just because he left it at my house by accident. Is that weird?'

Sarah took her hand. 'All of this is weird,' she said.

She noticed that one of the stacks had nothing on it. Thomas's, she supposed. After a while, she saw Nathaniel walk up to it and put something down. It was too small for her to see.

Malcolm walked to the front of the crowd and stood facing them. 'Thank you all for coming,' he said. 'We are here to remember the lives of Marcus, Will, Cole, Leon and Thomas. This is a small place. So to lose five of our people at once is a hard thing to bear. But we will bear it together.

'If anyone would like to speak about one of our lost brothers, please come forward.'

Sarah had thought there would be anger at the funeral. That people would not be able to restrain their fury at the men they had loved for taking such a stupid risk. But she was wrong.

Marcus's mother talked about how he'd always thrown himself headlong into danger. She talked about the time he almost got trampled by one of the bulls on their farm, because he was too heedless to take the long way around the field. The time he found a narrow cave in the cliffs and, in trying to explore it, got trapped for six hours.

'He always had me worried to distraction,' she said. 'But I could never be mad at him. He was so full of pluck. Willing to risk anything for adventure.'

Will's dad talked about how Will had stepped up when his mother had been so sick a few years earlier. 'He learned to cook,' he said. 'He even learned to bake so he could make her favourite lemon cake. I'm going to miss that cake.'

Cole's wife talked about how she'd met him, what their lives together had been like. Leon's son spoke about what an inspiration his dad had been.

No one stood up to speak for Thomas.

After a while, Malcolm stood again. 'Well,' he said, 'if that's all—'

'Wait,' came a voice. It was Nathaniel. 'I'll say something for him. For everyone,' he said, walking to the front. He looked around. 'I know this is not a simple thing to deal with. This is a grief with thorns. None of us knew, a year ago, what we would have to face. And if we'd known, we wouldn't have known how we could possibly get through it.

'It makes things complicated. How do we measure the grief at losing one person, at losing five people, against the grief at losing the entire world? I think if there's one thing to learn after this past year, it's that our griefs don't get dwarfed by larger tragedies. They're still their own.

'But the same is true of our joys. Our loves. The small stuff still matters, even at the end of the world.'

He cleared his throat and kept going.

'It would be easy, I think, to see this tragedy as a sign that we truly are alone. That all we can do is make the best of what we have here, on this island. But I think that would be a mistake. I think we should let the hope and determination of these five men spur us on.

'There is a world out there to rediscover. These men thought that was worth risking it all for. Carry their hope with you.

'We are not alone.'

Sarah felt a tear roll down her cheek as Nathaniel stepped back into the crowd.

Malcolm passed out tapers to Marcus's mother, Will's dad, Cole's wife and Leon's son. He kept the last for himself. They each stepped forward and set the tapers against the five stacks of driftwood.

The crowd watched for a while as the fires burned, and then slowly began to walk back to the village to raise a glass.

Nathaniel came up beside Sarah as she and Ana walked slowly along the beach.

'That was beautiful,' Sarah said. 'What you said.'

'Thanks.'

'What was it that you put on his fire?'

'Oh, that,' said Nathaniel. 'It was just his car key. I didn't really know him that well, but he seemed to really love that car.'

Sarah smiled and nodded as they walked on.

Chapter Thirty-one

Sarah was astonished at how quickly spring seemed to arrive after the funeral. It seemed like she blinked and the world went from grey and cold, to bright and warm. The snow had barely started to melt, and then suddenly it was gone, replaced by lush green glass with daffodils already beginning to bloom.

For a week or so there was nothing but beautiful weather and life springing forth that was entirely at odds with the mood in the village. The shock of the boat wreck had begun to abate, but it felt like people were still moving in slow motion. Moving quietly from one day to the next in a fog that didn't match the weather.

No one was ready when Graeme called a village meeting to plan the year ahead.

'I know we're all still reeling,' he said, 'and we all need to be patient with each other. But we also need to look to the future.

'There is a lot we need to discuss, and I'm not proposing we address every issue immediately. We need to take things one at a time. I'm proposing that we start with our farms.'

No one responded. The crowd was listening, but no one seemed to be deeply engaged. More so than they had been at any point so far, it seemed to Sarah that people just wanted to be told what to do.

Graeme continued. 'I think we would be wise to take stock of how our food stores lasted through the winter. That will give us an idea of what we need to produce in the coming year. If we are able to sow enough in the coming weeks, and if the harvest goes well, then hopefully we will have no need of a rationing system next winter, even if we are still unable to connect with the mainland.'

There was a small ripple across the crowd. Sarah wondered if anyone would want to try to reach the mainland now. Without Thomas to press the issue, and with such a catastrophic failure hanging over their heads, it seemed strange to bring it up.

'We know what crops we can't use ourselves,' Graeme continued, 'so we can use the space and time that would have gone to planting wheat, for example, and instead plant more fruits and vegetables. And maybe use a bit more space to try and increase our livestock.

'We know we need to grow things we can preserve and set aside, so we can prioritise those as well.'

He talked for a while longer, and the villagers listened and nodded and seemed to accept what they were told. But as they filed out of the hall, everyone seemed to feel flat and exhausted.

'It's just always going to be a grind, isn't it?' Ana said to Sarah as they walked away from the hall. 'It's like "Hooray, we survived, now we get to keep on trying to survive."'

'I don't know,' said Sarah. 'I think there's something invigorating about starting again fresh. We got through it all, and now we know how. Now we know what we need to do, and that we can do it. It makes me feel kind of strong. Like anything's achievable.'

Ana stopped walking and put a hand on Sarah's forehead. 'Well, you don't *feel* feverish,' she said.

'I'm serious,' said Sarah. 'This is when we really start to figure things out. Deliberately. We've been flailing for months, desperately just trying to stay afloat. Now it'll be different.'

'Hmm,' said Ana. 'I'm going to need to have a talk with Billie about you.'

Sarah rolled her eyes, but didn't press the issue. She didn't know how else to explain what she meant. She was sure things were going to be better this time. She could feel it.

Sarah reported to Graeme early the next morning. He seemed surprised to see her.

'Oh,' he said, 'we're not quite ready to start the proper work yet. I need a couple of days to figure everything out.'

'That's what I want to help with,' said Sarah. 'I think I can.'

Graeme smiled at her, but shook his head slightly. 'That's very good of you, Sarah. It's encouraging to see people so motivated. But how exactly did you think you would be able to help?'

Sarah was nonplussed. 'I thought there would be planning and things. Before the actual planting starts, I thought we'd have to figure out what to plant and where, and who to get on what tasks.'

Graeme gave a small chuckle. 'Of course, of course, we do have to do those things. But I'm not sure that's the right job for you. After all, do you know which crops are self-propagating? Which ones we don't rely on seeds shipped from the mainland to sow? Do you know what grows best in which types of soil? Which crops are more likely to fail, and therefore not worth the risk? Do you know what kind of attention will need to be paid to each different crop to ensure its success, and therefore what kind of labour we'll need to devote to them?'

Sarah swallowed and looked at the floor. She suddenly felt very small.

'It's extremely laudable that you're so ready to dig in and get some important work done,' said Graeme, making Sarah's skin crawl with embarrassment, 'but the one resource we have plenty of on this island is farming expertise. There is no shortage of people who can help plan our planting season, and they are already working on it. Why don't you ask your parents or your friend Ana what they need help with? I'm sure they'll have plenty of uses for you.'

Sarah felt fractious and angry with herself as she walked home. She knew her mothers would give her busywork to do if she was bored, but she also knew they didn't really *need* her help in the way that she wanted to be needed. They didn't have anything that would make her feel useful.

And Sarah needed to do something useful. There was an energy thrumming through her veins, and she knew that if she didn't get started on something, she wouldn't be able to release it. It wasn't physical energy, not something she could excise by hiking to the top of the hills. It was an eagerness to contribute, to put forth labour and see the fruits of it.

She tried to walk off her frustrations but even when she was physically exhausted the urge to do something substantial hummed in her veins.

'It's disgusting,' said Ana, when Sarah complained about this to her. 'You're making me feel like I should want to contribute something too. I'm going to have to start decorating the baby's room, and it's all your fault.'

Sarah laughed. 'I'll help you,' she said. 'Please let me help you. Do we have anything to decorate with?'

Ana shrugged. 'If we do, I am going to find it,' she said. 'If there is even one millilitre of lemon-yellow paint on this rock, I am going to track it down. I'm going to make stencils and sew blankets, and I don't even know what else.'

Sarah grinned at her. 'This is going to be the best baby's room of all time,' she said.

'Thank you. I think so.'

Sarah woke up a few days later to find only herself and Mam at home.

'Everything OK with you?' Mam asked mildly.

Sarah shrugged. 'I don't know. I just feel like I should be doing more. Like I *could* be doing more. I was ready to get stuck in, and now I just have to wait until Graeme lets me do something.'

'Ah,' said Mam. 'You're eager to spend your days hunched over in the dirt doing hard manual labour. I get it.'

Sarah laughed, then sighed. 'I just wanted to be useful.'

'Be useful, or feel useful?'

Sarah frowned. 'What's the difference?' she said.

Her mam smiled ruefully. 'You know, one of the things you learn as you get older is that you almost never get to be needed in the way you want to be needed.'

'What does that mean?' asked Sarah.

'You know, you'll have visions of yourself swooping into someone's difficult life and turning it around for them with profound speeches and an unerring sense of the best choices that person could make. But nine times out of ten, the most helpful thing you can do for someone who's going through it is clean out their fridge.'

'What?'

'Or, you know, do their laundry, bulk-cook some bolognese for them to heat up for their next five dinners. Ordinary things that help keep the wheels on their life while they deal with the real problems.'

'I don't think cleaning out fridges would be useful right now.'

Mam laughed. 'I'd appreciate your cleaning out ours, to be honest. My point is that to be really useful, you have to let go of what you want to do and look for what's actually needed. It's possible that right now, what's needed is for you to make sure you're rested and ready for the sowing when it starts.'

'But that's so . . .'

'Boring?' Mam said. 'Yes, well – very often, useful things are. But I have to say, I'm very impressed with you, Sarah.'

'With me? Why?'

'We were so worried, Moth and I, last year. We didn't know how to help you. You were so . . .'

'Angry?' supplied Sarah, her eyes wide, her head tilted to the side. 'Bitter?'

Mam laughed. 'Sure. And we understood. I know how hard it was for you to move here. I know you've never felt completely at home.'

Sarah looked at the ground. 'I tried to,' she said.

'I know. But you didn't. And that's OK. We felt bad for having had to make that decision for you. And we were happy for you that you were going to leave and find your own way out there, in the wider world. We were broken-hearted for ourselves, of course, but we were happy.

'And then everything happened, and you had everything that was ahead of you taken away. And that broke our hearts, too.'

Sarah felt a lump rising in her throat. She'd never really talked to Moth and Mam about this properly. She'd talked about plans and practicalities. She'd never asked how they felt about her leaving. She'd never been completely open about why she wanted to.

'But the last six months . . .' Mam continued. 'You've really changed. You've grown into someone I could have never imagined. You've always been fantastic, although I might be biased. But now there's something more to you. You're inspiring to me.'

'That's . . .' Sarah was overcome. 'I haven't been doing anything special,' she said. 'Just trying to help.'

Billie smiled softly. 'I know,' she said. 'I know you are. And you are helping. More than you realise.'

Sarah ran into Nathaniel a couple of days after her disappointing meeting with Graeme. She was walking slowly home from a visit with Ana, her hands in her pockets and her chin tucked into her scarf against the lingering chill of early spring. Dusk had fallen, and she didn't notice him immediately – he was standing still watching her when she did, and she got the impression he'd been waiting for her to catch up with him for a while.

'Oh,' said Sarah. 'Hi.' She looked down at her feet for a moment. She hadn't talked to Nathaniel since the funeral; she really didn't know what to say to him. Things had been weird between the two of them for a while – ever since he'd started hanging out with Thomas. She'd never understood their relationship, and after Thomas had died, it somehow felt like even more of a barrier between them.

'Are you heading home?' Nathaniel said asked her, and she nodded. 'Mind if I walk with you?'

They turned and started slowly down the street. Sarah was still searching for something to say.

'How's Ana?' Nathaniel said. 'She must only be a couple of months away from her due date.'

'Sure,' said Sarah, 'she's fine.' before stopping and turning to him. 'I'm sorry, you know. About Thomas. I know he was your friend.'

Nathaniel looked at her, his brow furrowed, then turned to keep walking. 'I don't know if we were friends, exactly.'

'Still,' said Sarah. 'You spent a lot of time with him, with all of them, and I . . . I'm just sorry.'

She glanced up at him as they walked, but he didn't look back at her. They walked in silence for a while, and Sarah chafed at the awkwardness, wondering if she'd been stupid to say anything.

'I couldn't figure out a way of convincing them they were wrong,' he said, finally. 'I tried. I guess I didn't try hard enough.'

Sarah was taken aback. It had never occurred to her that he might feel guilty about it. 'It wasn't . . .' She trailed off.

'I know it wasn't my fault,' said Nathaniel. 'I still don't know if there was anything I could have said. Probably not to Thomas. But maybe the others . . .' He shook his head a bit. 'They spent so much time hyping each other up. Convincing themselves it was the right thing to do. It's hard to compete with. And once I started expressing doubts, they acted like it was some betrayal. Like I'd pretended to agree with them and was finally showing my true colours or something. But I was just trying to say that it was worth taking a bit more time to make sure the boat was really sound.'

Sarah nodded. 'I was really scared,' she said. 'That day, I was really scared that you'd gone with them. That you'd . . .' She felt tears prickling in her eyes.

'I'm sorry,' said Nathaniel. 'I'm sorry I scared you. I didn't mean to.'

'You're just important to me,' said Sarah. 'You should know that.'

'I do. You're important to me, too.'

Sarah frowned and looked up at him. 'There's something here, isn't there? Between us?'

Nathaniel smiled slightly. 'There's loads here,' he said. 'You're my best friend. You're the most interesting person in Black Crag, and the only one who understands me at all.'

Sarah smiled back at him. 'That all?' she said.

He shook his head ruefully. 'I don't know if I can figure out what else, you know. Under these circumstances.'

Sarah laughed. 'I think that's probably enough to be going on with.'

'Sure,' he said. 'For the time being.'

They didn't speak again for a while, but it didn't feel awkward anymore.

'I still think they were right,' Nathaniel said, as they approached Sarah's house. 'They should have been more patient, but that doesn't mean the idea itself was wrong. We are going to have to figure out a way to get over there. Eventually.'

Sarah said goodbye and went inside, his words replaying in her head. Maybe he was right. But how were they supposed to do it? There were only two routes to the mainland and Thomas had failed at both. How would anyone else succeed?

Chapter Thirty-two

It's strange to mark the beginning of a new year in the middle of winter. The real beginning is, of course, spring. The season of new life, of stepping out of the darkness and the cold to confront the world anew. And this spring was the most important new beginning Black Crag had faced in perhaps its entire history.

The springs of the past seem to belong to another world. They would grow into a bustling time, with new seeds being shipped over from the mainland in astonishing quantities, with seasonal workers suddenly flooding the village to help with the planting. Lambs and pigs would be born and grow older and be butchered and shipped off to feed people in cities far away.

The spring of the previous year had been the strangest of all. The spring that changed as it faded, that shifted suddenly into the unforeseeable.

This spring was the first moment of the new future.

What they did over these months would define how they made it through the next year. Perhaps the one after that.

This spring was for deciding how they were going to keep living on through the end of the world.

Graeme knew he had a hard task ahead of him to bring the village together after the deaths of the five sailors. And he knew that they needed to come together if they wanted to keep surviving.

Thomas had been an agitator, he'd set himself against Graeme for reasons known only to himself, but he had been right on some points. And those points would need to be addressed.

Graeme called together a small team of people to meet over dinner. There was Helen, who Graeme knew to be an experienced diver. Walter, who had managed to get the electricity working again after the power cut. And there was Francis, whose small dinghy was now the best boat available to them.

'We need to talk about the turbines,' Graeme said. 'Apart from the one outage in the winter, they seem to be operating as they should, but we need to check them out, try and figure out how the system works, and see if we can come up with a plan should anything go more seriously wrong.'

The group looked at each other nervously.

'I'm not sure we're capable of this, Graeme,' said Walter.

'I'm not sure we are, either,' said Graeme. 'But we're the only option. So we need to at least try. God willing, the system will hold for at least another year, and it may well hold for several. But if we can avoid being caught out and having to scramble again, then that would be better for everyone.'

'But where do we even start?' said Helen.

'We do have some blueprints of the village's electrical system,' said Graeme. 'So Walter, I'll need you to familiarise yourself with that. Try and find places that might be vulnerable, and do what you can to shore them up, but also note where will be the first places to look if there's a problem.

'Helen, I need you to put together a team of whoever you think can handle a dive out at the turbines. We need to check what condition they're in, and see if we can learn about the cable system that runs to us here. Only take those you're sure can handle it; this isn't the time for anyone to test their mettle. I think you'll need to do some practice dives close to shore to make sure everyone is fit, and that whatever equipment you have is stable.'

Helen was shaking her head, worried. 'I'm not sure we'll have enough oxygen tanks for serious investigation,' she said. 'And we won't be able to get more. And I haven't been diving since the fire, I would need some smaller dives first to make sure my arm isn't going to hold me back.'

'Well, figure out how much we have, and what kind of exploration we can do. If you're not up to diving yourself, you're still the best person to take the lead on this, make sure the other divers are capable. We are operating on a better-than-nothing understanding for this.'

Francis was frowning. 'This is all very well,' he said. 'But whatever we manage to learn about the grid and the turbines . . . It's all still going to be temporary. Eventually, there will be wires that need to be replaced. And we won't have replacements. Eventually, we will lose power.'

Graeme nodded. 'We will,' he said. 'If we never do make contact with anyone on the mainland, if we truly are alone here, then yes, eventually the electrical system will break down, and we will have to learn to live without it. But I would like to give us as much time as possible to prepare for that.'

'But how are we going to prepare for that?' said Helen.

Graeme gave a small smile. 'Don't worry about that. Your job is buying us time. I have another team for the rest.'

*　　*　　*

Graeme watched the planting start with satisfaction. He was sure the plan he had made would make the coming year easier than the last one, and he was relieved to see people coming together to make it happen.

There were a few people he asked to do more, after they'd finished their days out in the field. He felt guilty about asking when they'd already done so much, but he knew he couldn't wait around.

He asked Jeremy, Malcolm, Seonaid and Ana to come and meet with him at the end of a long day. Ana was the only one with any energy to spare – she had been excused from the planting thanks to her pregnancy.

'Thank you for giving me what little energy you have left,' he said. 'But we need to start planning for the winter. For the coming winter, and every one after that.'

Malcolm laughed darkly. 'No pressure, then,' he said.

'We have plenty of time to get things in place,' said Graeme. 'We have the whole summer. But I don't want to waste time; I want to be ready to go as soon as the planting is done. We need to be ahead of this, if only for our own peace of mind.'

'Graeme, what are you talking about?' said Seonaid.

'I've put together a team to maintain the electrical system for as long as possible,' said Graeme. 'But the reality is, all we're going to be able to do is buy time. We need to be prepared to do without it as well.'

There were a few tense glances around the table.

'Jeremy, you already started trying to make sure everyone has working fireplaces. How is that going?'

Jeremy nodded. 'There's still a lot to do,' he said. 'Some places are easy, just needed a clean out. But some need extensive repairs. And a few need something new put in. A lot could do with better insulation as well.'

'OK, well, put together a team who can get started the moment the seed is in the ground,' said Graeme. 'And let everyone know what the schedule is for this as soon as possible. I want them to be reassured that we won't be caught out again. That they can feel safe in their own homes.'

Jeremy nodded slowly.

'The other thing you may not have thought of is whether people will be able to use their fires for cooking. Heating water. Those kinds of things,' Graeme went on.

Jeremy's eyes snapped up to meet his. 'I had not thought of that,' he said slowly.

'Well,' said Graeme. 'Start thinking of it. Malcolm, I know you've done a bit of open-fire cooking. Can you help with that?'

Malcolm frowned. 'Roasting a pig over a spit isn't the same as knowing how to do day-by-day cooking in a domestic fireplace,' he said.

'Well, figure something out,' said Graeme. 'And we might need to have an education programme. Teach people how to cook at home without burning the house down.'

'I'm not sure I'm qualified for that,' said Malcolm.

'No one else is, either. You're the best we've got, so you'll have to manage somehow.'

Malcolm looked a bit surprised, but nodded.

Seonaid leaned forward. 'What do you want me to do, Graeme?' she said.

He turned to her. 'I'm hoping you and Ana can take on the other big problem. Light. We don't have many candles on the island, and we can't get more. We'll need to regress a bit, go back to tallow perhaps.'

Seonaid was nodding slowly, but Ana looked baffled.

'I have some history books that might have something about that,' said Seonaid. 'But it will take some trial and error, and it's not like we can keep butchering cows just to make candles.'

'Oh god,' said Ana. 'Is that what they're made from?'

Seonaid laughed. 'I knew you weren't listening in that class,' she said. She turned back to Graeme. 'The candles on their own won't be enough. We'll need candlesticks, maybe even wall sconces, that kind of thing.'

Graeme nodded. 'I'll get some of the better carpenters working on it,' he said.

As each day passed, more crops were laid down. More plans were made. Graeme could feel the energy shifting.

Each problem solved – each problem even given the possibility of a solution – gave a burst of confidence to the community. They were pulling together.

There were still questions to be answered. The petrol supplies were dwindling fast as the tractors ploughed the fields. There wouldn't be any left for the harvest. There were rowing boats in need of repair, in order to keep a supply of fish coming in.

And there was still an undercurrent of uncertainty. How long could they keep it up on their own? How long would they have to?

But for now, there was a spirit that was carrying them through. There was hope for the future.

Elliot

It was when the chill of early spring was still in the air, but the relief of having survived the winter was everywhere, that Elliot Harrison almost died.

He'd been running up and down the beach with his friends, daring each other to plunge into the freezing ocean water, when he'd suddenly dropped to his knees, gasping for air. He'd known he should be careful – his asthma medication had run out a month earlier – but the joy of the sun and the excitement of his friends had been contagious.

When his parents got to him, he was blue in the face and a small, panicked crowd had gathered.

His mam wrapped him in a blanket and held him upright, talking in low, soothing tones, as she carried him into the nearby pub. She ordered Malcolm to bring a bowl of boiling water and helped Elliot breathe in the steam, keeping a hand on his chest to warm him. Slowly, his breathing calmed until he was able to drink some tea.

The incident made clear to everyone how precarious their position was. They could grow enough food to survive, but they couldn't replenish their depleted medical supplies.

There was a limit to what they could do on their own. And no one was coming to save them.

Chapter Thirty-three

It was the same spot on the beach where she'd found the arm. That was where she heard them.

It was her first day off from the planting in a while, so she'd taken her time to ease into the morning, moving slowly around the house, lingering over her breakfast. And then, after lunch, she'd set off on one of her old walks.

The day had been clear, with a crisp breeze coming down from the hills, but the sun was setting as she walked, and she knew it would get cold quickly once the light faded. But that was OK. She welcomed the thought of a long, moonlit walk back alone.

The sound came up through her feet. A feeling more than a sound. The vibration working through her bones.

It continued as she looked around, getting stronger, louder, building until it felt like the sound was surrounding her.

And then there they were. Streaming across the grassland. Horses. Dozens of them, galloping across the land, shaking their heads in the dying light. They poured on to the sand and ran along the beach towards her, and her heart stopped in her chest.

The horse at the front, a gleaming chestnut, saw her and it let out a neigh and veered to the left, pulling the herd back to the grasslands and away again. But one was slow to keep up. He trotted towards Sarah, shook out his mane, and circled around her once before cantering away again after the herd.

Sarah remained breathless on the sand for a few minutes after the horses had disappeared. She almost thought it had been a dream, but the sand around her was still all stirred up.

She turned to go after the horses, but thought better of it. It was getting dark; she needed to get back home. But her mind was humming.

She knew there had once been horses on the farms, years before. Before even her mother had been born. But slowly, people had given them up, using the land for crops or cows instead. Sarah had always been disappointed that there were no horses; she'd thought a farm without a horse was a waste when she was a kid.

But no one else seemed to question it. They took a lot of upkeep, and it was easier to get around the farms on dirt bikes anyway.

But now . . .

Now they could be exactly what the village needed.

She was excited to tell her parents about what she'd seen, but it did not go as she'd imagined. At first, no one believed her.

'But where would they have come from?' said Mam. 'There are no horses on the island.'

'I don't know,' said Sarah. 'But they were there.'

'I'm not saying they weren't, kid,' said Mam. 'I'm just confused.'

'I don't understand why,' said Sarah. 'I saw them. They were there. One of them came right up to me.'

'OK, love,' said Moth. 'No one's disagreeing.' But she didn't seem convinced.

'I guess they came along the road,' said Sarah. 'They must be from the mainland.'

'I guess they must,' said Mam.

There was an awkward silence. Sarah didn't know why no one else was as excited as she was.

'Don't you see?' she said. 'This could change everything. We're about to run out of petrol; this could be the answer to that.'

'Oh, hon,' said Moth. 'I mean, it's possible. But we don't know where these horses have come from. I know there used to be herds of wild horses seen to the north from time to time, it's possible they've made their way across the isthmus. And training wild horses is extremely difficult to do. And these are adult horses. They won't like being corralled, they won't like being put to work. I imagine even an experienced trainer would struggle – most work horses are trained from birth.'

'Not to mention we don't have the equipment for that,' said Mam. 'You can't just hitch the back of a tractor to a couple of horses and hope for the best. You need custom-designed stuff.'

Sarah rolled her eyes in frustration. 'You guys are giving up before we've even tried,' she said. 'Maybe it won't work, but what do we have to lose?'

Moth and Mam looked at each other, and then back at Sarah.

'We just want you to be realistic,' Moth said. 'We don't want you getting overwrought.'

'I'm not overwrought!' said Sarah, indignant.

'You sure don't *sound* overwrought,' said Elliot with a smirk.

'OK,' said Mam. 'That's enough. Sarah, tell Graeme about

the horses. But don't count on them being the solution to all our problems.'

Sarah did tell Graeme about the horses, and he was only slightly less pessimistic than Moth and Mam.

'They're wild beasts, Sarah,' he said. 'They're not going to be easy to even get near, let alone train.'

'They didn't seem afraid of me,' said Sarah.

'They may not be afraid, but that doesn't mean they'll let you harness them or put them to work.'

For some reason, Sarah felt more flattened by Graeme's caution than she had by her parents'. Moth and Mam were easy to dismiss as overly cautious – parents were supposed to keep you safe, and part of that was letting you know when you were going too far.

But Graeme . . . she'd expected him to see the same possibilities she had. She was disappointed that he hadn't seemed to. But he'd told her that he could spare her from the planting for a few days if she wanted to see if she could approach the horses again.

'There are plenty of people helping out,' he said. 'And if you did manage to work a miracle with those horses, then there's no denying that would be useful.'

She didn't talk to anyone else about them yet. She knew word would spread, but part of her thought it would be better if the story was coming from her parents and Graeme. They'd tell it as an example of a beautiful happenstance, rather than the possible salvation of the village.

As hopeful as Sarah was about what the horses could mean for them all, she didn't want to spread that hope too far and be responsible for disappointment. She didn't want to make this something the village would count on, even if she couldn't stop herself from counting on it.

So she attempted to lower her expectations as she prepared for her second meeting with them.

Chapter Thirty-four

Sarah packed a bag with a few precious carrots and some of the last sugar cubes from the pantry.

She tried to talk herself down, to convince herself that they wouldn't come near her, that they wouldn't even be there anymore, that they would have gone back to wherever they'd come from. That all she'd ever have of them was the memory, and that before long, even she wouldn't be sure they hadn't been a dream.

She talked to herself the whole way along the beach, trying to build her hopes into a more realistic shape, but she couldn't help the anticipation rising in her chest.

She got to the point on the beach where she'd seen them. The sand had been smoothed out by the tide, which had risen and fallen in between, but she knew she was around the right spot. This part of the beach had been burned into her brain by the arm. She walked slowly along the edge of the sand, right where it met the grass, where the tide didn't reach it, and finally she found a spot where the grass had been flattened by hooves.

She followed the flattened grass for a while, and eventually she found a patch of mud. Most of it had been churned up but there were a couple of clear hoofprints. They sent a bell ringing in her head, but for a moment she couldn't figure out why.

She stared at the prints for what felt like an age, wondering why they seemed so important. And then it hit her.

They had horseshoes. The horses were shod. They weren't wild at all.

That's why they hadn't seemed all that afraid of her; that's why one of them had come right up to her. He'd probably assumed she'd had a treat for him.

Her pulse raced; her mind hummed with excitement. If they weren't wild, they wouldn't need training at all. They'd just need to get used to people again. They'd just need to learn to trust them.

Sarah followed the path of flattened grass for another half hour or so before she saw them. They were just ahead, at least forty of them, grazing around a patch of trees.

She stood completely still, breathing deeply. Finally, she started stepping forwards, moving slowly, trying not to startle them. She was a few feet away when one of them noticed her. It watched her for a couple of minutes and then gave a snort, before turning and ambling away.

As the first horse moved, a few others looked up and saw her too. Some of them trotted away immediately, while others watched her for a while, waiting for her to get closer, before they, too, moved away.

Sarah took out a chunk of carrot from her bag and held it out in front of her as she continued to move slowly forwards. A couple of the horses took a step or two towards her, before moving away again. She was slowly driving them away towards the hills, like a very inefficient sheepdog.

Sarah stopped moving and dropped her hands to her sides. She took a deep breath. She'd known this would take patience.

She decided to stop trying to get close to the horses. She'd just be here, near them. Letting them get used to her.

She sat on the ground, her legs crossed, and placed the chunk of carrot out in front of her. She waited.

At one point, on the other side of the trees, she saw one of the horses start to run, and she was immediately worried that they'd all join in. That they'd leave without her ever having got close to one of them. The horse ran in a circle and slowed down again, walking over to a clump of grass to graze upon. As Sarah was breathing a sigh of relief, something knocked against her shoulder.

She jumped and then turned, willing herself to move slowly. There was a horse standing beside her. The same one that had circled her yesterday, a sandy bay. He batted his nose against the side of her face and then bent down to eat the chunk of carrot.

Slowly, Sarah pulled another bit of carrot out of her bag and held it out on the palm of her hand. He gently took it from her and munched it.

Carefully, trying to move slowly and fluidly, Sarah stood. The horse stayed with her. She put out a hand and laid it on his nose and slowly started to stroke him.

He gave a gentle whicker, and Sarah started to relax. She ran a hand down his neck and over his shoulders, and felt tears welling in her eyes.

This could work, she was sure of it.

She felt a surge of adrenaline run through her, and she spun around to see if there was another horse close by she could approach. But the sudden movement startled the bay, and before she was aware what was happening, he'd turned and lashed out with his back hooves, catching her between her shoulders.

Sarah flew through the air, landing on her front a few feet away, her left arm crushed awkwardly underneath her. She lay there stunned for a moment, before slowly rolling on to her back. She could see the horse still standing a few feet away, placidly pulling up clumps of grass with his teeth.

She sighed and went to stand, but when she put her hands on the ground to push herself up, pain shot through her left elbow. Sarah yelled out, tears starting in her eyes. She took a few deep breaths to pull herself together, and then stood, holding her injured arm close to her body. She gathered up her bag and rolled her head around a couple of times. The jolt of the kick was still reverberating through her, and she could feel a headache starting to grow.

She sighed and began the long trudge towards home.

'Well, it's not broken,' Billie said a couple of hours later, as she and Sarah sat at the kitchen table. 'It would be a lot more swollen if it was.'

She'd carefully poked and prodded at Sarah's arm, bending it back and forth, listening to Sarah's gasps of pain.

'Are you sure?' said Sarah. 'It really hurts.'

'I'm sure it does,' her mam replied. 'Look, I'm a GP in a small farming community. Most of my job is small injuries like this. Sprained ankles, bruised hips, wrenched elbows, broken ribs, dislocated shoulders.'

'OK, OK, I get it.'

'You're going to be fine,' said Billie, pushing her chair back from the table. 'You just need to rest that arm for a couple of weeks. I'll grab you a sling from the surgery. Oh, and I don't want you going back out there.'

Sarah stared at her. 'Mam! I have to. Especially now; it's not like I can help with the planting like this.'

'Oh, but you can train wild horses?' Billie scoffed.

'Oh, Mam, I forgot! They're not wild. They're shod; they've all been shod.'

Billie just looked at her with a raised eyebrow.

'Don't you see?' Sarah continued. 'They must have been farm horses, somewhere on the mainland. They're already trained.'

Billie shook her head slightly. 'Even if they are, they've been living wild for months now. Who knows how they'll respond to being back among humans?'

'But maybe they'll want to live on farms again, where they'll be fed oats and carrots and nice things instead of just grass all the time. Where they'll be given blankets when it's cold.'

Sarah could tell her mam was trying not to look to sceptical. 'Either way,' Billie said, 'you can't train them until your arm's healed. And I don't want you out there alone – you could have been hurt much more seriously than you were, and we wouldn't have known where to look for you. '

'Mam, I'm fine. And it's not like I need both arms to get them used to having me around. I can do this.'

'What you can do is rest and recover. I'm not saying never go out there again, ever – just not until your arm's a bit better. And not on your own.'

Sarah rolled her eyes, but didn't say anything.

She stayed near home the next day to appease her mam, but she had no intention of staying away from the horses for long. She knew she should have been more careful, she knew it was her fault she'd been hurt, and she was sure she could stop it happening again. And if she was right, the horses could change everything.

She explained it all to Arthur that afternoon on the jetty, feeling a little embarrassed at her own fervour as she outlined her plans, and nervous that he'd pour cold water on them the way Graeme and her parents had. To her surprise, he grew a little misty-eyed and nostalgic.

He told her his father had had the last horses on the island. 'The land here's always been a bit rocky for horses. A lot broke their legs, needed either extensive rehabilitation or . . . Well, they were risky and expensive.

'By the time I was a kid, all the farms were using tractors and the like. My dad, too, but he kept a couple of horses on hand because he liked to have them around. His dad and his grandad had been expert trainers, you know. Horses were in the blood.'

Sarah stared at him. 'Do you know how to train them?' she asked.

Arthur frowned and looked out over the water. 'I remember a few things my dad taught me,' he said. 'Not sure I'd call that knowing.'

'I'd call that knowing more than anyone else in Black Crag,' said Sarah, and Arthur just shrugged. There was a light in his eyes, though, and a faraway look on his face, and Sarah could feel a grin spreading across her own face in response to it.

Arthur could come with her, and Billie would have nothing to complain about. He'd teach her what his father had taught him, and they'd be able to bring the horses home in no time.

Over the next couple of weeks, Sarah and Arthur started making trips to find the horses. Sarah had been worried the walk would be hard on Arthur, but he didn't seem to mind it. The horses weren't always in the same place, but their tracks were pretty easy to follow. There were no other large animals on this part of the island to confuse them with.

After a few visits, the bay started coming forward to meet them when he saw them approaching, although the others still tended to move away. Sarah started calling the bay Terry, and hoped that by the time she ran out of carrots, he'd like her for herself.

She knew she had to be careful with him. She'd been on pony rides a few times as a child, but she'd never learned to ride properly. She'd discovered how easy it was to spook him, and she knew that it would be easy for her to get seriously hurt. She had been lucky that day – his hooves could have just as easily caught her in the head as the back, he could have kicked a lot harder than he did, she could have landed on a rock instead of soft grass.

She knew she had to take this slowly, but she was determined, and now she had Arthur to help her. Together, they spent a couple of days just trying to get him acclimated to them, stroking the horse, talking to him, letting him get used to them. After a few days, with Arthur's encouragement, Sarah put an arm over the horse's back for a while, and strolled alongside him as he meandered around the field.

A couple of days after that, she climbed up on a tree stump and leaned across Terry's back, trying to keep herself steady on her feet while putting a decent amount of weight on him. He didn't seem to mind, and Sarah was elated.

He seemed to like her company. He seemed to trust her. And the more time she spent with him, the more the other horses seemed to trust her too. They didn't move away from her quite as quickly. A couple of them had let her and Arthur stroke their noses.

This was working, she thought to herself. This was going to work.

At the beginning of the second week, they took the biggest step yet. Sarah hadn't told her parents what she was planning – she knew Billie would have insisted she wait until her arm was fully healed. But it was already feeling so much better, and Sarah was too impatient to wait. She had to try.

She spent an hour or so with Terry, talking to him softly, walking with her arm over his back, Arthur observing from a few feet away. Eventually, Sarah brought the horse to the tree stump. She climbed on top of it, but this time, instead of just leaning on him, she brought a leg up and hoisted herself on to his back.

She held her breath for a few seconds. Part of her was sure he would immediately throw her off, but instead he stood there placidly. Sarah took a few deep breaths. It was much higher up than she'd realised. She gave Terry a nudge in the sides with her heels, and he began to slowly walk forwards.

She laughed aloud with joy and surprise. Without a bridle, she couldn't direct him, but she let Terry take her on a slow, plodding tour of the trees for a while, before she slid awkwardly down. She gave him a hug in joy and he seemed unperturbed.

She turned to Arthur glowing, and he gave a small, stoic nod.

She walked home in triumph, her heart soaring. She chattered non-stop to Arthur, wondering if any of the farms had any old gear lying around that they could use. It would be old, it might be damaged, but it might be enough.

Arthur didn't say much in reply, just nodded along with Sarah's chatter, but there was an energy to him that hadn't been there before. Sarah wondered if he, too, had been wanting to feel useful. If the arrival of the horses, and what they could mean for Black Crag, had given him as much purpose as it had her.

Chapter Thirty-five

Graeme had a saddle and bridle that was still in reasonably good condition, and some oil treatment to help improve it. Sarah spent an evening polishing the leather and cleaning some small spots of rust on the buckles.

She was worried about trying them out. She knew they would make it easier to ride Terry, but she didn't know if he'd like it. But he accepted both the saddle and bridle placidly. He seemed to enjoy being ridden, although it took Sarah a while to get used to it.

Her muscles ached after the smallest time spent riding, and she still wasn't confident in the saddle, although Arthur said she was doing fine. He said it would take a while to feel natural, and that Terry would let her know immediately if she was doing anything he didn't like.

'How would he do that?' she'd asked, a little apprehensive.

Arthur had shrugged. 'Refuse to move. Throw you off. That kind of thing,' he'd said, which Sarah did not find encouraging.

Arthur wasn't trying to ride himself – he claimed he was too old to relearn, at least when they were practising so far from the doctor – but he remembered a fair bit about riding from his youth, and they had help from an old book on horses Moth had found at the school.

Sarah spent a couple of weeks getting used to riding Terry, and then she decided it was time to take things up a notch.

Because Sarah had a plan.

After she was more or less comfortable – if not confident – riding, she and Arthur brought Jeremy and Beth out to see the horses. They both spent a couple of days letting the horses get used to them, and then Jeremy lifted Beth carefully on to a small black mare, before pulling himself up on to a tall grey horse.

Ana was too pregnant to come out, but Sarah brought Nathaniel and Malcolm's son, Neil. Again, they spent a few days getting to know the horses, before trying to ride one.

For their first expedition, they headed towards the hills, away from the village.

Sarah led alongside Nathaniel, while Beth and Jeremy stayed in the rear. They rode for almost an hour, and to Sarah's delight, most of the horses came with them, cantering out alongside, shaking their heads in the joy of the run.

And when Sarah rode Terry in a wide circle, turning around to go back, again the other horses followed.

She thrilled to the power of it, to the possibilities her success held.

This is it, she thought. *This is the answer.*

While Sarah and her team had been concentrating on getting the horses accustomed to people, Graeme had put another band of people to work on the farms.

One of the tractors had broken down early in the planting and was sitting useless on the sidelines. Graeme had it dismantled and refitted to a makeshift harness designed to be pulled by a team of two horses.

He'd elected to just make one, to start with. They had enough petrol, just about, to get through the spring, and then they'd have summer to figure out if the homemade horse-drawn system could work before they replicated it with the rest of the tractors.

It was a big ask, but not as big as getting the harvest in with no mechanical help whatsoever.

The news of the horses had spread like wildfire, and Sarah had had to put in place strict rules to stop people converging on them before they were ready. She hadn't told anyone where the horses were, and she'd made sure the others knew not to tell either, but she still felt that it was important to make sure no one tried to follow them.

She called a town meeting to talk through everything that was happening, to counter some of the rumours, and to confirm her plan for the horses.

'This is a delicate operation,' she said. 'These aren't creatures we can control, or that we should want to control. We're hoping we'll be able to work with them. We're hoping we can train them to work for us. But in order to do that, we need them to feel safe with us. We can't all rush them at once.

'We have to be prepared to get to know them slowly, like we do with each other.'

'Are you sure you're the best person to be in charge of this?' someone asked. 'Aren't you a little young?'

'I'm not sure of anything,' said Sarah. 'But I've spent a lot of time with the horses recently, and I think I'm coming to understand them. It's taken time. It does take time. You all have to be prepared for it to take time.'

She outlined her plan for bringing the horses into the village, and while there were a few questions, no one argued. Those that didn't necessarily think she was the best person for the job at least trusted that Graeme trusted her.

That seemed to be enough.

In the end, it was a full six weeks after Sarah first saw the horses before she brought them home. She and the others had spent every day with them, had ridden them, had befriended them.

They were never going to be any more ready than they were.

Finally, they set off. Sarah in front on Terry, with Nathaniel beside her on a horse he was calling Burt. Neil rode back and forth along the edges, on his horse, Bellows. And Beth and Jeremy were at the back, on horses they'd called Lady and Tramp.

Sarah led them across the grassland, back to the beach where she'd first seen them. She turned and rode along the strip of sand. The same strip she'd walked down nearly a year ago, carrying a diseased-looking severed arm.

She kept the horses at a walking pace. They had people to meet along the way.

Stationed along the beach were Sarah's friends, family and neighbours.

Seonaid and Billie. Elliot and his friends. Ana and her mother. Arthur. Malcolm, a look of pride in his eyes as he saw Neil helping guide the horses home.

They were spaced out and under strict instructions not to rush forwards, but to wait for the horses to come to them. In turn, they each let the horses surround and pass them, putting their hands up to stroke those who seemed willing.

Sarah knew it was an impressive sight – and a symbol of

hope. Her heart swelled as she saw her home come into view, as she brought the future to it.

As they drew past the village, she turned up onto the road, leading the herd carefully into the paddock that had been prepared for them. She rode past Graeme, standing beside the open gate, and he nodded his head to her, tears in his eyes.

Sarah and Arthur set up a programme for getting the wider village used to the horses, and the horses used to the wider village. There were only a few saddles and bridles, all of which were in various states of wear, but those who wanted to try to ride were given slots to try with one of Sarah's initial team.

Mostly, she wanted people to get used to leading the horses. That would be what was most useful when it came time to harvest.

Also important was getting the horses used to the tractor attachments. Jeremy started focusing on that, picking out a couple of the steadier, more placid horses to try first. Sarah concentrated on learning to ride well herself, while helping others do the same. Both of them deferred to Arthur in all things.

The three of them spent evenings together ostensibly to mark the progress of the villagers and the horses. Sarah had suggested it would be a good idea to track which horses seemed well suited to each different task, and which villagers were most to be trusted with them. More often than not, though, they ended up gossiping and swapping stories.

Arthur showed himself to be full of stories of Black Crag. There was a spark to him that hadn't been there before the horses arrived, and he slipped more easily into the past. He shared all the village scandals of his childhood, revealing secrets about Sarah's grandparents and great-grandparents that made her shriek in shock and cackle with laughter.

Jeremy, who had no relatives to hear scandalous stories about, had a knack for asking Arthur just the right questions to get him off on wild tangents about the youthful antics of Black Crag's older residents, somehow managing to get to the juiciest histories.

Sarah found her ideas about the village undergoing a drastic change – she'd never realised there was so much room for drama in such a tiny place.

The Sky, Once More

There was a growing sense among the villagers that the world was ordinary again. That it was safe. If they'd put conscious thought towards it, though, they would have recognised this sense of safety was an illusion.

Everyone knew they were running out of crucial supplies. Parents were urging caution on their children, aware that accidents held more peril now than they used to. The care with food had become habitual, and the idea of wasting anything was an anathema.

But the feeling of doom that had maintained an ambient presence in everyone's minds was abating, and there was one clear reason for it. The sky overhead was relentlessly blue.

The strange tint was still there if you looked to the east, but it had retreated so far that it felt completely removed from Black Crag. It had been months since anyone had feared its approach, and it seemed inevitable that one day soon it would be gone completely.

If people were thinking about what that meant, they weren't owning up to it. There was still too much to fear in asking the question of what things looked like on the mainland, and too much to focus on right in front of them.

People let themselves concentrate on immediate priorities,

and allowed their slowly growing optimism to hover in the background, helping them get through each day without coalescing into tangible thought.

Thought could wait.

Chapter Thirty-six

Ana was growing closer to her delivery date, and she was so tired that Sarah felt a little guilty for having any energy herself at all. She'd drop past Ana's house in the evenings – when she herself was exhausted by a full day of working with the horses – and still felt like a toddler on a sugar high compared to her friend.

Ana had taken to sitting on the floor with her back against the wall, claiming it was the only way she could relax that wasn't lying down.

'If I sit on the couch, I feel like I have to be actively holding my pelvis in the right position the whole time,' she'd said. 'It's exhausting.'

She was sitting there, eyes half-closed, listening to Sarah repeat Arthur's most recent stories, when she let out a sudden gasp.

Sarah looked over at her, laughing, initially taking the gasp as the logical reaction to the news that Mrs Wallace from down the street, who had several times told them off for walking past her house too loudly, had once got drunk and rode a pig through the village centre, half-dressed and singing 'Jingle Bells' at the top of her lungs.

But Ana had gone suddenly pale. Her eyes were closed and

she was breathing rapidly. 'I think I need to lie down,' she said. 'Can you help me to my bed?'

But when Sarah grasped her by the waist and helped her move, Ana gave a cry and shook her head. Sarah lowered her back down to the ground, and grabbed some cushions to put under her head.

'Is it . . . are you having contractions?' she asked.

Ana gulped and shook her head. 'It can't be,' she said. 'This can't be normal.' She closed her eyes, taking deep breaths. 'There's something wet,' she said. 'I think . . . Did my waters break?'

But when Sarah looked at the bright cotton of Ana's skirt, she saw a dark red circle blooming.

The world felt completely silent as Sarah flew through the village. It was like time had stopped. All she could hear was her own breath catching in her throat. When she got home, her mam took one look at her face and stood up.

'Ana?' she asked.

Sarah nodded mutely, and felt tears spill from her eyes. She was vaguely aware of Moth saying she'd run round to Beth's in case she was needed, before she turned and left again, shivering slightly as her mam hurried beside her.

'Has her water broken?' Mam was saying, 'Are her contractions coming fast or slow?'

Sarah shook her head and took a couple of shaky breaths before she tried to reply. 'I don't . . . She isn't . . . There was blood. There's blood. I'm sorry.'

'It's OK, love. We just need to stop by the surgery to get some things. It seems like I should assess her at home before I try to move her there.'

As soon as they walked through the door of Ana's home, Sarah knew something was very wrong. Ana's dad was sitting in his chair by the window, his face tight and drawn. He'd clearly been waiting for them, but didn't say much as he nodded them through to the room beyond. Ana's mother was hovering over her daughter, who was lying on the floor, her face so pale that for a moment, Sarah thought she was already dead.

But as the door closed behind Sarah and her mam, Ana's eyes flickered open and she looked over to them. 'Something's wrong,' she said quietly.

'So it seems,' said Billie, in a calm, breezy voice. 'But don't you worry, we're going to sort it out.'

She directed Ana's mum to get some water ready for boiling in the kitchen in case she needed to sterilise something.

'Shouldn't I stay with . . .' Ana's mum started to protest, but trailed off.

'I'm going to give Ana an anaesthetic,' Billie replied. 'You want to make sure you and her father are rested for when she wakes up.'

Ana's mum nodded a few times, still staring down at her daughter, before heading out of the room.

'Now, Sarah,' said Billie, as she began pulling tools and vials out of her bag, 'do you think you can give me a hand until Beth gets here?'

'What?' said Sarah. Her voice felt like it was coming from very far away.

'It would just mean handing things to me when I ask for them. Beth should be here before I need to start – well, before things get beyond your capabilities.'

Sarah nodded and took a shaky breath. 'I think so,' she said.

Billie nodded briskly as she pulled on a pair of gloves. 'Now Ana,' she said, 'I'm going to give you something to put you to sleep in a moment, but first I need to make sure I know what we're dealing with, so I'm going to ask you a few questions. Do you think you can manage that?'

Ana nodded. Billie started with a few questions about the nature of the pain and when it had started, if anything had been feeling strange or painful over the last couple of weeks, if it hurt when Billie pressed here, or when she pressed here.

'Is the baby OK?' Ana asked.

Billie sighed. 'I don't know,' she said. 'But we're going to do everything we can.'

Ana closed her eyes again, and Sarah wasn't sure if she'd really heard Billie's answer.

Sarah tried to keep her eyes on the supplies her mam had laid out in front of her, desperate to avoid seeing whatever was happening to her friend. When she heard doors opening and Beth's voice cut through, she gasped with relief.

'Perfect timing, Beth,' Billie said, 'We're just about ready to give Ana an anaesthetic.' She looked over at Sarah. 'Thank you, love,' she said. 'You did really well. I'll see you at home later.'

But once Sarah had left the room, she found she couldn't go any further. She sank to the floor by the door and took some heaving breaths. One or two silent tears rolled down her cheeks as she struggled to get her breathing under control. She wished she'd asked how long it would be. But what kind of answer could there be to that? How long until what?

The idea that something could go wrong with Ana's pregnancy, that it could hurt her, had never been something Sarah had taken seriously. There were kids in Black Crag who'd been born in their own homes, with no need for hospitals. She'd known that there were things that could go wrong, of course; she'd just assumed they wouldn't happen to Ana. Not to her friend.

Sarah sat, her back to the wall, her head in her hands, for hours, concentrating on breathing in and out, willing Ana to be OK.

It felt like it had been an eternity when Sarah suddenly heard a thin cry from the next room. For a brief moment, she was confused – in her fear for Ana, she'd almost forgotten about the baby.

Her heart skittered in her chest, and she stood up, staring across the room at Ana's parents, who'd been sitting still as statues for as long as she had. Ana's mum stood as well, and started towards the door. Before she could get to it, it opened, and Beth stepped out, a bundle in her arms. The baby was covered in slime and still crying. Beth gave Sarah a small smile, before crossing the room to Ana's parents.

They had a brief conversation, their voices too low for Sarah to hear, and then Beth passed the baby to its grandmother, before heading back into the closed room that held the new mother. Sarah stared after her for a moment, then back at Ana's mum, who was gazing down at the baby in her arms as it whimpered and quietened.

After a moment, she looked up at Sarah. There were tears in her eyes. 'They don't know,' she said. 'The baby's OK, but they don't know . . .'

'Oh,' said Sarah.

'It's a girl.'

337

Sarah nodded mutely, somehow aware that this was not the response she was supposed to be giving to the arrival of her best friend's daughter.

Ana's dad was staring around the room as if not really seeing it. Ana's mum rested a hand briefly on his shoulder, before carrying the baby away to get it cleaned up. Sarah walked to the window, looking out at the street. She was suddenly full of nervous energy she didn't know what to do with. She wished she could be more useful. Whatever her mam and Beth were doing on the other side of the door, surely another pair of hands would have been helpful to them. Maybe there was still something she could do? She could hand them things they needed, she could sterilise things, she could take away used cloths and bandages.

But at the image of bloodied cloths, and the thought of where the blood was coming from, Sarah felt suddenly faint. She dropped into a chair and pulled her knees into her chest.

It was another three hours before Billie emerged from the back room. By then, the baby had been washed, clothed and fed, and was lying in a bassinet between her grandparents. Billie crossed the room, walking straight over as Ana's parents stood to meet her.

Sarah held her breath as she waited for her mam to speak.

'She's going to be OK,' Billie said, after what felt forever, and Sarah was suddenly shaking all over.

'It'll still be a while before she wakes up, but I want to be here when she does. I'm going to leave Beth with her while I take Sarah home, and then, if it's possible, I'd like to stay here overnight, just as a precaution.'

*　　*　　*

Moth was waiting for them when they walked through the door. She pulled each of them into a hug, before stepping back and grabbing Billie by the shoulders and looking intently at her face.

'Are you OK?' she asked.

Billie swallowed hard and nodded. 'Yeah,' she said. 'I'm OK. It was . . .' She glanced at Sarah. 'We'll talk later. Ana's OK and the baby's OK, but I'm going to head back and stay for the night so I'm close if I'm needed. I just wanted to bring Sarah home.'

'Of course,' said Moth. 'Maybe have a shower before you head back? And something to eat?'

Billie nodded again and walked slowly out of the room.

Sarah felt ashamed. She hadn't considered what this must have been like for her mam. She'd just seen her as the doctor, as the person who knew what she was doing. But Billie wasn't a gynaecologist, she wasn't a surgeon. It must have been terrifying for her. Maybe it still was.

Moth was looking at her. 'I think you should probably head to bed,' she said.

'I'm not tired,' said Sarah.

Moth smiled. 'Maybe not,' she said. 'But I think having a lie-down will do you good.'

Sarah shrugged and headed to her bedroom, more because she couldn't think of a reason not to than because she felt like she needed to rest. But within a minute of letting her body sink into her bed, she was fast asleep.

Chapter Thirty-seven

The news of the arrival of Poppy Hope Martin was like lightning to the village of Black Crag. There was a crackling energy and excitement in the air. People traded in stories of Ana and her daughter. Because of the trauma of the birth and the slow pace of Ana's recovery, not many people had been admitted in to meet the new resident, and those few that had were called upon over and over again to aver that Poppy was, indeed, the most beautiful baby Black Crag had ever seen.

There was also rampant speculation about the nature of the birth, although no one knew the details. In sympathy with Ana's difficult experience, people shared what felt like every pregnancy story they'd ever heard. Those who had given birth themselves went into great detail about their own experiences, and everyone suddenly remembered an astounding amount about the pregnancies of their friends and relatives, all the way down to cousins several times removed. Sarah heard more talk of torn perineums and displaced pelvises than she'd ever imagined possible.

It was a week before Sarah herself found out what had happened in that room. Her mam wouldn't tell her; she said it was private information that only Ana had the right to share.

The first few times Sarah went to visit Ana, her friend was

still very weak. All the energy she had was devoted to the baby. She'd lie there, propped up on pillows, the baby in her arms, her eyes half-closed as Sarah chatted to her about nothing important.

But every day she recovered a little, and finally she was well enough to sit up in bed and stay awake for a few hours at a time. Finally, Sarah felt like it was OK to ask about that day.

Ana smiled sadly. 'Your mam is amazing,' she said. 'A proper superhero, really. I could have died.' She looked down at Poppy, sleeping in her bassinet beside them. '*She* could have died.' Ana looked back at Sarah. 'I can't have any more children,' she said.

Sarah was stricken. Ana had always wanted children, always said she was determined to have a big family. Sarah had always been a bit jealous that her friend's greatest ambition was something so easy to achieve. She'd never considered that it might not happen.

Ana went on. 'There was a rupture,' she said. 'Billie said she didn't have the skill to deal with it, so the only way to save my life was to perform a hysterectomy. She was very apologetic. Said that if I'd been in a hospital, it probably would have been different.'

'Oh, Ana,' said Sarah. 'I'm so sorry.'

'No, it's OK,' said Ana. 'I mean, I'm sad about it. But I'm OK. Poppy's OK. And we wouldn't be without your mam. I'm sad about hypothetical other children, but it doesn't compare to how happy I am about the one that's here.'

Sarah frowned. 'But it wasn't just the children you wanted,' she said. 'It was the life. Your life was supposed to be different.'

Ana laughed properly at that. 'Well, aren't you ridiculous? As if any of us have the lives we were supposed to.'

Sarah laughed a bit too, but shook her head. 'But yours, what you wanted – that was still possible, even after everything.'

Ana shrugged. 'Or maybe it was never going to happen, even without everything. I had an emergency hysterectomy – maybe I would have anyway. It doesn't always take some great disaster that cuts off contact with the whole world for someone's life to not go the way they'd planned. And that's OK. That's normal. Probably we're all pretty bad at planning our lives anyway, and we'd be much better off being open to whatever happens. Or doesn't.'

Sarah could feel a change in the air as she walked around the village in the weeks after Poppy's birth, even after the crack-ling excitement of the first few days had eased. Ana was up and about again, although under strict orders to take it easy, and seeing her push her baby around in the sunshine seemed to act like a healing balm on the villagers. The sight was both calming and invigorating; the energy on the island went from a sense of desperation and panic to one of tranquil determination.

But Poppy wasn't the only thing that was affecting the mood. The planting had gone well; it was almost over. A new harvest, catered expressly for their needs, would be ready for them in a few months. There wouldn't be any need to ration so strictly over the winter, with the planning done so far in advance.

Graeme's different project groups were working hard, and giving people more confidence. There was a growing sense that if something went wrong, they would be able to figure out how to deal with it, that there were ways of preventing disaster.

It was starting to feel like life was possible again. Not just survival, but life.

Sarah breathed it in like it was oxygen. It was intoxicating. This simple shift in attitude. This realisation that small joys were still possible.

That life could still be wonderful.

The burden of having inspired the village by the act of becoming a parent did begin to wear on Ana after a while. Sarah went to visit her every day, but there was always someone else there, someone who had just happened to find their old baby clothes or picture books, and had just dropped by to see if Ana could use them.

And then they'd stay for half an hour, staring at the sleeping baby with tears in their eyes.

There was something strange about it. They would stroke Poppy's cheek and close their eyes as if in benediction. They would grasp Ana's hand and tell her thank you, as if she'd saved their own lives.

After a while, Ana started begging Sarah to take her on one of her big walks, to show her the fens or the hills.

'Can you walk that far?' said Sarah. 'I mean, will you be OK?'

'Of course I can,' said Ana. 'I'm fine.' Then she grimaced. 'OK, maybe not that far. I just want to get out for a while, go somewhere with no other people. Maybe I'll wear a mask so people don't know it's me. I don't need to be dragged into another discussion about booties and the redemption of humanity.'

Sarah laughed. It was strange to see her friend so changed and yet so much the same.

They walked through the village, stopping every so often because someone needed to talk to Ana. Eventually, they found their way to their favourite spot at the end of the jetty. The place where they knew no one could overhear them.

'You must be exhausted,' said Sarah.

'Oh, you have no idea,' said Ana.

'I've heard babies are like that.'

Ana shook her head. 'The baby's fine,' she said. 'Poppy's a dream. It's everyone else. They're going to drive me to an early grave.'

'Yeah,' said Sarah. 'There are a lot of them.'

'It's not the number,' Ana said, staring out over the water. 'Well, it is. There are a lot; there are way too many. But it's more the way they are. What they say to me.'

'What do you mean? I thought they were all being really nice. A bit too nice, to be honest.'

'Exactly,' Ana said, nodding emphatically. 'That's what I mean. They're too nice, and it's too much pressure.'

Sarah thought back to the people she'd seen in Ana's house. She could understand it being annoying, but it didn't feel like pressure. No one seemed to want anything from her.

Ana was looking at her. 'You don't get it,' she said. 'I can see you don't get it. Maybe I'm being a bitch.'

'You're not,' said Sarah. 'I mean, you're right, I don't get it. But you just had a baby, so even if you were being a bitch, I think that would be fine.'

Ana sighed, leaning back on her hands. 'People are treating me like I'm a saint or something. Like Poppy is this miracle that's going to save them. Save us all. Like everything is going to be OK now, because I got knocked up by some idiot I didn't even like, who then went and got himself killed.' Ana looked out over the ocean. 'Part of me wishes I was as deluded as they are,' she went on. 'If I could convince myself that they're right, then everything would be so much easier.

'I chose to stay pregnant. I didn't have to do that. I chose it because I thought it was what I wanted.'

Sarah stared at her, chewing on her lip. 'Are you saying you regret it? That you wish you'd asked Billie for an abortion?'

Ana swallowed and looked down at the worn wood of the jetty. She didn't speak for a while.

'It's not that I don't love Poppy,' she said eventually. 'She's fantastic. And I love being her mother. Everyone tells you that you'll love your children, but they don't tell you that you'll *like* them, you know? I *like* her. I think she's the coolest. And it's fun, even when it's hard. It's fun and interesting.' She glanced up at Sarah. 'For me, I mean,' she said quickly. 'I'm not saying it would be for everyone.' She put a hand up to her face and rubbed her eyes. 'I just can't stop thinking,' she said, 'why have I done this to her? Why have I brought her into this? I'm raising a daughter – for what? For nothing. There's nothing for her here. There's nothing for her anywhere. She's going to grow up and grow old and die here, all alone, and what is the point of that?'

Sarah took a while to reply. The water lapped against the jetty. The sun was warm on the back of her neck.

'We don't know that,' she said. 'Things can change. Faster than you'd think they could.'

'Yeah, well,' said Ana. 'Right now, it's feeling like a pretty outside chance.'

Sarah didn't say anything. There was an idea she was turning over in her mind, but she wasn't ready to share it with anyone yet, not even with Ana. Especially not with Ana.

She had to think it through properly for herself first.

Chapter Thirty-eight

Sarah knew there was one person she had to talk to before she made any decisions, more than anyone else. She found Arthur leaning against a paddock fence, looking across at the horses. He looked over at her as she came up beside him, and then turned back to the animals grazing on the far side of the paddock.

'I have to ask you something,' she said.

He nodded silently.

'I know you don't want to talk about it. But . . .' The question she hadn't asked hung in the air between them.

'You want to know what happened. That day.'

Sarah nodded.

'You're going to go over,' he said. 'You think that if the horses made it here, then. they could take you back.'

Sarah nodded. She took a moment before saying more. 'If we're going to try to get there, we need to know what to be afraid of. We need to know what's not safe.'

Arthur was silent for a long time. Sarah wondered if he would ever answer her. She knew she couldn't press him. She couldn't imagine how difficult it must be to retrace the path of that day. In all the stories he'd told her about his life on the mainland, he'd never even come close to the present. The most recent ended a solid two or three years earlier. It seemed clear that he was trying to give the events that had led him to Black Crag, alone, in a damaged and sinking ferry, as wide a berth as possible.

The two of them stood, side by side, watching the horses. Sarah settled into the silence, resisting the urge to glance sideways at Arthur. To check if he was building up the strength to talk, or simply trying to ignore what she'd asked. Then, after what might have been an hour or five minutes, he spoke.

'It was like a drum beat in the sky,' he said. 'Not the sound of a drum beat – there was no sound at all – but the feeling. Do you know? Something travelling through the air, a kind of pressure. It happened and was gone, and for a while it seemed like nothing. But then the fields . . .'

The strange, soundless beat in the sky occurred at six forty-seven in the morning, the day after the end of that vast, endless storm. It reverberated across the villages, the towns, the cities – then named, now never spoken of – and dissipated so quickly you'd almost think you'd imagined it.

Then . . . If you'd been out in the farmland, you would have noticed it immediately, but further from the fields, it took a little longer to register. It was like heat rising from the earth, but wrong. Stronger.

All the fields, just a couple of weeks after planting, with new growth beginning to poke through, began giving off a strange sheen. A sickening green, shot through with a dirty purple. It was eerie and unsettling to look at, and it smelled of charged electricity.

Arthur might have taken longer to see it if he'd been at

home. He wasn't. He'd decided to drive the two hours to a neighbouring village to drop off some supplies to his son and daughter-in-law, who had a new baby – their second. He'd been on the road by quarter past six. He always was an early riser.

When the strange thump pounded, he thought at first something was wrong with his truck. He pulled over to check, but as he stepped out of the cab, he could feel it still pulsating in the air around him. It faded within a couple of minutes, but left him feeling unnerved. He drove more slowly the rest of the way, but nothing else happened, and by the time he arrived, he wasn't sure he hadn't imagined it.

He spent an hour or so making the exhausted parents breakfast and doing a load of laundry for them, playing with their older child, and then started the journey back at around quarter past ten.

When he was just over halfway home, he noticed the strange haze over the fields around him. He rolled up the windows, without really knowing why. He dropped in on his wife at the pharmacy she worked at, and she said she hadn't noticed anything strange.

But by mid-afternoon, the atmosphere in the village had shifted. There were rumours of people getting sick, of farmers dropping in their fields. Arthur turned his radio on to check the news, but all they were saying was that there were unsubstantiated reports coming from various places across the country: talk of a strange infection that spread quickly.

At five to four, a plane careened across the sky in the distance, towards the city, tipping drunkenly to the right.

At four-thirty, Arthur could hear noise coming from the street. He looked out the window and saw people running in all directions, pushing at each other, scrambling desperately to get away from something they didn't understand. At four forty-one, he heard the first gunshot.

He left his house, trying to walk calmly, unthreateningly, through the streets, staying out of everyone's way. When he got to the pharmacy, the door was hanging from its hinges. At first, he thought no one was inside, but then he heard a moan from behind the counter. He walked towards it and looked down. The head pharmacist, Henry, was lying on the floor, bleeding profusely from a wound in his side. His eyes flickered as he looked up at Arthur.

'I don't think they even knew what they wanted,' he said faintly. He coughed, and blood bubbled in the corner of his mouth. 'She's . . .' he went on. 'She was . . .' But before he could say more, he coughed again and was still.

Arthur stood breathless for a moment, then turned quickly back to look at the rest of the small shop. She was in the corner to the left of the door. A bundle on the floor. Arthur ran to her and lifted her up. Empty eyes stared back at him. The back of her head was matted with blood.

The world spun away for a moment, and then snapped back into focus. He darted out of the pharmacy, then, remembering the sick-looking air, dashed back in. He found a box of surgical masks and grabbed a handful, putting two on immediately.

He ran for his truck, no longer trying to remain inconspicuous, unthreatening. He didn't see the fist until it hit him. He fell to the ground in a daze, looking as if through water at the man who was stealing his truck.

'Wait,' Arthur said, 'I have to get to my son.'

'We've all got people to get to,' the man said. He grabbed

Arthur by the shirtfront and dug in his pockets until he found the keys. Arthur tried to grapple them back, but the man punched him again, and his head bounced against the concrete. He didn't know how long he was unconscious, but by the time he came to, no one was around – and the truck was gone.

He staggered towards the edge of the village, trying to get to the highway that would take him to his son. But as the streets opened up around him, he saw in the distance a massive fire. It looked like the whole village was ablaze.

Arthur looked around him hopelessly for a moment. If he could find another car, he could try and get there, try and help. And then he noticed a figure lying in the long grass on the side of the road. He crept closer to it to get a better look. At first, he thought the person was wearing a mask. One of those cheap rubber monster masks where the paint starts flaking off it the moment you take it off the shelf. But as he edged nearer the figure he saw the truth. The person's skin had mottled and hardened. It was a sickening yellow-pink colour and had split in places, showing bruised-looking flesh beneath it. The person's eyes were wide and staring, the whites stained a strange pink, shot through with red.

Arthur felt blank terror for the first time that day. His grief at his wife's death, his fears for his son and grandchildren, everything vanished into the white noise of survival. He turned and ran, faster than he'd run in years, heading straight for the dock.

He barely took in what was happening around him, the fights, the fires, bodies already lying in the street. When he got to the dock, he could see people grappling for control of the fishing boats, but he couldn't tell if anyone had tried to get to his ferry. It was behind a locked gate that didn't seem to have been tampered with or broken.

It was soon clear that people had found another way on board. There was a group of people fighting on the deck, while another couple were trying to break into the cabin. Arthur saw one swing a crowbar at the window, but he knew that wouldn't work – the glass was reinforced.

'Let me through,' he said, running up to the cabin door. 'I have a key.'

One of the men turned to him, a fist raised in preparation.

Arthur raised his hands in front of him. 'Look,' he said, 'do you know how to pilot this thing? I can get us out of here.'

The man looked at him for a moment, before nodding and stepping aside. As Arthur unlocked the door, he could hear the fight continuing. There was a woman yelling, but he couldn't tell what she was saying.

There was a gunshot from outside, and Arthur threw himself through the door. There were more gunshots, some from further away. It seemed like there was a shoot-out between those on the boat and someone else on the dock, or on the shore. Arthur tried to stay low, to keep his body shielded and out of sight of the windows as he started up the ferry.

The engine jumped to life and the ferry started rumbling under his feet. He slowly eased it out, away from the dock, and pressed forward into the ocean ahead. As the dock grew slowly smaller behind him, he took what felt like his first breath in hours. He walked out of the cabin and on to the deck.

There was blood everywhere. He hadn't counted exactly how many people had been fighting on the deck, so he couldn't be sure, but it seemed like at least a couple of them must have fallen overboard – or been pushed. There were three bodies splayed on the deck; they looked like they'd been pulverised in places. Arthur didn't know much about guns, but whoever had been shooting at them had clearly chosen a particularly brutal weapon.

There was one person still standing. The man who'd been swinging a crowbar at the window. He and Arthur stood staring at each other for a few minutes. Arthur looked briefly back at the shore, to see how far they'd moved away from it and, when he looked back, he noticed something. The man's fingers were a strange colour. Mottled. Pink. It looked like the skin was hardening.

The man noticed the direction of his gaze and looked down. He froze, staring at his own hand. Arthur slowly backed away, until he reached the door of the cabin. He shut himself in and locked the door, but the man hadn't moved. He didn't seem to notice that Arthur had left.

Eventually, the man shifted his weight, and Arthur glanced around the cabin, wondering if there was anything he could use as a weapon. But the man didn't show any sign of trying to get in after him. He walked to the back of the boat, where a row of seats was attached to the deck, and sat down, looking back to where the sun was beginning to set above the village that had until today been home.

Arthur turned away from him, facing out into the open sea.

After an hour or so, he noticed that the ferry was listing slightly to the side. He went outside to see if he could find the problem, keeping his eyes carefully turned away from the back of the boat. He walked to the side of the ferry and leaned over the railing. He could see a small eddy swirling around the side of the boat.

As he moved to go below deck, he couldn't stop himself from glancing to the back. The man with the crowbar was slumped sideways in his seat, unmoving.

Arthur made his way down into the engine room and, for a moment, closed his eyes in despair. Two holes had been blasted into the side of the boat, presumably by whoever had been shooting at the group on the deck as the ferry pulled away. The water was already ankle-deep.

It would be easier to just give up, he thought to himself for a moment. *Why shouldn't I just give up?*

But something beyond thought propelled him. He pulled out a tarpaulin and tied it across the wall, pushing sandbags up against it to hold it in place. He knew it wouldn't slow the water that much. All he could do was hope it would be enough.

Enough to get him to Black Crag.

'I'll never forgive myself,' Arthur said.

Sarah turned to look at him, her brow furrowed. 'For getting away?'

Arthur wasn't looking at her. He wasn't looking at the horses. His head was turned away, towards the hills in the distance.

'For going in the wrong direction. For going to the sea instead of to my family.'

'Do you think you could have made it to them? Do you think there was something you could've done to help them?'

'Doesn't matter,' said Arthur. 'I would better have died trying.'

Sarah was silent. She couldn't think of anything to say. She thought perhaps there was nothing anyone could say.

'You can tell people,' Arthur said, after a while. 'I don't mind people knowing. But I don't want to say it all again.'

Sarah nodded. 'Thank you,' she said. 'For telling me.' She hesitated for a moment, before continuing. 'Do you think . . .' She trailed off, trying to find the right way to phrase her question.

But Arthur knew what she meant. 'I don't know,' he said. 'Well, I have some thoughts. But I don't know if they're accurate; I have no way of knowing anything, really. But there was this colour over the fields, and it spread all over the land and into the sky. After I got here, it kept spreading. Growing brighter. Growing closer. Those first couple of months, I was terrified it was going to reach us here, too. And then it stopped spreading, and eventually it began to fade. It's almost gone now. I think another week or two, and there'll be no trace of it.

'Whatever it was that happened, I think it's stopped happening. I don't think that you'll go over there and get sick. That doesn't mean I think it's safe.'

'Well,' said Sarah. 'Nothing's safe.'

'No.'

Sarah hesitated for a moment, biting her lip. 'Do you want me,' she said, 'when we get over there, do you want us to try and find—'

'No,' Arthur said quickly, almost breathlessly. 'I can't hope that they're alive. The chances are so small . . . And if they're not, then I don't think I could cope with knowing how . . .'

He let his sentence trail to nothing.

Chapter Thirty-nine

Sarah took a day for herself before she talked to anyone else.

She spent it walking. Not one of her usual walks. Not to the cliffs or along the beach or across the fields. She walked the streets. She took in the sights of the small village she'd hated for so long. The village that had felt like a prison she was never going to escape. The village that it had taken the apocalypse to make into her home.

She ran her hand over the wall of the school. She passed by the hall and the pub. She walked out onto the jetty and looked back at it all. Alive to her in a way it had never been before.

And then she went to find Nathaniel and Graeme.

The three of them sat talking for hours. They made lists and consulted maps. They talked through goals and hopes and contingencies. They agreed on a time frame.

That was the easy bit.

The next day, Sarah made her family dinner and had it waiting for them when they all got home. She sat them down and poured her parents each a glass of Malcolm's blackcurrant wine. His stockpile had finally run out, and he was now experimenting with making his own.

'Ooh, are we letting that become a thing?' Mam said.

'Trust me,' said Sarah. She took a deep breath. 'I have something to tell you all. And I hope you'll understand.'

She looked around at them. Her parents looked confused and worried. Her brother looked bored.

'I'm leaving,' she said.

'You're moving out?' said Moth. 'Where will you go?'

Sarah shook her head. 'I'm leaving Black Crag.'

Everyone stared at her.

'I've talked it over with Graeme. Nathaniel and I – we're going to try to get to the mainland. We're going to see what's out there.'

There was silence for a moment. And then, 'How?' said Mam.

'On horseback. The horses must have got to us over the isthmus. We're going to try and retrace their steps.'

Moth shook her head slightly. 'Why? What's made you want to leave?'

Sarah frowned slightly and looked down at her plate. She didn't know how to explain it cleanly, all the things that had happened that led to this moment. Ana's fears for Poppy. Elliot's asthma attack. The way everyone was trying so hard to get by without support or help.

'We may be able to keep going on our own here for a while,' she said. 'A couple of years maybe. But we need more than that. More than a couple of years. More than survival.'

'When are you going?' Moth asked, swallowing hard.

'In a few days,' said Sarah. 'It's not set entirely, but we want to go as soon as possible. We want to be able to explore as much as we can, and make it back before the weather gets bad. We're hoping to find a boat over there so we can load it up with supplies to bring home.'

'And Graeme thinks this is a good idea?' asked Mam.

Sarah nodded. 'He thinks it's time. We think – Arthur thinks, and we agree – that the sky clearing up means it's probably safe over there now. And Graeme always knew someone would have to go eventually. With the horses he thinks we can make it across.'

Moth was shaking her head. 'I don't like it,' she said. 'How can you know you'll be OK?'

'I don't,' said Sarah. 'But we've made a lot of plans. We've thought it through as well as we can, and I can go over all of that with you.'

'Don't we get a say in this?' said Mam.

'You're welcome to try and persuade me,' said Sarah. 'But I know this is the right thing for me to do. We're doing the best we can on our own here. But it's time to find out if someone else is out there.'

Elliot was silent. He was staring at the table, biting his lip.

Moth and Mam looked at each other, and then back at Sarah.

'I don't know what to say,' said Moth.

'I'm sorry,' said Sarah. 'I know it's a lot. And you have some time to get used to the idea. I'm not vanishing in an instant.'

'We just feel like we should be protecting you from this, kid,' said Mam. 'It shouldn't be your responsibility to put yourself in danger like this.'

Sarah shrugged. 'But it is.'

Mam nodded silently. Tears were rolling down Moth's face. Elliot was still staring at the table.

Mam picked up her glass and drained it. 'God,' she said, pulling a face. 'It really is revolting.' She poured herself another glass.

*   *   *

357

Sarah was lying on her bed staring at the ceiling later that night, when there was a knock on her bedroom door. She turned to look as it opened. Elliot was standing there. His eyes were red.

'I don't want you to go,' he said.

Sarah smiled sadly. 'I know, pal,' she said. 'But I'll be back.'

'You'd better be.'

Chapter Forty

When Sarah had made up her mind, the plan to head to the mainland had still felt amorphous and hypothetical, and it took her aback how quickly it solidified into something real, something that was happening.

Graeme called a meeting the day after Sarah had talked to her family to tell the rest of the village about the plan.

He related Arthur's account of his last day on the mainland, and explained why the changing colour of the sky gave them reason for optimism. He talked through Thomas's unsuccessful attempt in the Autumn, outlining how they planned to address his failures. He stressed the milder weather of Spring, and the fact that Sarah and Nathaniel would be on horseback, rather than on foot.

There were a few questions raised, but not as many as Sarah had expected. And after the meeting was over, most people rallied around Sarah and Nathaniel to make sure they'd have everything they need.

Once preparations began in earnest, Sarah found herself focusing on them almost obsessively. She could feel the other side of her decision, the sacrifice of it, sitting in the back of her mind, but she couldn't bring herself to look at it too closely. She had to concentrate on making it to the mainland; she couldn't think too hard about leaving her family.

And there was a lot to think about. They didn't know how easily she and Nathaniel would be able to find food, so they had to figure out how much they could carry with them without being overloaded. There was camping equipment to be checked over for damage, and clothing for all weather eventualities to be packed. And every day, they spent as much time as they could with the horses, getting used to the feeling of riding for hours at time.

Sarah was so focused on the preparations, that it came as a complete surprise when Beth and Jeremy announced they wanted to get married.

'What, now?' she said, when Jeremy told her. They'd spent the day with the horses and a few large rucksacks full of rope, trying to get them used to carrying heavy loads. As the light began to fade, they'd begun to pack things away. They were in the middle of shovelling horse manure from the paddock into wheelbarrows to be taken to a compost heap. It didn't really seem like the time.

Jeremy laughed. 'Not right this second, no. But yes, now, I think. This weekend. We, ah . . . We wanted to do it before you left. Because, well, I was wondering if you would be my best man. Best woman.'

Sarah felt a sob rise in her throat. 'Oh my god,' she said. 'Of course I will.'

They walked together back to the village and, as they walked past Billie's surgery, Beth came running out the front door.

'Did you ask her?' she cried.

'He asked me,' said Sarah. 'Congratulations. I won't hug you – I'm revolting – but I'm so happy for you.'

Beth beamed. 'I'm happy for me, too,' she said.

It felt like the first wedding Black Crag had ever seen. There was an uncertainty, a tentativeness to the enthusiasm with which the village came together. There were sparkling eyes and shy smiles, hushed laughter and blissful silences. Every attempt at joy thus far had come with a sense of grim determination, a refusal to give in to the despair of circumstance. But now, for the first time, it was as if people were allowing themselves to actually think about the future – a future where there was still life and love.

Before Sarah knew what was happening, the hall was covered with flowers. Sarah and Moth managed to cobble together a semblance of a wedding cake, while Ana's mother altered her own wedding dress to fit Beth.

Sarah felt strange digging into her wardrobe for a nice dress to wear for the wedding. It had been such a long time since she'd thought about dressing up at all. She dug out the make-up she hadn't touched in a year, and it felt like her hands weren't her own as she brushed colour across her eyes.

Her heart ached in her chest when she saw the hall filled with people, all dressed up in a way they hadn't had a chance to be in so long.

Mam glanced at her and chuckled. 'It's early to be crying yet,' she said. 'Wait for the vows, at least.'

Sarah gave a wobbly smile. 'I hadn't thought of things like this still being able to happen,' she said. 'It hadn't occurred to me to think about it, but I guess I assumed there was no room for weddings anymore.'

Mam smiled back at her. 'Ah,' she said. 'Whatever else is going on, people always find ways to love.' Then she shrugged. 'And to hate, but we don't have to think about that right now.'

Sarah walked to the front of the hall and looked out over the assembled guests. She wasn't the only one who was already in tears.

Jeremy and Beth walked in together, both radiating joy and peace. They made it up to the front of the hall and stood gazing at each other. Graeme stood between them and began the service.

'The one constant of the human condition,' he said, 'is hope. Even in the most disastrous of times, we cannot help it. There is something within us that remains convinced that there is a future worth fighting for. Worth living for.

'Choosing to love another person is a wonderful expression of that hope. Committing to work together as one to build a future that you're not sure you can even imagine.

'I want to thank you, Beth and Jeremy, for allowing us all to share in your hope and your love.'

Sarah heard someone break into open sobs.

Jeremy smiled at Graeme, and then turned to Beth. 'Beth,' he said. 'You're amazing, and I'm so glad I met you. Even though it took the end of the world to make that happen.' He looked out at the crowd. 'Not that I'm thankful for the end of the world, or anything,' he said quickly, before turning back to Beth. 'But I am thankful for you. You have made this world brighter than I ever thought it could be.'

Beth swallowed and took a shaky breath. 'Jeremy,' she said, 'I don't know if Graeme's right. That hope is a constant condition. I do know that if he is, I had forgotten how to find mine. Until you. You are my hope.'

Graeme took them through their vows, and tears flowed freely around the room.

Sarah looked out over the crowd and she caught sight of Nathaniel, sitting a few rows from the front. He was staring at Beth and Jeremy as they pledged their hearts to each other, and there was a wistful, pained look on his face. He noticed Sarah watching him and flashed her a sad smile.

Sarah felt her heart throb again as she looked over the crowd. She'd worked so hard to be comfortable here, and she thought she finally was. She felt like what she did here mattered. Like she was building something valuable.

But as she looked at the crowd, as she watched Beth and Jeremy have their first kiss as husband and wife, she knew it wasn't enough. These two had been lucky, she knew. They had found the life they wanted and needed here. And the whole village was coming together to keep that life safe – for them and for everyone else for whom it was enough.

But it wasn't enough for everyone. It never would be.

The party moved to the pub, where Malcolm was serving his blackcurrant wine. It only took an hour or so before people were telling each other that it was actually not that bad – and in fact, was entirely drinkable.

Greta was at the piano, banging out some upbeat music with more enthusiasm and less skill than was normal for her.

Beth and Jeremy spun dreamily in the centre of the room, while other dancers whirled around them. Sarah dragged Elliot out onto the floor, ignoring his embarrassed protests.

'Shut up,' she cried, 'and dance with your sister.'

There was a pain in her chest she hadn't yet started to examine, but she let herself be swept away by the joy and energy of the night. She looked around at the crowd and let the sight of them buoy her. Her parents swirling around in each other's arms. Nathaniel attempting to get a dance battle going among a group of kids. Graeme, sitting to the side, beaming out across the crowd.

She kept dancing for what felt like hours, until she noticed how exhausted she was, and threw herself into a seat across from Ana, who was cradling a sleeping Poppy in her arms.

'Oh god,' Sarah said. 'I haven't danced like that in forever.'

Ana smiled at her, then sighed. 'I can't believe you'll be gone in a few days,' she said.

Sarah swallowed and looked down, her eyes suddenly hot. 'Maybe only briefly,' she said. 'Remember when Thomas and Marcus tried to get across the isthmus? They had to turn back after a few days.'

Ana gave a low, sad laugh. Talking about Marcus was still strange. 'They were on foot,' she said. 'And they'd thought about it for around ten minutes before deciding to go. They were bafflingly unprepared, when you think about it. You, you've been planning now for ages. You're going to make it.'

'Maybe,' said Sarah. 'Right now, it seems crazy to be going. To be putting ourselves in that kind of danger, when we could stay here and help out with everything.'

'Don't make me persuade you to go when I really want you to stay,' said Ana, laughing properly now. 'That's not fair at all.'

Sarah sniffed and brushed a tear from her cheek. 'I'll be back,' she said, nodding slightly as if to convince herself. 'Eventually, I'll make it back.'

'I know,' said Ana. 'We'll all be waiting for you.'

*   *   *

And then the time had come.

It was a bright, still day, and Sarah and Nathaniel were standing at the edge of the village, surrounded by their friends and family. Their community.

Sarah's parents held her tight one last time. Elliot gave her a restrained nod, and she grabbed him and pulled him in for a hug.

Then she pulled herself up on to Terry's back. Nathaniel was beside her, astride Burt, leading a third horse who was loaded up with – hopefully – everything they'd need.

She looked around her home one last time. And then she turned and headed into the unknown.

The Future

So it had been like this.

A village isolated for a year. Surviving just to keep on surviving. Grieving and hoping and living for a future they couldn't imagine.

A new baby, born with the hope of her community on her shoulders. And two explorers, barely grown, sent forth to find . . . answers? Help? No one really knew. They were sent to find something.

The summer bloomed mellow and warm. Seeds put forth life.

And always, there were eyes on the horizon. Watching to the east for a boat to cross. Looking to the south for travellers on horseback.

Waiting for whatever answers had been found.

Acknowledgements

Thank you to my agent Claudia Young, and everyone at Greene & Heaton. Thank you Areen Ali, Alex Clarke, and Headline team – Felicia Hu, Serena Arthur, Ella Gordon.

Thanks, as always, to Jamie Drew. To my family – Sharron, Peter, Christy, Joyia, Eli, Tineke, Sean, James, Sam, Theo, Libby, Will.

Thank you to Dolly, Norma, Mike, Duncan, Celly, Hue, Emma, Conor, Oliver, Jeffrey, Mary, Sarah, Ella, Caroline, Griff, other Mike, Adam, Cal, Charlotte, Amy, Daisy, other Amy, Mel, and the dozen or so other people who's names will pop into my head one night soon, making me sit bolt upright in bed and break into a cold sweat at the realisation that I forgot to put them on this list.

I love you all.

© Jamie Drew

Janina Matthewson is originally from Christchurch, New Zealand and now lives in London. She trained as an actress and also studied English, history and linguistics. Her first novel, *Of Things Gone Astray*, was published by The Friday Project in 2015. She co-authored (with Jeffrey Craner) her latest novel, *You Feel It Just Below the Ribs*, which was published by HarperCollins US in November 2021. She also co-writes the cult-hit podcast, *Within the Wires*, with season nine coming soon. She has also written for *Murmurs*, *The Cipher*, and *Passenger List*.